THE
IMMORTALS

THE IMMORTALS

JAMES GUNN

Pocket Books
New York   London   Toronto   Sydney

An *Original* Publication of Pocket Books

POCKET BOOKS, a division of Simon & Schuster, Inc.
1230 Avenue of the Americas, New York, NY 10020

Designed by Jaime Putorti

Cover design by John Vairo, Jr.
cover photograph by Lorraine Molina/Photonica

Manufactured in the United States of America

INTRODUCTION

James Gunn's *The Immortals* is elegant, innovative—and chilling. Gunn's take on immortality is simple enough, yet mythic—it's all in the blood.

More blood.

Mutated blood.

With the right blood, you can live forever . . .

A man is born who is resistant to the disease of aging, and anyone with enough money on this Earth wants to know where he is, where his children are . . .

Because they could be tickets to immortality. Rich old men hankering for life everlasting. For the blood is the life . . .

I don't know about you, but all that scares the bejesus out of me. We've seen it before, of course; it's now the core of one of the great themes of imaginative literature, the vampire. One difference here is that it is not the upper class monster who conveys an unwanted deathlessness on a hapless commoner, but the hapless and elusive commoner who carries the highly desired trait.

James Gunn does it as straight science fiction, with a strong scientific underpinning. Very convincing. Clinical, medical noir. They should film it in black and white.

And that makes *The Immortals* a classic.

—Greg Bear

PREFACE

THE IMMORTALS

Story ideas come at unexpected times and develop in unexpected ways, and sometimes have lives of their own.

The idea for *The Immortals* came to me during my second stint as a full-time writer. The first was a twelve-month period back in 1948–49 after I had given up the idea of becoming a playwright and then of becoming a radio writer. I sold several stories (the first ten under the pseudonym of Edwin James) but not enough to live on and decided to return to the University of Kansas to get a master's degree in English. Two years later I took a job as an editor for Western Printing & Lithographing Company of Racine, Wisconsin. It published paperback books and Disney comics for Dell and Little Golden Books for Simon and Schuster. I was supposed to create a science-fiction line. But when I attended my first World Science Fiction Convention (and my first convention of any kind) in Chicago in 1952 and learned from my agent, Frederik Pohl, that he had sold four stories for me, I decided to return to full-time writing.

Halfway through that period of about two and a half years, I came up with the idea for *The Immortals*. Science fiction's appeal is its sense of wonder, its series of "what-ifs?" One day I began wondering about how humanity might actually achieve immortality. Those ideas are starting points, they develop into stories through research. Some creatures, I found, never die from natural causes. Another source suggested that people age because our circulatory system is inefficient; it doesn't provide food for the cells when they need it, or remove the by-products of oxidation. What would happen if someone were born with a better circulatory system? And what if that improvement were capable of being transmitted to someone else through a blood transfusion? And what if the rejuvenating power might reside in a blood protein like the gamma globulins that provide passive immunity against infection when they are injected into other people (such as pregnant women, so that they don't catch German measles)? Then the rejuvenation itself might be only temporary, lasting only about thirty to forty-five days, like the passive immunity conferred by gamma globulins. Those were the what-ifs that set off a process of story creation.

I sat down and wrote "New Blood," which my agent sent to John Campbell, editor of *Astounding Science Fiction*. It was published in the November 1955 issue. By then I had finished the second story in the series "Donor." Campbell wasn't interested in more stories about immortal blood, so I sold it to *Startling Stories;* it was scheduled for publication in the winter issue of 1955—but the fall issue was the last *(Startling Stories* wasn't the only magazine I helped kill). I resold it to *Fantastic Stories of the Imagination*, where it appeared in the November 1960 issue.

By the time "New Blood" was published, I had moved my family from Kansas City back to Lawrence, Kansas, and had been asked to teach a couple of sections of English composition at the University of Kansas. Before the semester was over, I was invited to become managing editor of the University's *Alumni Magazine*. I made a deal with the university to work only three weeks a month during the summers so I could use the fourth for writing. During the first summer I wrote "Medic," which Bob Mills published in the July 1957 issue of *Venture Science Fiction* as "Not So Great an Enemy." The second summer I wrote "The Immortals," which Fred Pohl published in *Star Science Fiction #4* in 1958.

By that time, Bantam Books had launched its science fiction line. I had already sold them *Station in Space* and *The Joy Makers*. The third book Dick Roberts accepted was *The Immortals*. It was published in 1962.

On the other side of the continent, Robert Specht, an aspiring screenwriter, was working in the Los Angeles office of Bantam Books. Each month a stack of paperback books arrived from the East Coast; one month Specht picked *The Immortals* to take home with him and, he later told me, decided immediately that he wanted to make it into a movie.

Four years later he was story editor for Everett Chambers on the *Peyton Place* television series, and he persuaded Chambers to go in with him to obtain the film and television rights to *The Immortals*. They contacted my agent, who by then was Harry Altshuler (Fred Pohl had gone out of the agenting business). We agreed upon a two-year option with modest payments every six months. I got three checks but the fourth never came. I wrote Bob Specht, who said that Chambers had dropped out, that he had tried the novel on every producer, director, and major actor in Hollywood without success, but that some new possibilities had opened up. We agreed upon a new contract that—to everyone's surprise—actually developed into a film.

ABC had decided that it would make its own television films rather than renting them from Hollywood and use them on what it called the ABC-TV Movie of the Week. Suddenly TV scripts were in demand, and Bob Specht sold Paramount on *The Immortals*. It was filmed in the spring of 1969 as *The Immortal*, featuring Christopher George, Barry Sullivan, Ralph Bellamy, Carol Lynley, and Jessica Walter, directed by Joseph Sargent, and broadcast the following September. It was scheduled to be the first film in the new ABC series, but at the last moment was edged out by *Seven in Darkness* with Milton Berle.

Apparently the film rated well ("It ranked fourth in the eighty-city Nielsens," Bob told me later), although, to be sure, the film had changed the focus from the social change created by the reality of immortality for a few to a chase story in which Christopher George was pursued by rich and powerful aging people lusting for his blood. ABC decided to commission an hour-long series, also called *The Immortal*, for the following year. Only Christopher George was carried over from the film (Bob Specht didn't even get considered for story editor), and ABC decided to play the series for adventure instead of science fiction. But I won't go into that.

During the interim Bob Specht called and said that ABC wanted a novelization of the screenplay to promote the series. I was offered one-third of the royalties and said, "Go ahead." At the last minute I was phoned by Bantam to say that it couldn't find a writer to do the novelization, so I wrote it myself. It may have been the only time that the author of a novel wrote the novelization of the script (our director of Special Collections called it "cruel and unusual punishment"). My consolation is that it was easy money: I wrote it in six days so that it could be published before the series started in September 1970.

Flash forward about twenty-five years. Some interesting things happened in the interim: Bantam Books reprinted the novel in 1968 and Pocket Books in 1979, and it got translated into Italian, Japanese, German, Portuguese, and French, and reprinted in Great Britain. But then, in the mid-1990s I got a telephone call from a woman who said she was calling from Disney Pictures and was looking for the person who owned the feature film rights to *The Immortals*. "You've found him," I said. Back in 1968, Paramount, when it took over the contract from Bob Specht, had elected to buy only the television rights, not the more costly feature-film rights.

That began a series of Hollywood experiences (which Vonda N. McIntyre has characterized as "hysterical enthusiasm followed by total silence"). Touchstone Pictures, a Disney subsidiary, was interested in making a feature film ("we see it as a major motion picture with a major star and a major director such as Sidney Pollack or James Cameron," the Touchstone president told me, when I visited him with my agent, Dorris Halsey). But whoever at Disney was enthusiastic about the project got fired, and Disney did not renew the option. Before the Disney option had expired, however, another producer was already pursuing the rights (tipped off, we heard, by a screenwriter who had been asked by Touchstone to offer a "take" on the film), and he took over the feature-film rights on the same terms. But then he, too, did not renew the option. A third and then a fourth producer took options and were unsuccessful. Now the novel is once more under option, to Warner Bros.

During all this film hope and hype, I resold the reprint rights to Pocket Books and, at the editor's request, updated some of the material and added a new 20,000-word section in the middle. The Touchstone president had commented (perceptively, I thought) that it was really the doctor's story, so I filled in a middle section about Dr. Russell Pearce's search for the *elixir vitae*.

People have not yet discovered immortality, although a recent article in *The New York Times* speculated that by 2,200 people may be living for six hundred years. But until then our only immortality may lie in progeny and books.

James Gunn
Lawrence, Kansas

TO RICHARD

Light breaks where no sun shines;
Where no sea runs, the waters of the heart
Push in their tides.
Light breaks where no sun shines
And death shall have no dominion.

—DYLAN THOMAS

PART I

NEW BLOOD

The young man was stretched out flat in a reclining hospital chair, his bare left arm muscular and brown on the table beside him. The wide, flat band of the sphygmomanometer was tight around his bicep, and the inside of his elbow, where the veins were blue traceries, had been swabbed with alcohol and betadine.

His eyes followed the quick efficiency of the phlebotomist. Her movements were as crisp as her white uniform.

She opened the left-hand door of the big refrigerator and from the second shelf removed a double plastic bag connected by plastic tubing. There was a hole at the bottom for hanging the bags from an IV pole. The plastic bag was empty, flat, and wrinkled. A syringe needle on a length of clear, plastic tubing was attached.

The technician removed the protective plastic cap from the needle and stretched out the tubing. She inspected the donor's inside arm where it had been sterilized and deadened with lidocaine. The vein was big and soft, and she slipped the needle into it with practiced skill. Dark red blood raced through the tube and into one of the plastic bags. Slowly a pool gathered at the bottom and the wrinkles began to smooth.

The technician stripped a printed label with the date

and a number from a sheet of nonstick paper and pressed it on the plastic bag. At the bottom she put her initials.

"Keep making a fist," she said, glancing at the bag.

When the bag was full, she closed a clamp on the tube and removed the needle from the donor's arm, replacing it with a cotton ball and a plastic bandage.

"Keep that on for an hour or so," she said.

She drained the blood in the tubing into test tubes, sealed them, and applied smaller labels on them from the same preprinted sheet of paper before she placed them on a rack in the refrigerator.

The tubing and needle were carefully discarded in a waste disposal canister with a plastic lining.

"The typing will be done at the center," the technician said. "If you're really O-neg, you might make a bit of money from time to time. That's the only kind that we have to buy when we can't get enough donations."

The donor's youthful lips twisted at the corners.

"I'll need your name and address for the records," the technician said briskly, turning to the computer on her desk and typing a number into it. After the young man had given it and she had typed it in, she said, "We can have you notified when the results come back. The lab checks for AIDS, hepatitis, venereal and other blood-carried diseases. All confidential, of course. If you like, we can put your name in our professional donor's file."

Without hesitation the young man shook his head.

The technician shrugged and handed him a slip of

paper. "Thanks anyway. Stay seated in the waiting room for ten minutes. There's some orange juice, coffee, and muffins that you can have while you wait. The paper is a voucher for fifty dollars. You can cash it at the cashier's office—by the front door as you go out."

For a moment after the young man's broad back had disappeared from the doorway, the technician stared after him. Then she shrugged again, turned, and put the unit of blood onto the refrigerator's top left-hand shelf.

A unit of whole blood—new life in a plastic bag for someone who might die without it. Within a few days the white cells will begin to die, the blood will decline in ability to clot. With the aid of refrigeration, the red cells will last—some of them—for three weeks. After that the blood will be sent to the separator for the plasma, if it has not already been separated for packed red blood cells, or sold to a commercial company for separation of some of the plasma's more than seventy proteins, the serum albumin, the gamma globulins. . . .

A unit of blood—market price: $50. After the required tests, it will be moved to the second shelf from the top, right-hand side of the refrigerator, with the other units of O-type blood. But this blood was special. It had everything other blood had, and something extra that made it unique. There had never been any blood quite like it.

Fifty dollars? How much is life worth?

The old man was eighty years old. His body was limp on the hard hospital bed. The air-conditioning was so muffled that the harsh unevenness of his breathing was loud. The only movement in the intensive care unit was the spasmodic rise and fall of the sheet that covered the old body.

He was living—barely. He had used up his allotted three-score years and ten, and then some. It wasn't merely that he was dying—everyone is. With him, it was imminent.

Dr. Russell Pearce held one bony wrist in his firm, young right hand and looked at the monitors checking blood pressure, heart function, pulse, oxygen level. . . . Pearce's face was serious, his dark eyes steady, his pale skin well molded over strong bones.

The old man's face was yellow over a grayish blue, the color of death. The wrinkled skin was pulled back like a mask for the skull. Once he might have been handsome; now his eyes were sunken, the closed eyelids dark over them, his mouth was a dark line, and his nose was a thin, arching beak.

There is a kinship in old age, just as there is a kinship in infancy. Between the two, men differ, but at the extremes they are much the same.

Pearce had seen old men in the nursing units, Medicaid patients most of them, picked up on the North Side when they didn't wake up in their cardboard boxes or Dumpsters, filthy, alcohol or drug addicts many of them. The only differences with this man were a little care and a few billion dollars. Where this man's hair was groomed and snow-white, the other's was yellowish-gray, long, scraggly on seamed, thin necks. Where this man's skin was scrubbed and immaculate, the other's had dirt in the wrinkles, sores in the crevices.

Gently Pearce laid the arm down beside the body and slowly stripped back the sheet. The differences were minor. In dying, people are much the same. Once this old man had been tall, strong, vital. Now the thin body was emaciated; the rib cage struggled through the skin, fluttered. The old veins stood out, knotted, ropy, blue, varicose, on the sticklike legs.

"Pneumonia?" Dr. Easter asked with professional interest. He was an older man, his hair gray at the temples, his appearance distinguished, calm.

"Not yet. Malnutrition. You'd think he'd eat more, get better care. Money is supposed to take care of itself."

"It doesn't follow. As his personal physician, I've learned that you don't order around a billion dollars."

"Anemia," Pearce went on. "Bleeding from a duodenal ulcer, I'd guess. We could operate, but I'm not sure he'd survive. Pulse weak, rapid. Blood pressure low. Arteriosclerosis and all the damage that entails."

Beside him a nurse made marks on a chart. Her face was smooth and young; the skin glowed with health.

"Let's have a blood count," Pearce said to her briskly. "Urinalysis. Type and cross-match two units of blood, packed RBCs if you can get them, and administer one unit when available."

"Transfusion?" Easter asked.

"It may provide temporary help. If it helps enough, we'll give him more, maybe strengthen him enough for the operation."

"But he's dying." It was almost a question.

"Sure. We all are." Pearce smiled grimly. "Our business is to postpone it as long as we can."

A few moments later, when Pearce opened the door and stepped into the hall, Dr. Easter was talking earnestly to a tall, blond, broad-shouldered man in an expensively cut business suit. The man was about Easter's age, somewhere between forty-five and fifty. The face was strange: It didn't match the body. There was a thin, predatory look to its slate-gray eyes.

The man's name was Carl Jansen. He was personal secretary to the old man who was dying inside the room. Dr. Easter performed the introductions, and the men shook hands. Pearce reflected that the term *personal secretary* might cover a multitude of duties.

"Doctor Pearce, I'll only ask you one question," Jansen said in a voice as flat and cold as his eyes. "Is Mister Weaver going to die?"

"Of course he is," Pearce answered. "None of us escapes. If you mean is he going to die within the next few days, I'd say yes—if I had to answer yes or no."

"What's wrong with him?" Jansen asked. His tone sounded suspicious, but that was true of everything he said.

"He's outlived his body. Like a machine, it's worn out, falling to pieces, one part failing after another."

"His father lived to be ninety-one, his mother ninety-six."

Pearce looked at Jansen steadily, unblinking. "They didn't accumulate several billion dollars. We live in an age that has almost conquered disease, but its pace has inflicted a price. The stress and strain of modern life tear us apart. Every billion Weaver made cost him five years of living."

"What are you going to do—just let him die?"

Pearce's eyes were just as cold as Jansen's. "As soon as possible we'll give him a transfusion. Does he have any relatives, close friends?"

"There's no one closer than me."

"We'll need two pints of blood for every pint we give Weaver. Arrange it."

"Mister Weaver will pay for whatever he uses."

"He'll replace it if possible. That's the hospital rule."

Jansen's eyes dropped. "There'll be plenty of volunteers from the office."

When Pearce was beyond the range of his low, penetrating voice, Jansen said, "Can't we get somebody else? I don't like him."

"That's because he's harder than you are," Easter said. "He'd be a good match for the old man when he was in his prime."

"He's too young."

"That's why he's good. The best geriatrician in the Middle West. He can be detached, objective. All doctors need a touch of ruthlessness. Pearce needs more than most; he loses every patient sooner or later. He's got it." Easter looked at Jansen and smiled ruthfully. "When men reach our age, they start getting soft. They start getting subjective about death."

*   *   *

The requisition for one unit of blood arrived at the blood bank. The hospital routine began. A laboratory technician, crisp in a starched white uniform, came from the blood bank on the basement floor. From one of the old man's ropy veins she drew five cubic centimeters of blood, almost purple inside the slim barrel of the syringe.

The old man didn't stir. In the silence his breathing was a raucous noise.

Back at the workbench, she dabbed three blood samples onto two glass slides, one divided into sections marked A and B. She slipped the slides onto a light-box with a translucent glass top; to one sample she added a drop of clear serum from a green bottle marked "Anti-A" in a commercial rack. "Anti-B" came from a brown bottle; "Anti-Rho" from a clear one. She rocked the box back and forth on its pivots. Sixty seconds later the red cells of the samples marked A and B were still evenly suspended. In the third sample the cells had clumped together visibly.

She entered the results on her computer: patient's name, date, room, doctor. . . . Type: O. Rh: neg.

She pushed another key. A list of blood available wrote itself across the screen, grouped by types. The technician opened the right-hand door of the refrigerator and inspected the labels of the plastic bags on the second shelf from the top. She selected one and put samples of the donor's and patient's blood into two small test tubes.

A drop of donor's serum in a sample of the patient's blood provided the major crossmatch: the red cells did not clump, and even under the microscope, after centrifuging, the cells were perfect, even, suspended circles. A drop or two of the patient's serum in a sample of the donor's blood and the minor crossmatch was done.

On the label she wrote:

FOR
LEROY WEAVER 9–4
ICU DR. PEARCE

She telephoned the nurse in charge that the blood was ready when needed. The nurse came for the blood in a few minutes. She and the lab tech checked the name of the recipient, the blood type, and the identifying numbers of the blood unit and initialed the tag that hung from the bag. The lab tech stripped one copy for her file, and the nurse carried the bag away. At the nurses' station she removed another copy and filed it in a drawer. Then, with a second nurse, she went to ICU and attached a copy of the tag to the patient's chart before both reviewed the doctor's orders and the patient's identity, and compared the numbers on the patient's identification bracelet with those on the unit of blood and on the tag.

Dr. Pearce studied the charts labeled "Leroy Weaver." He picked up the report from the hematology laboratory. Red cell count: 2,360,000/cmm. Anemia, all right. Worse than he'd even suspected. That duodenal ulcer was losing a lot of blood.

The transfusion would help. It would be temporary, but everything is, at best. In the end it is all a matter of time. Maybe it would revive Weaver enough to get some solid food down him. He might surprise them all and walk out of this hospital yet.

Pearce picked up the charts and reports and walked down the long, quiet corridor, rubbery underfoot, redolent of the perennial hospital odors: alcohol and anesthetic, fighting the ancient battle against bacteria and pain. He opened the door of the intensive care unit and walked into the coolness.

He nodded distantly to the nurse on duty in the room. She was not one of the hospital staff. She was one of the three full-time nurses hired for Weaver by Jansen.

Pearce picked up the clipboard at the foot of the bed and looked at it. No change. He studied the old man's face. It looked more like death. His breathing was still stertorous; his discolored eyelids still veiled his sunken eyes.

What was he? Name him: Five Billion Dollars. He was Money. At this point in his life he served no useful function; he contributed nothing to society, nothing to the race. He had been too busy to marry, too dedicated to father. His occupation: accumulator. He accumulated money and power; he never had enough.

Pearce didn't believe that a man with money was necessarily a villain. But anyone who made a billion dollars or a multiple of it was necessarily a large part predator and the rest magpie. Pearce knew why Jansen was worried. When Weaver died, Money died, Power died. Money and Power are not immune from death, and when they fall they carry empires with them.

Pearce looked down at Weaver, thinking these things, and it didn't matter. He was still a person, still human, still alive. That meant he was worth saving. No other consideration was valid.

Three plastic bags hung from the IV pole—one held a five-percent solution of glucose for intravenous feeding, another held saltwater, the third held dark life fluid itself. Plastic T-joints reduced multiple plastic tubes into one that passed through an IV pump fastened to the pole and plugged into the nearest outlet. The plastic tube from the IV pump entered a catheter inserted into the antecubital vein swollen across the inside of the patient's elbow.

"The blood bank didn't have any packed RBCs in O-neg," the nurse said. "We had to get whole blood."

Pearce nodded and the nurse closed the clamp to the intravenous feeding and released the clamp closing the tube from the saline solution before doing the same for the bag of blood. There was a brief mixture of fluids, and then it was all blood, running slowly through the long, transparent tubing with its own in-line filter into the receptive vein, new blood bringing new life to the old, worn-out mechanism on the hard hospital bed.

New blood for old, Pearce thought. *Money can buy anything.* "A little faster."

The nurse adjusted the pump. Occasionally the pump beeped a warning, and the nurse made further adjustments. In the bag the level of the life fluid dropped more swiftly.

Life. Dripping. Flowing. Making the old new.

The old man took a deep breath. The exhausted laboring of his chest grew easier. Pearce studied the old face, the beaklike nose, the thin, bloodless lips, looking cruel even in their pallor. New life, perhaps. But nothing can reverse the long erosion of the years. Bodies wear out. Nothing can make them new.

Drop by drop the blood flowed from the bag through the tubing into an old man's veins. Someone had given it or sold it. Someone young and healthy, who could make more purple life stuff, saturated with healthy red cells, vigorous white scavengers, platelets, the multiple proteins; someone who could replace it all in less than ninety days.

Pearce thought about Richard Lower, the seventeenth-century English anatomist who performed the first transfusion, and the twentieth-century Viennese immunologist, Karl Landsteiner, who made transfusions safe when he discovered the incompatible blood groups among human beings.

Now here was this old man, who was getting the blood through the efforts of Lower and Landsteiner and some anonymous donor; this old man who needed it, who couldn't make the red cells fast enough any longer, who couldn't keep up with the rate he was losing them internally. What was dripping through the tubes was life, a gift of the young to the old, of the healthy to the sick.

The old man's eyelids flickered.

*　　*　　*

When Pearce made his morning rounds, the old man was watching him with faded blue eyes. Pearce blinked once and automatically picked up the skin-and-bone wrist again. "Feeling better?"

He got his second shock. The old man nodded.

"Fine, Mister Weaver. We'll get a little food down you, and in a little while you'll be back at work."

He glanced at the monitors on the wall and studied them more closely. Gently, a look of surprise on his face, he lowered the old arm down beside the thin, sheeted body.

He sat back thoughtfully beside the bed, ignoring the bustling nurse. Weaver was making a surprising rally for a man in as bad shape as he had been. The pulse was strong and steady. Blood pressure was up. Somehow the transfusion had triggered hidden stores of energy and resistance.

Weaver was fighting back.

Pearce felt a strange and unprofessional sense of elation.

The next day Pearce thought the eyes that watched him were not quite so faded. "Comfortable?" he asked. The old man nodded. His pulse was almost normal for a man of his age; his blood pressure was down; his oxygen level was up.

On the third day Weaver started talking.

The old man's thready voice whispered disjointed and meaningless reminiscences. Pearce nodded as if he understood, and he nodded to himself, understanding the process that was reaching its conclusion. Arteriosclerosis had left its marks: chronic granular kidney, damage to the left ventricle of the heart, malfunction of the brain from a cerebral hemorrhage or two.

On the fourth day Weaver was sitting up in bed talking to the nurse in a cracked, sprightly voice. "Yessirree," he said toothlessly. "That was the day I whopped 'em. Gave it to 'em good, I did. Let 'em have it right between the eyes. Always hated those kids. You must be the doctor," he said suddenly, turning toward Pearce. "I like you. Gonna see that you get a big check. Take care of the people I like. Take care of those I don't like, too." He chuckled; it was an evil, childish sound.

"Don't worry about that," Pearce said gently, picking up Weaver's wrist. "Concentrate on getting well."

The old man nodded happily and stuck a finger in his mouth to rub his gums. "You'll git paid," he mumbled. "Don't *you* worry about that."

Pearce looked down at the wrist he was holding. It had filled out in a way for which he could remember no precedent. "What's the matter with your gums?"

"Itch," Weaver got out around his finger. "Like blazes."

On the fifth day Weaver walked to the toilet.

On the sixth day he took a shower. When Pearce came in, he was sitting on the edge of the bed, dangling his feet. Weaver looked up quickly as Pearce entered, his eyes alert, no longer so sunken. His skin had acquired a subcutaneous glow of health. Like his wrist and arm, his face had filled out. Even his legs looked firmer, almost muscular.

He was taking the well-balanced hospital diet and turning it into flesh and fat and muscle. With his snowy hair he looked like an ad for everybody's grandfather.

The next day his hair began to darken at the roots.

"How old are you, Mister Weaver?" Pearce asked.

"Eighty," Weaver said proudly. "Eighty my last birthday, June 5. Born in Wyoming, boy, in a mountain cabin. Still bears around then. Many's the time I seen 'em, out with my Pa. Wolves, too. Never gave us no trouble, though."

"What color was your hair?"

"Color of a raven's wing. Had the blackest, shiniest hair in the county. Gals used to beg to run their fingers through it." He chuckled reminiscently. "Used to let 'em. A passel of black-headed kids in Washakie County before I left."

He stuck his finger in his mouth and massaged his gums ecstatically.

"Still itch?" Pearce asked.

"Like a Wyoming chigger." He chuckled again. "You know what's wrong with me, boy? In my second childhood. That's what. I'm cutting teeth."

During the second week Weaver was removed from intensive care to a private suite and his mind turned to business, deserting the long-ago past. A telephone was installed beside his bed, and he spent half his waking time in short, clipped conversations about incomprehensible deals and manipulations. The other half was devoted to Jansen, who was so conveniently on hand whenever Weaver called for him that Pearce thought he must have appropriated a hospital room.

Weaver was picking up the scepter of empire.

While his mind roamed restlessly over possessions and ways of keeping and augmenting them, his body repaired itself like a self-servicing machine. His first tooth came through—a canine. After that they appeared rapidly. His hair darkened almost perceptibly; and when a barber came in to trim it, Weaver had him remove all the white, leaving him with a crewcut as dark as he had described. His face filled out, the wrinkles smoothing themselves like a ruffled lake when the wind has gentled. His body became muscular and vigorous; the veins retreated under the skin to become gray traceries. Even his eyes darkened to a fiery blue.

The lab tests were additional proof of what Pearce had begun to suspect. Arteriosclerosis had never thickened those veins; or else, somehow, the damage of plaque buildup had been repaired. The kidneys functioned perfectly. The heart was as strong and efficient a pump as it had ever been. There was no evidence of a cerebral hemorrhage.

By the end of that week Weaver looked like a man of thirty, and his body provided physical evidence of a man in his early, vigorous years of maturity.

"Carl," Weaver was saying as Pearce entered the room, "I want a woman."

"Any particular woman?" Jansen answered, shrugging.

"You don't understand," Weaver said with the impatience he reserved for those immediately dependent on his whims. "I want one to marry. I made a mistake before; I'm not going to repeat it. A man in my position needs an heir. I'm going to have one. Yes, Carl—and you can hide that look of incredulity a little better—at my age!" He swung around quickly toward Pearce. "That's right, isn't it, Doctor?"

Pearce shrugged. "There's no physical reason you can't father a child."

"Get this, Carl. I'm as strong and as smart as I ever was, maybe stronger and smarter. Some people are going to learn that very soon. I've been given a second chance, haven't I, Doctor?"

"You might call it that. What are you going to do with it?"

"I'm going to do better. Better than I did before. This time I'm not going to make any mistakes. And you, Doctor, do you know what you're going to do?"

"I'm going to do what I've always done: my job, as best I can."

Weaver's eyes twisted to Pearce's face. "You think I'm just talking. Don't make that mistake. You're going to find out why."

"Why?"

"Why I've recovered like I have. Don't try to kid me. You've never seen anything like it. I'm not eighty years old anymore. My body isn't. My mind isn't. Why?"

"What's your guess?"

"I never guess. I know. I get the facts from those who have them, and then I decide. That's what I want from you—the facts. I've been rejuvenated."

"You've been talking to Doctor Easter."

"Of course. He's my personal physician. That's where I start."

"But you never got that language from him. He'd never commit himself to a word like *rejuvenation.*"

Weaver glowered at Pearce from under dark eyebrows. "What was done to me?"

"What does it matter? If you've been 'rejuvenated,' that should be enough for any man."

"When Mister Weaver asks a question," Jansen interjected icily, "Mister Weaver wants an answer."

Weaver brushed him aside. "Doctor Pearce doesn't frighten. But Doctor Pearce is a reasonable man. He believes in facts. He lives by logic, like me. Understand me, Doctor! I may be thirty now, but I will be eighty again. Before then I want to know how to be thirty once more."

"Ah." Pearce sighed. "You're not talking about rejuvenation now. You're talking about immortality."

"Why not?"

"It's not for humans. The body wears out. Three-score years and ten. That—roughly—is what we're allotted. After that we start falling apart."

"I've had mine and a bit more. Now I'm starting over at thirty. I've got forty or fifty to go. After that, what? Forty or fifty more?"

"We all die," Pearce said. "Nothing can stop that. Not one man born has not come to the grave at last. There's a disease we contract at birth from which none of us recovers; it's invariably fatal. Death."

"*Suppose somebody develops a resistance to it?*"

"Don't take what I said literally. I didn't mean that death was a specific disease," Pearce said. "We die in many ways: accident, infection—" *And senescence,* Pearce thought. *For all we know, that's a disease. It could be a disease.* Etiology: *Virus, unisolated, unsuspected, invades at birth or shortly thereafter—or maybe transmitted at conception.*

Incidence: *Total.*

Symptoms: *Slow degeneration of the physical entity, appearing shortly after maturity, increasing debility, failure of the circulatory system through arteriosclerosis and heart damage, decline in the immunity system, malfunction of sense and organs, loss of cellular regenerative ability, susceptibility to secondary invasions. . . .*

Prognosis: *100% fatal.*

"Everything dies," Pearce went on without a pause. "Trees, planets, suns . . . it's natural, inevitable. . . ." *But it isn't. Natural death is a relatively new thing. It appeared only when life became multicellular and complicated. Maybe it was the price for complexity, for the ability to think.*

Protozoa don't die. Metazoa—sponges, flatworms, coelenterates—don't die. Certain fish don't die except through accident. "Voles are animals that never stop growing and never grow old." Where did I read that? And even the tissues of the higher vertebrates are immortal under the right conditions.

Carrel and Ebeling proved that. Give the cell enough of the right food, and it will never die. Cells from every part of the body have been kept alive indefinitely in vitro. *Differen-*

tiation and specialization—that meant that any individual cell didn't find the perfect conditions. Besides staying alive, it had duties to perform for the whole. A plausible explanation, but was it true? Wasn't it just as plausible that the cell died because the circulatory system broke down?

Let the circulatory system remain sound, regenerative, and efficient, and the rest of the body might well remain immortal.

"When we say something's natural, it means we've given up trying to understand it," Weaver said. "You gave me a transfusion. Immunities can be transferred with the blood, Easter told me. Who donated that pint of blood?"

Pearce sighed. "Donor records are confidential."

Weaver snorted derisively.

The blood bank was in the basement. Pearce led the way down busy, noisy corridors, cluttered with patients in wheelchairs waiting for X rays and other tests, and others on gurneys being maneuvered to labs or back to their rooms.

"If you're smart," Jansen told him on the stairs, "you'll cooperate with Mister Weaver. Do what he asks you. Tell him what he wants to know. You'll get taken care of. If not—" Jansen smiled unpleasantly.

Pearce laughed. "What can Weaver do to me?"

"Don't find out," Jansen advised.

The blood bank was clean and efficient and, for the moment, empty except for the phlebotomist. When Jansen asked for the information about Weaver's transfusion, she keyed in Weaver's name on her computer.

"Weaver?" she said. "Here it is. On the fourth." Her finger traveled across the screen. "O-neg."

Pearce said to the technician, "Have you had any donations from Mister Weaver's office?"

"None that have identified themselves."

"You're just making difficulties," Jansen said. "There's no such rule about replacing blood, but don't worry: You'll get your blood tomorrow. Who was the donor?"

"That information cannot be released," the technician said.

"We can get a court order here within two hours," Jansen replied.

"Go ahead," Pearce said. "I'll take responsibility."

The technician pressed another key and the array of data shifted on the computer screen. "Marshall Cartwright," she said. "O-neg. Kline: Okay. Now I remember. That was the day after our television appeal. We ran low on O-neg, and our usual donor list was exhausted. The response was limited."

"Remember him?" asked Jansen.

She frowned and turned her head away to stare out the window. "That was the third. We have more than twenty donors a day. And that was over a week ago."

"Think!" Jansen demanded.

"I *am* thinking," she snapped. "What do you want to know?"

"What he looked like. What he said. His address."

"Was there something wrong with the blood?"

Pearce grinned suddenly. "'Contrariwise,' said Tweedle-dee."

A brief smile slipped across the technician's face. "We don't get many complaints like that. I can give you his address easy enough." She punched some keys on her computer. "Funny. He sold his blood once, but he didn't want to do it again.

"Cartwright. Marshall Cartwright. Abbot Hotel. No phone listed."

"Abbot," Jansen said thoughtfully. "Sounds like a flop joint. Does that bring anything back?" he asked the technician insistently. "He didn't want his name on the donor's list."

Slowly, regretfully, she shook her head. "What's all this about anyway? Weaver? Isn't that the rich old guy up in 305 who made such a miraculous recovery?"

"Right," Jansen said, brushing the question away. "We'll want copies of the computer entries."

"You can have the computer entries as soon as the technician can have them run off," Pearce cut in.

"In the next hour," Jansen said.

"In the next hour," Pearce agreed.

"That's all, then," Jansen said. "If you remember anything, get in touch with Mister Weaver or me, Carl Jansen. There'll be something in it for you."

Something in it, something in it, Pearce thought. *The slogan of a class.* "What's in it for the human race? Never mind. You got what you came for."

"I always do," Jansen said brutally. "Mister Weaver and I—we always get what we come for. Remember that!"

Pearce remembered while the young-old man named Leroy Weaver grew a handsome set of teeth, as white as his hair was black, and directed the course of his commercial empire from the hospital room, chafed at Pearce's delay in giving him the answer to his question, at the continual demands for blood samples, at his own enforced idleness, and slyly pinched the nurses during the day. Pearce did not inquire into what happened at night.

Before the week was over, Weaver had discharged himself from the hospital and Pearce had located a private detective.

The black paint on the frosted glass of the door read:

JASON LOCKE
Private Investigations

But Locke wasn't Pearce's preconception of a private eye. He wasn't tough—not on the outside. The hardness was inside, and he didn't let it show.

Locke was middle-aged, graying, his face firm and tanned, a big man dressed in a well-draped tropical suit in light cocoa; he looked like a successful executive. But business wasn't that good: The office was shabby, the furniture was little better, and there was no secretary or receptionist.

He was just the man Pearce wanted.

He listened to Pearce and watched him with dark, steady eyes.

"I want you to find a man," Pearce said. "Marshall Cartwright. Last address: Abbot Hotel."

"Why?"

"What difference does it make?"

"I have a license to keep—and a desire to keep out of jail."

"There's nothing illegal about it," Pearce said, "but there might be danger. I won't lie to you; it's a medical problem I can't explain. It's important to me that you find Cartwright. It's important to him—it might mean his life. It might even be important to the world. The danger lies in the fact that other people are looking for him; if they spot you they might get rough. I want you to find Cartwright before they do."

"Who is 'they'?"

Pearce shrugged. "Pinkerton, Burns, International—I don't know. One of the big firms, probably. Maybe a private outfit."

"Is that why you don't go to them?"

"One reason. I won't conceal anything, though. The man hiring them is Leroy Weaver."

Locke looked interested. "I heard the old boy was back on the prowl. Have you got any pictures, descriptions, anything to help me spot this man Cartwright?"

Pearce looked down at his hands. "Nothing except the name. He's a young man. He sold a pint of blood on the third. He refused to have his name added to our professional donor's file. He gave his address then as the Abbot."

"I know it," Locke said. "A fly trap on Ninth. That means he's left town, I'd say."

"Why do you say that?"

"That's why he sold the blood. To get out of town. He wasn't interested in selling it again; he wasn't going to be around. And anyone who would stay at a place like the Abbot wouldn't toss away a chance at some regular, effortless money."

"That's what I figured," Pearce said. "Will you take the job?"

Locke swung around in his swivel chair and stared out the window across the light standards, transformers, and overhead power lines of Twelfth Street. It was nothing to look at, but he seemed to draw a decision from it. "Two hundred fifty dollars a day and expenses," he said, swinging back. "Fifty more if I have to go out of town."

That was the afternoon Pearce discovered he was being followed.

He walked along the warm autumn streets, and the careless crowds, the hurrying, anonymous shoppers, passed on either side without a glance and came behind, and conviction walked with him. He moved through the air-conditioned stores, quickly or dawdling over a display of deodorants at a counter, casually glancing behind in a way calculated to conceal his unease, seeing nothing but sure that someone was watching.

The symptoms were familiar. They were those of paranoia, of people in that wistful, tormented period of middle age when potential has turned to regret and one looks for someone or something to blame besides oneself. Pearce had never expected to share them: the sensitivity in the back of the neck and between the shoulder blades that made him want to shrug it away, the leg-tightening desire to hurry, to run, to dodge into a doorway, into an elevator. . . .

Pearce nodded to himself and lingered. When he went to his car, he went slowly, talked to the parking lot attendant for a moment before he drove away, and drove straight home.

He never did identify the man or men who shadowed him, then or later. The feeling lasted for weeks, so that when it finally vanished he felt strangely naked and alone.

When he got to his apartment, the phone was ringing. That was not surprising. A doctor's phone rings a dozen times as often as that of ordinary people.

Dr. Easter was the caller. The essence of what he wanted to say was that Pearce should not be foolish; Pearce should cooperate with Mr. Weaver.

"Of course I'm cooperating," Pearce said. "I cooperate with all my patients."

"That isn't what I meant," Dr. Easter said. "Work with him, not against him. You'll find it's worth your while."

"It's worth my while to practice medicine the best way I can," Pearce said evenly. "Beyond that no one has a call on me, and no one ever will."

"Very fine sentiments," Dr. Easter agreed pleasantly. "The question is: Will Mister Weaver think you are practicing medicine properly? That's something to consider."

Pearce lowered the phone gently into the cradle, thinking about the practice of medicine, about being a doctor—and he knew he could never be happy at anything else. He turned over in his mind the subtle threat Easter had made; it could be done. The specter of malpractice was never completely absent, and a power alliance of money and respectability could come close to lifting a license, or at least of making practice too expensive. Malpractice insurance premiums were already steep—a number of his colleagues, particularly in obstetrics, had left their professions as a result, or practiced defensive medicine in a way that sent hospitalization and Medicare costs soaring—and a lawsuit, won or lost, might send his rates beyond his income.

He considered Easter, and he knew that it was better to risk the title than to give away the reality.

The next week was a time of wondering and waiting, and of keeping busy—a problem a doctor seldom faces. It was a time of uneventful routine.

Then everything happened at once.

As he walked from his car toward the front door of the apartment house, a hand reached out of the shadows beside an ornamental evergreen and pulled him into the darkness.

Before he could say anything or struggle, a hand was clamped tight over his mouth, and a voice whispered in his ear, "Quiet now! This is Locke. The private eye, remember?"

Pearce nodded as well as he could. Slowly the hand relaxed. As his eyes adjusted to the darkness, Pearce made out Locke's features. His face was heavily, darkly bearded, and something had happened to his nose. Locke had been in a brawl; the nose was broken, and the face was cut and bruised.

"Never mind me," Locke said huskily. "You should see the other guys."

As Pearce drew back a little, he could see that Locke

was dressed in old clothes looking like hand-me-downs from the Salvation Army. "Sorry I got you into it," he said.

"Part of the job. Listen. I haven't got long, and I want to give you my report."

"It can wait. Come on up. Let me take a look at that face. You can send me a written re—"

"Nothing doing," Locke said heavily. "I'm not signing my name to anything. Too dangerous. From now on I'm going to keep my nose clean. I did all right for a few days. Then they caught up with me. Well, they're sorry, too. You wanta hear it?"

Pearce nodded.

For a while Locke had thought he might get somewhere. He had registered at the Abbot, got friendly with the room clerk, and finally asked about his friend, Cartwright, who had flopped there a couple of weeks earlier. The clerk was willing enough to talk. Trouble was, he didn't know much, and what little he knew he wouldn't have told to a stranger. Guests at the Abbot were likely to be persecuted by police and collection agents, and the clerk had suspicions that every questioner was from the health department.

Cartwright had paid his bill and left suddenly, no forwarding address given. They hadn't heard from him since, but people had been asking about him. "In trouble, eh?" the clerk asked wisely. Locke nodded gravely.

The clerk leaned closer. "I had a hunch, though, that Cartwright was heading for Des Moines. Something he said—don't remember what now."

Locke took off for Des Moines with a sample of

Cartwright's handwriting from the Abbot register. He canvassed the Des Moines hotels, rooming houses, motels. Finally, at a first-class hotel, he noticed the name "Marshall Carter."

Cartwright had left the Abbot on the ninth. Carter had checked into the Des Moines hotel on the tenth. The handwritings seemed similar.

Locke caught up with Carter in St. Louis. He turned out to be a middle-aged salesman of photographic equipment who hadn't been near Kansas City in a year.

End of the trail.

"Can anyone else find him?" Pearce asked.

"Not if he doesn't want to be found," Locke said. "A nationwide search—an advertising campaign—they'd help. But if he's changed his name and doesn't go signing his new one to a lot of things that might fall into an agency's hands, nobody is going to find him. That's what you wanted, wasn't it?"

Pearce looked at him steadily, not saying anything.

"He's got no record," Locke went on. "That helps. Got a name check on him from the bigger police departments and the FBI. No go. No record, no fingerprints. Not under that name."

"How'd you get hurt?" Pearce asked, after a moment.

"They were waiting for me outside my office when I got back. Two of 'em. Good, too. But not good enough. 'Lay off!' they said. Okay. I'm not stupid. I'm laying off, but I wanted to finish the job first."

Pearce nodded slowly. "I'm satisfied. Send me a bill."

"Bill, nothing!" Locke growled. "Five thousand is the

price. Put the cash in an envelope, take it out a little at a time to avoid notice, and mail it to my office—no checks. I should charge you more for using me as a stakeout, but maybe you had your reasons. Watch your step, Doc!"

He was gone then, slipping away through the shadows so quickly and silently that Pearce started to speak before he realized that the detective was not beside him. Pearce stared after him for a long, speculative moment before he turned and opened the front door.

Going up in the elevator, he was thoughtful. In front of his apartment door, he fumbled the key out absently and inserted it in the lock. When the key wouldn't turn, he took it out to check on it. It took a moment for the realization to sink in that the door was already unlocked. Pearce turned the knob and gave the door a little push. It swung inward quietly. The light from the hall streamed over his shoulder, but it only lapped a little way into the dark room. He peered into it for a moment, hunching his shoulders as if that might help.

"Come in, Doctor Pearce," someone said softly.

The lights went on.

Pearce blinked once. "Good evening, Mister Weaver. And you, Jansen. How are you?"

"Fine, Doctor," Weaver said. "Just fine."

He didn't look fine, Pearce thought. He looked older, haggard, tired. Was he worried? Weaver was sitting in Pearce's favorite chair, a dark-green leather armchair beside the fireplace. Jansen was standing beside the wall switch. "You've made yourself right at home, I see."

Weaver chuckled. "We told the manager we were

friends of yours, and of course he didn't doubt us. Solid citizens like us, we don't lie. But then, we are friends, aren't we?"

Pearce looked at Weaver and then at Jansen. "I wonder. Do you have any friends—or only hirelings?" He turned his gaze back to Weaver. "You don't look well. I'd like you to come back to the hospital for a checkup—"

"I'm feeling fine, I said." Weaver's voice lifted a little before it dropped back to a conversational tone. "We wanted to have a little talk—about cooperation."

Pearce looked at Jansen. "Funny—I don't feel very talkative. I've had a hard day."

Weaver's eyes didn't leave Pearce's face. "Get out, Carl," he said calmly.

"But, Mister Weaver—" Jansen began, his gray eyes tightening.

"Get out, Carl," Weaver repeated. "Wait for me in the car."

After Jansen was gone, Pearce sank down in the armchair facing Weaver. He let his gaze drift around the room, lingering on the polished darkness of the music center and the slightly lighter wood of the desk in the corner. "Did you find anything?" he asked.

"Not what we were looking for," Weaver replied.

"What was that?"

"Cartwright's location."

"What makes you think I'd know anything about that?"

Weaver clasped his hands lightly in his lap. "Can't we work together?"

"Certainly. What would you like to know—about your health?"

"What did you do with those samples of blood you took from me? You must have taken back that pint I got."

"Almost. Part of it we separated. Got the plasma. Separated the gamma globulin from it with zinc. Used it on various animals."

"And what did you find out?"

"The immunity is in the gamma globulin. It would be, of course. That's the immunity factor. You should see my old rat. As frisky as the youngest rat in the lab."

"So it's part of me, too?" Weaver asked.

Pearce shook his head slowly. "That's just the original globulins diluted in your blood."

"Then to live forever I would have to have periodic transfusions?"

"If it's possible to live forever," Pearce said, shrugging.

"It is. You know that. There's at least one person who's going to live forever—Cartwright. Unless something happens to him. That would be a tragedy, wouldn't it? In spite of all precautions, accidents happen. People get murdered. Can you imagine some careless kid spilling that golden blood into a filthy gutter? Some jealous woman putting a knife in that priceless body?"

"What do you want, Weaver?" Pearce asked evenly. "You've got your reprieve from death. What more can you ask?"

"Another. And another. Without end. Why should some nobody get it by accident? What good will it do him? Or the world? He needs to be protected—and used.

Properly handled, he could be worth—well, whatever men will pay for life. I'd pay a million a year—more if I had to. Other men would pay the same. We'd save the best men in the world, those who have demonstrated their ability by becoming wealthy. Oh, yes. Scientists, too—we'd select some of those. People who haven't gone into business—leaders, statesmen . . ."

"What about Cartwright?"

"What about him?" Weaver blinked as if recalled from a lovely dream. "Do you think anyone who ever lived would have a better life, would be better protected, more pampered? Why, he wouldn't have to ask for a thing! No one would dare say no to him for fear he might kill himself. He'd be the hen that lays the golden eggs."

"He'd have everything but freedom."

"A much overrated commodity."

"The one immortal man in the world."

"That's just it," Weaver said, leaning forward. "Instead of only one, there would be many."

Pearce shook his head from side to side as if he had not heard. "A chance meeting of genes—a slight alteration by cosmic ray or something even more subtle and accidental—and immortality is created. Some immunity to death—some means of keeping the circulatory system young, resistant, rejuvenated. 'Man is as old as his arteries,' Cazali said. Take care of your arteries, and they will keep your cells immortal."

"Tell me, man! Tell me where Cartwright is before all that is lost forever." Weaver leaned farther forward, as if he could transmit his urgency.

"A man who knows he's got a thousand years to live is going to be pretty darned careful," Pearce said.

"That's just it," Weaver said, his eyes narrowing. "He doesn't know. If he'd known, he'd never have sold his blood." His face changed subtly. "Or does he know—now?"

"What do you mean?"

"Didn't you tell him?"

"I don't know what you're talking about."

"Don't you? Don't you remember going to the Abbot Hotel on the evening of the ninth, of asking for Cartwright, of talking to him? You should. The clerk identified your picture. And that night Cartwright left."

Pearce remembered the Abbot Hotel all right, the narrow, dark lobby, grimy, infested with flies and roaches. He had thought of cholera and bubonic plague as he crossed it. He remembered Cartwright, too—that fabulous creature, looking seedy and quite ordinary, who had listened, though, and believed and taken the money and gone . . .

"I don't believe it," Pearce said.

"I should have known right away," Weaver said, as if to himself. "You're smart. You would have picked up on it right off, maybe as soon as I woke up, and you would have realized what it meant."

"Presuming I did. If I did all that you say, do you think it would have been easy for me? To you he's money. What do you think he would have been to me? That fantastic laboratory, walking around! What wouldn't I have given to study him! To find out how his body worked, to try to synthesize the substance. You have your drives, Weaver, but I have mine."

"Why not combine them, Pearce?"

"They wouldn't mix."

"Don't get so holy, Pearce. Life isn't holy."

"Life is what we make it," Pearce said softly. "I won't have a hand in what you're planning."

Weaver got up quickly from his chair and took a step toward Pearce. "Some of you professional men get delusions of ethics," he said in a kind of muted snarl. "Not many. A few. There's nothing sacred about what you do. You're just craftsmen, mechanics—you do a job—you get paid for it. There's no reason to get religious about it."

"Don't be absurd, Weaver. If you don't feel religious about what you do, you shouldn't be doing it. You feel religious about making money. That's what's sacred to you. Well, life is sacred to me. That's what I deal in, all day long, every day. Death is an old enemy. I'll fight him until the end."

Pearce propelled himself out of his chair. He stood close to Weaver, staring fiercely into the man's eyes. "Understand this, Weaver. What you're planning is impossible. What if we all could be rejuvenated? Do you have the slightest idea what would happen? Have you considered what it might do to civilization?

"No, I can see you haven't. Well, it would bring your society tumbling down around your pillars of gold. Civilization would shake itself to pieces like an unbalanced flywheel. Our culture is constructed on the assumption that we spend two decades growing and learning, a few more producing wealth and progeny, and a final decade or two decaying before we die.

"Look back! See what research and medicine have done in the past century. They've added a few years—just a few—to the average lifespan, and our society is groaning at the readjustment. Think what forty years more would do! Think what would happen if we never died!

"There's only one way something like this can be absorbed into the race—gradually, so that society can adjust, unknowing, to this new thing inside it. All Cartwright's children will inherit the mutation. They must. It must be dominant. And they will survive, because this has the greatest survival factor ever created."

"Where is he?" Weaver asked.

"It won't work, Weaver," Pearce said, his voice rising. "I'll tell you why it won't work. Because you would kill him. You think you wouldn't, but you'd kill him as certainly as you're a member of the human race. You'd bleed him to death, or you'd kill him just because you couldn't stand having something immortal around. You or some other warped specimen of humanity. You'd kill him, or he'd get killed in the riots of those who were denied life. One way or another he'd be tossed to the wolves of death. What people can't have they destroy."

"Where is he?" Weaver repeated.

"It won't work for a final reason." Pearce's voice dropped as if it had found a note of pity. "But I won't tell you that. I'll let you find out for yourself."

"Where is he?" Weaver insisted softly.

"I don't know. You won't believe that. But I don't know. I didn't want to know. I'll confess to this much: I told him the truth about himself, and I gave him some money, and I told him to leave town, to change his name, hide—anything, but not be found; to be fertile, to populate the earth. . . ."

"I don't believe you. You've got him hidden away for yourself. You wouldn't give him a thousand dollars for nothing."

"You know the amount?" Pearce asked.

Weaver's lip curled. "I know every deposit you've made in the last five years, and every withdrawal. You're small, Pearce, and you're cheap, and I'm going to break you."

Pearce smiled, unworried. "No, you're not. You don't dare use violence, because I just might know where Cartwright is hiding. Then you'd lose everything. And you won't try anything else because if you do I'll release the article I've written about Cartwright—I'll send you a copy— and then the fat would really be in the fire. If everybody knew about Cartwright, you wouldn't have a chance to control it, even if you could find him. You're big and powerful, but there are people in this world and groups and nations that could swallow you and never notice."

Weaver rose from the chair and said, "You wouldn't do that. Then there would be thousands of people looking for Cartwright, not just one." He turned at the door and said, calmly, "But you're right—I couldn't take the chance. I'll be seeing you again."

"That's right," Pearce agreed and thought, *I've been no help to you, because you won't ever believe that I haven't got a string tied to Cartwright.*

But you're not the one I pity.

*   *   *

Two days after that meeting came the news of Weaver's marriage with a twenty-five-year-old girl from the country club district, a Patricia Warren. It was the weekend sensation—wealth and beauty, age and youth.

Pearce studied the girl's picture in the Sunday paper and told himself that surely she had got what she wanted. And Weaver—Pearce knew him well enough to know that he had got what he wanted. Weaver's heir would already be assured. Otherwise, Weaver would never risk himself and his empire in a woman's hands. Tests were reliable even as early as this.

The fourth week since the transfusion passed uneventfully, and the fifth week was only distinguished by a summons from Jansen, which Pearce ignored. The beginning of the sixth week brought a frantic call from Dr. Easter. Pearce refused to go to Weaver's newly purchased mansion.

A screaming ambulance brought Weaver to the hospital, clearing the streets ahead of it with its siren and its flashing red light, dodging through the traffic with its precious cargo: money in the flesh.

Pearce stood beside the hard hospital bed, checking the pulse in the bony wrist, and stared down at the emaciated body. It made no impression in the bed. In the silence the harsh unevenness of the old man's breathing was loud. The only movement was the spasmodic rise and fall of the sheet that covered the old body.

He was living—barely. He had used up his allotted three-score years and ten and a bit more. It wasn't merely that he was dying. Everyone is. With him it was imminent. The pulse was feeble. The gift of youth had been taken away. Within the space of a few days Weaver had been drained of color, drained of fifty years of life.

He was an old man, dying. His face was yellowish over grayish blue, the color of death. It was bony, the wrinkled skin pulled back like a mask for the skull. Once he might have been handsome. Now his eyes were sunken, the closed eyelids dark over them; his lips were a dark line, and his nose was a thin, arching beak.

This time, Pearce thought distantly, there would be no reprieve.

"I don't understand," Dr. Easter muttered. "I thought he'd been given another fifty years—"

"That was his conclusion," Pearce said. "It was more like forty days. Thirty to forty days—that's how long the gamma globulin remains in the bloodstream. It was only a passive immunity. The only person with any lasting immunity to death is Cartwright, and the only ones he can give it to are his children."

Easter looked around to see if the nurse was listening and whispered. "Couldn't we handle this better? Chance needs a little help sometimes. With semen banks and artificial insemination we could change the makeup of the human race in a couple of generations—"

"If we weren't all wiped out first," Pearce said and turned away.

He waited, his eyes closed, listening to the harshness of Weaver's breathing, thinking of the tragedy of life and death—the being born and the dying, entwined, all one, and here was Weaver who had run out of life, and there was his child who would not be born for months yet. It was a continuity, a balance—a life for life, and it had kept humanity stable for millions of years.

And yet—immortality? What might it mean?

He thought of Cartwright, the immortal, the hunted man. While men remembered, they would never let him rest, and if he got tired of hiding and running, he was doomed. The search would go on and on—crippled a little, fortunately, now that Weaver had dropped away— and Cartwright, with his burden, would never be able to live like other men.

He thought of Cartwright, trying to adjust to immortality in the midst of death, and he thought that immortality—the greatest gift, surely, that a man could receive—demanded payment in kind, like everything else. For immortality, you must surrender the right to live.

You're the one I pity, Cartwright.

"Transfusion, Doctor Pearce?" the nurse repeated.

"Yes," he said. "Might as well." He looked down at Weaver once more. "Type and crossmatch two units of blood and administer one unit when available. We know his type already—O negative."

PART II
DONOR

The search had been organized to last a hundred years. Half of that period was already gone, and the search was no nearer success than when it had started. Only the ultimate desperation can keep hope alive without periodic transfusions of results.

The National Research Institute was unique. It had no customers and no product. Its annual statement was printed all in red. And yet the tight-lipped donors made their contributions regularly and without complaint. Whenever one of them died, his estate was inherited by the Institute.

The purpose of the Institute was learning, but not education. It had an omnivorous appetite for information of all kinds, particularly old information recorded on paper or the newer kind coded into on or off electronic markers: vital statistics, newspaper accounts, hospital records, field reports. . . . A Potomac of data flowed through the gray, bombproof, block-square building near Washington, D.C., reduced to innocuous signals from which computers would make esoteric comparisons or draw undecipherable conclusions.

Possibly only one man in the Institute knew its function. The thousands of other employees, many of whom were not listed on the payroll, performed their duties blindly, accepted their generous salaries, and asked no questions. If they wished to keep their jobs, that is.

The Institute survived on hope and thrived on death.

The main computer room was confusion that seemed to escape growing into chaos only by accident. Mail was opened, entered, stapled, and passed along assembly lines. Old newspapers were scanned by machines, key words identified by computers, and then checked, line by line, by human readers. Computer disks of all kinds were inserted into waiting receptacles and their information, like DNA, transformed into identical copies with new meaning. Copy boys raced along the aisles on roller skates. Clerks blue-penciled and clipped and commented to the computers. Operators punched electrons out of blank atoms. . . .

Edwin Sibert threaded his way between the desks with a taut feeling of excitement, as if he were on his way to a rendezvous with the world's most desirable woman. The copy room was old to him; he had spent six months there without learning anything. He didn't glance at it as he climbed the steps behind the office set over the copy room like a guardroom over a prison yard.

The outer office was lined with locked filing cabinets; their contents were meaningless. A colorless, elderly filing clerk puttered among the papers in one of them.

"Hello, Sanders," Sibert said carelessly.

The desk by the door leading into the inner office was equipped with a switchboard, a scrambler, an automatic recorder, and a lovely dark-haired secretary. Her eyes had widened as Sibert entered.

"Hello, Liz," he said, his voice as effective as his appearance. "Locke in?" He moved past her to the door without waiting for an answer.

"You can't, Ed—" she began, springing to her feet, "Mister Locke will—"

"—be very angry if he doesn't get my news immediately," Sibert finished. "I've found the key, Liz. Get it—Locke, key? A poor thing but mine own." He drew skillful fingers along the smooth curve of her throat and jaw.

She caught his hand, held it to her cheek for a moment. "Oh, Ed!" she said brokenly. "I'm—"

"Be good, Liz," he said cheerfully, his blue eyes smiling gently in his expressive face. "Maybe—a little later—who knows?"

But there would be no "later"—they both knew that. He had wasted a month on her before he was sure she knew nothing. He pulled his hand free and opened the door and stepped into the inner office.

Beyond Locke was an entire wall of one-way glass. From here the director of the Institute could watch the copy room or, if he wished, switch to indirect observation of the other rooms and offices of the windowless building. Locke was talking to someone on his private phone.

"Patience is our greatest asset," he said. "After all, Ponce de León . . ."

Sibert turned his head quickly, but he caught only a glimpse of a face that great age had unsexed. It was wrinkled and gray and dead except for the eyes that still burned with life and desire.

"Interruption," Locke said smoothly. "Call you back." The screen set into the wall opposite him went dark as he touched the arm of his executive chair. "Sibert," he said, "you're fired."

Locke was no youngster himself, Sibert thought. He was pushing ninety, surely, though he looked fit and vigorous. Medical care had kept his body healthy; geriatrics and hormone injections had kept his shoulders broad, his muscles firm and unwithered. Perhaps surgery had replaced his old heart and several other organs, but they could not rejuvenate his aging arteries and his dying cells.

"Right," Sibert said briskly, another man than the one who had spoken to the secretary in the outer office. "Then you won't be interested in my information—"

"Maybe I was hasty," Locke said. His lips framed the unfamiliar words awkwardly. "If your information is important, I might reconsider."

"And a bonus, too?" Sibert prompted.

"Maybe," Locke growled, his eyes small. "Now, what's so earth-shattering that it can't come through channels?"

Sibert studied Locke's face. It had not spent all its days in an office. There were scars around the eyes and a long one down one cheek almost to the point of the jaw; the nose had been broken at least once. Locke was an old bear. He must be careful, Sibert thought, not to tease him too much.

"I think I've found one of Marshall Cartwright's children."

Locke's face writhed for a moment before he got it

back under control. "Where? What name is he using? What's he—"

"Slow down," Sibert said calmly. He deposited his lean young body in the upholstered chair beside the desk and leisurely lit a cigarette. "I've been working in the dark for five years. Before I give anything away, I want to know what I've got."

"You're well paid," Locke said coldly. "If this pans out, you'll never have to worry about money. But don't try to cut yourself into the game, Sibert. It's too big for you."

"That's what I keep thinking about," Sibert mused. "A few hundred thousand bucks—what's that to an organization that spends at least one hundred million a year? Fifty years of that is five billion dollars. Just to find somebody's kids."

"We can get the information out of you."

"Not in time. And time is what you don't have. I left a letter. If I don't get back soon, the letter gets delivered. And Cartwright's kid is warned that he is being hunted. . . ."

"Let me check that statement with truth serum."

"No. Not because it isn't true. You might ask other questions. And it would take too long. That's why I couldn't wait for an appointment. Try to squeeze the information out if you want to." He lifted his right hand out of his jacket pocket; a tiny, ten-shot plastic automatic was in it. "But it might take too long. And you might lose everything just when everything is within your grasp. You might die. Or I might die."

Locke sighed heavily and let his heavy shoulders relax. "What do you want to know?"

"What's so important about Cartwright's kids?"

"Barring accidents, they'll live forever."

The middle-aged man walked slowly through the station, his face preoccupied, his hands thrust deep in his jacket pockets. He retrieved an overnight bag from a locker and took it to the nearest washroom, where he rented a booth. He never came out of the washroom. A reservation on the Talgo express to Toronto was never picked up.

A young man with a floppy hat and a conquistador beard caught a taxi outside the station and left it in the middle of a traffic jam in the business section, walked quickly between the immovable cars until he reached the adjacent street, where he caught a second taxi going in the opposite direction. At the airport, he picked up a no-show reservation on the first outgoing flight.

At Detroit he caught a jet to St. Louis. There he changed to a slow, two-dozen-seat transport to Wichita. There he hired an old, two-seater jet, filed a flight plan, and proceeded to ignore it. Two hours later he set down at Kansas City's nearly deserted International Airport and caught a decrepit bus down the old interstate and across the crumbling New Hannibal Bridge to the downtown shopping district.

The section was decaying. Business had followed the middle class into the suburbs. Buildings and shops had not been repaired for a decade. Only a few people were on the street, but the young man with the beard did the best he could, ducking through arcades, waiting in doorways, and finally edging into a department-store elevator just before the doors closed. The car creaked upward. When it reached the fifth floor, only the young man was left. The young man walked swiftly through the floor to the men's room.

Two minutes later he flushed an ugly, black mass of hair down the toilet, buried a hat under a heap of paper towels, and grinned at his reflection in the mirror. "Greetings, Mister Sibert," he said gaily. "What was it Locke said to you?"

"You were an actor, weren't you, Sibert?"

"Once. Not a very good one, I'm afraid."

"What made you quit?"

"It couldn't give me what I want."

"What's that?"

"If your psychologists didn't find out, I won't tell them. That would make your job too easy."

"Your mistake, Sibert. A live actor—even a poor one—is better than a dead adventurer. That's what you'll be if you try to set up something on your own. We've got you, Sibert—trapped in plastic, like that solidograph, and in measurements and film and ink. Wherever you try to hide, we'll dig you out. . . ."

"If you can find me, Locke," Sibert said to the mirror. "And you've lost me for the moment."

He raced down the firestairs to the Main Street entrance, went through the used-clothing stores, up the escalators, down the stairs, and out a side entrance onto Twelfth Street. As an eastbound bus elevated itself on its pads and pulled away from the stop, Sibert slid between the closing doors. A mile past City Hall he got off, ran through two alleys, and swung into a cruising taxi.

"Head west. I'll tell you when to stop," he said, a bit breathlessly.

The cabby gave him a quick, sharp glance in the rearview screen, swung the creaky '44 Mercedes around on a forward wheel, and started west. In that glance Sibert compared the man's features with the picture in the rear seat's holographic projection. For whatever assurance it brought, they matched.

When he dismissed the taxi, he waited until it rolled out of sight before he turned north. The street was deserted; the sky was clear. He walked the five blocks briskly, feeling a sick excitement grow as the apartment buildings of Quality Towers grew tall in front of him. He couldn't see the Y where the Kansas River flowed into the Missouri. Smoke from the industrialized Bottoms veiled the valley.

In the early days of the city, the bluff of Quality Hill had been a neighborhood of fine homes, but it had made the cycle of birth and death twice. As the city had grown out, the homes here had degenerated into slums. They had been razed to provide space for Quality Towers, but fifty years of neglect and declining revenues and irresponsible tenants had done their work. It was time to begin again, but there would be no new beginning. A wave of smog drifted up over the bluff and sent Sibert into a fit of coughing.

Money was leaving the city. Those who could afford it were seeking a cleaner, healthier air and the better life in the suburbs, leaving the city to those who could not escape. They could die together.

Sibert turned in the doorway and looked back the way he had come. There was no one behind him, no one visible for blocks. His eyes lifted to the hill rising beyond the trafficway. The only new construction in all the city was there; it had been that way for years.

Hospital Hill was becoming a great complex. In the midst of the general decay, it was shiny and new. It reached out and out to engulf the gray slums and convert them into fine, bright magnesium-and-glass walls, markets of health and life.

It would never stop until all the city was hospital. Life was all. Without it, everything was meaningless. The people would never stint medicine and the hospitals, no matter what else was lost. And yet, in spite of the money contributed and the great advances of the science of health and life in the last century, it was becoming increasingly more expensive to stay as healthy as a man thought he ought to be.

Perhaps some day it would take more than a man could earn. That was why men wanted Cartwright's children. That—and the unquenchable thirst for life, the unbearable fear of death—was why men hunted those fabulous creatures.

Men are like children, Sibert thought, *afraid of the long dark. All of us.*

He shivered and pushed quickly through the doorway.

The elevator was out of order as usual. Sibert climbed the stairs quickly. He stopped at the fifth floor for breath, thankful that he had to go no higher. Stair-climbing was dangerous, heart-straining work, even for a young man.

But what made his heart turn in his chest was the sight of the woman standing in front of a nearby door and the long, white envelope she held in her hands.

A moment later Sibert leaned past her and gently detached the envelope from her fingers. "This wasn't to be delivered until six, Missus Gentry," he chided softly, "and it's only five."

"I got a whole building to take care of," she complained in an offended whine. "I got more to do than run up and down stairs all day delivering messages. I was up here, so I was delivering it, like you said."

"If it hadn't been important, I wouldn't have asked."

"Well"—the thin, old face grudgingly yielded a smile—"I'm sorry. No harm done."

"None. Good night, Missus Gentry."

As the landlady's footsteps faded down the uncarpeted, odorous hallway, lighted only by a single bulb over the stairwell, he turned to study the name printed on the door: Barbara McFarland.

He added a mental classification: Immortal.

The quick, sharp footsteps came toward the door and stopped. Fingers fumbled with locks. Sibert considered retreat and discarded the notion. The door opened.

"Eddy!" The young woman's voice was soft, surprised, and pleased. "I didn't know you were back."

She was not beautiful, Sibert thought analytically.

Her features were ordinary, her coloring neutral. With her mouse-brown hair and her light brown eyes, the kindest description was "attractive." And yet she looked healthy, glowing. Even radiant. That was the word. Or was that only a subjective reflection of his new knowledge?

"Bobs," he said fondly, and took her in his arms. "Just got in. Couldn't wait to see if you were all right."

"Silly," she said tremulously, seeming to enjoy the attention but showing a self-conscious necessity to minimize it. "What could happen to me?" She drew back a little, smiling up into his eyes.

His gaze dropped momentarily, then locked with hers. "I don't know, and I don't want to find out. Pack as much as you can get in one bag. We're leaving."

"I can't just pick up and walk out," she said quickly, her eyes puzzled. "What's the—"

"If you love me, Bobs," he said in a low, tight voice, "you'll do as I ask, and no questions. I'll be back in half an hour at the latest. I want you to be packed and ready. I'll explain everything then."

"All right, Eddy."

He rewarded her submission with a tender smile. "Get busy, then. Lock your door. Don't open it for anybody but me." He pushed her gently through the doorway and pulled the door shut between them and waited until he heard a bolt shot home.

His room was at the end of the hall. Inside, a tidal wave of weariness crashed over him. He let himself slump into a chair, relaxing completely. Five minutes later he pulled himself upright and ripped open the letter he had retrieved from Mrs. Gentry. It began:

Dear Bobs:
If I am right—and you will not receive this letter un-less I am—you are the object of the greatest man-hunt ever undertaken in the history of the world. . . .

He glanced through it hastily, ripped it to shreds, and burned them in the ashtray. He crushed the ashes into ir-retrievable flecks, and sat down in front of the desk and a portable computer. His fingers danced over the keys and a series of words formed on the screen:

Near this nation's capital, in a seven-story bombproof building, is the headquarters of an orga-nization which spends $100,000,000 a year and has not produced a single product of value. It has been spending for fifty years. It will continue for fifty more if it does not achieve its purpose before then.

It is hunting for something.

It is hunting for immortality.

If you have read this far, you are the third man besides the founders of this corporation to know the secret. Let it be a secret no more.

The organization is the National Research Insti-tute. It is hunting for the children of Marshall Cartwright.

Why should Cartwright's children be worth a search that has already cost $5,000,000,000?

Marshall Cartwright is immortal. It is believed that his children have inherited his immunity.

This fact alone would be unimportant were it not for the additional fact that the immunity factor is carried in the bloodstream. It is one of the gamma globulins which resist disease. Cartwright's body manufactures antibodies against death itself. His circulatory system is kept constantly rejuvenated; with abundant food, his remaining cells never die.

In the bloodstream. And blood can be transfused; gamma globulin can be injected. The result: new youth for the aged. Unfortunately, like all gamma globulins, these provide only a passive immunity which lasts only as long as the proteins remain in the bloodstream—thirty to forty days.

For a man to remain young forever, like Cartwright, he would need a transfusion from Cartwright every month. This might well be fatal to Cartwright. Certainly it would be unhealthful. And it would be necessary to imprison him to make certain that he was always available.

Fifty years ago, through an accidental transfusion, Cartwright learned of his immortality. He ran for his life. He changed his name. He hid. And it is believed that he obeyed the Biblical injunction to be fruitful and replenish the earth.

This was his goal: to spread his seed so widely that it could not be destroyed. This was his hope: that the human race might eventually become immortal.

In no other way could he hope to survive for more than a few centuries. Because he could be killed by accident or by man's greed. If he were ever discovered, his fate was certain.

Cartwright has disappeared completely, although his path has been traced up to twenty years ago. In the Institute office there is a map on which glows the haphazard wanderings of a fugitive from mankind's terrible fear of death. Agents have worked and reworked that path for children that Cartwright may have fathered.

If one is found, he will be bled—judiciously—but his primary function will be to father more children so that there will eventually be enough gamma globulin to rejuvenate almost fifty men.

Once there were one hundred. They were the wealthiest men in the world. Now over half of them have died, their estates going—by mutual arrangement—to the Institute for the search.

Already these men are exercising a vast influence over the governments of the world. They are afraid of nothing—except death. If they succeed, it will not matter if Man becomes immortal.

He will have nothing to live for.

Sibert read it over, making a few corrections, and grinned. He pushed a key and a printed version rolled out of the computer. He folded the sheets in half and then twice in the opposite direction. On a small envelope he wrote in ink: I entrust this to you, your conscience, and your honor, as a journalist. Do not open this envelope for thirty days. If I send for it before that time—verifying my request by repeating this message—I will expect you to return it unopened. I trust you.

He sealed the typewritten sheets inside the envelope. On a larger one he wrote: MANAGING EDITOR, KANSAS CITY STAR.

There was no use trusting public servants anymore. It was not just that they could be bought, but that they were on the open market. Perhaps newspapers and their staffs could be bought, too, but purchasers had to know which of them had information worth the buying.

He checked the tiny automatic to make sure that the chamber was full and the safety was off, then slipped it back into his jacket pocket. Cautiously he opened the door, inspected the dark hallway, and frowned. The single light over the stairwell had gone out.

He slipped into the hall, the stamped envelope in his hand held under his jacket to shield the whiteness. At the top of the stairs he hesitated and then turned to the mail chute. He fished a coin out of his pocket and dropped it into the slot. For a few seconds it clanked against the side of the chute as it fell.

The chute was clear. With a gesture of finality, Sibert shoved the letter through the slot.

"Insurance, Eddy?"

Sibert whirled, his hand thrust deep into his jacket pocket. Slowly he relaxed against the wall as a shadow detached itself from the shadows beside the stairs and moved toward him, resolving into a lean, dark-faced man with thin lips curling in a gently deprecatory smile.

"That's what it is, Les," Sibert said easily. "What are you doing up here?"

"Now, Eddy," Les protested mildly, "let's not play games. You know what I want. The kid, Eddy."

"I don't know what you're talking about, Les."

"Don't be cute, Eddy. Locke sent me. It's all over."

"How did you find me?"

"I never lost you. I'm your shadow, Eddy. Did you ever learn that poem when you were a kid:

"I've got a little shadow
That goes in and out with me,
And what can be the use of him
Is more than I can see."

"Locke may be old, Eddy, but he ain't dumb. He's pretty cute, in fact. He knows all the tricks. You shouldn't oughta cross him, Eddy. Everybody's got a shadow. I got a shadow, too, I guess. I wonder who he is. I didn't have to follow you, Eddy. Locke let me know you were coming home. Now, Eddy, the kid. Where is he?"

So that was why Les had that front apartment on the first floor, Sibert thought ruefully. *And that was why he sat there hour after hour in the dark with his door ajar.*

"You know better than that, Les. I can't tell you. I know too much."

"That's what Locke said," Les told him softly. "The kid's in the building, Eddy, we know that. Maybe right on this floor. You wouldn't let him get far away. And you'd hurry back to him, first thing. I'd like to make it easy on you, boy. But if you want us to do it the hard way—"

His lifting hand held a vest-pocket gun.

Sibert squeezed the automatic in his pocket. It exploded twice, thunderous in the uncarpeted hallway. Surprise blanked Les's bony face; pain twisted as he leaned toward Sibert, his shoulders hunching, his gun hand coming down over his abdomen to hold in the pain. In grotesque slow motion he folded forward onto the floor.

Sibert was bringing his gun out, patting the tattered hole in his pocket to smother the flames, as a third shot shook the hall. Flame spurted down the stairs. The bullet flung Sibert back against the mail chute. His left hand clutched his chest as he triggered three quick shots toward the flash.

In the silence that followed, someone sighed. Like a sack of old bones, a body tumbled down the stairs from the landing above. It stopped at the bottom and leaned its head tiredly against the wall.

The wrinkled old face framed in gray hair was very dead. Through the pain Sibert smiled at it. "What a delightful hostelry you keep, Missus Gentry," he said softly.

He started to chuckle, but it turned into a fit of coughing. A pink froth stained his lips. Someone was slapping him in the face. Someone kept saying, "Eddy! Eddy!" Over and over. His head weaved as he tried to get away, tried to force his eyes open.

Behind him was the mail chute. He was still leaning

against it, but he felt disembodied, as if he were somewhere else receiving these odd sensations distantly, attenuated and distorted. He had blacked out for a moment, he thought feverishly. Give him a few minutes; he'd be all right.

"Eddy!" The voice was getting hysterical. "What's happened? You're bleeding!"

"Hello, Bobs," Sibert said weakly. "Funny thing—" He began to laugh, but it brought back the coughing. When the spell was over, his hand was freckled with blood. It sobered him. "You're—dangerous companion, Bobs," he panted. "Come on—got to get out of here."

He caught her arm and tried to start for the stairs. She held him back. "You're hurt. You need a doctor. We can't go anywhere until you've had medical attention. And these bodies—one of them is Missus Gentry—"

"Lovely woman, Missus Gentry," Sibert said. "Especially dead. Shot me, she did. Come on, Bobs—no time. Explanations later. They're—after you."

She let him pull her to the head of the stairs. There he sagged. She took his right hand and pulled it across her shoulders; she put her left arm around his waist. She was surprisingly strong. Together, his left hand clinging desperately to the handrail, they descended the never-ending stairs, down and around and down, until, at last, they came to the bottom and his knees buckled.

The broad first-floor hall was blurred like an old photograph. Sibert frowned, trying to bring it into focus, thinking: *This is what it is like to grow old, to have the senses fail, the muscles weaken, the living organs and functions of the body die inside. And finally death.*

Someone was talking. Barbara again, trying to make him say something. "Where do we go now?" she kept saying.

He tried to think, but thought was torture. "Hide. Anyplace. Trust nobody. Everyone—against us."

And then there was no memory at all, only the irony that stayed with him, that edged his dreams about a young man who went hunting for life but found the dark companion instead. He woke to a pearl-gray mustiness and thought it was a dream. He was alone. His chest burned. He pressed it with his hand. When he brought it away, the hand was dark. He tried to make out the color in the dimness, but it was too difficult. It dripped unconsciousness into his eyes.

The second time was reality. This time he was sure. He was in a basement. He raised himself on one elbow, finding the strength in some hidden reservoir. He was lying on a cot. Barbara knelt beside him. Kneeling beside the cot was a white-coated stranger. He had a syringe in his hand.

"Get away from me!" Sibert shouted hoarsely. "It's no use—"

Gently Barbara pushed him back. "It's a doctor, Eddy. I got a doctor."

He lay back, feeling stronger, watching. Maybe the man was a doctor. Maybe he was something else, too. Everyone was suspect.

He sneaked his hand down his side, but the pocket was empty. The gun was gone. The syringe was slipped back into its case, and the case was deposited in its slot in the black bag. That meant the injection had already been given, Sibert thought.

"I've done all I can," the doctor said sullenly. "I've patched the holes in his shoulder, but there's no way to patch the holes in his lung. Only time can do that, and the proper care. I think it's too late now. The man's dying. It's a wonder to me he isn't in shock already."

"Would a transfusion help?" Barbara asked quietly.

"At this stage, I doubt it. No point in pouring water into a sieve. Besides, I've no blood with me. If you would let me get him to a hospital—"

"Use my blood."

"Impossible! There's no equipment here for typing and crossmatching, not to mention the unsanitary conditions—"

"I said, 'Use my blood.'" Barbara's voice was hard.

Sibert looked at her. She had a gun in her hand—his gun. It pointed unwaveringly at the doctor, Barbara's knuckles white where they gripped the handle.

The doctor frowned uncertainly. "What's your blood type?" he asked Sibert.

"O negative," Sibert said. His voice seemed a long way off.

"Yours?" the doctor said, turning toward Barbara.

"What does it matter? If you don't use it, he dies anyway."

That was callous, Sibert thought vaguely. He had not suspected that Barbara could be so hard.

Silently the doctor removed a small square box from his bag. *A fractionating machine,* Sibert thought. The doctor brought out plastic tubing equipped with needles and fastened them to the box. . . .

"Whole blood," Barbara said, "not just the plasma!"

Things were getting distant. Sibert felt weak again, and old and used up. He fought to stay conscious.

Barbara sank down beside the cot, the gun steady in her right hand. The basement was dark and dirty, littered with trash, the accumulation of decades of neglect.

Dimly, Sibert felt the doctor swab his arm and the distant pressure of the needle. But as the blood began to flow, he felt stronger. It was like liquid life.

"That's a liter," the doctor said.

"All right. Shut it off."

"I'll have to report this, you know. That's a gunshot wound."

"It doesn't matter. We'll be gone by then."

"Try to move this man again, and he'll die of shock."

The voices were fading. He was going to sleep again, Sibert realized with dismay. He struggled against the rich, black tide, but it was hopeless.

Just before he went under, he saw the doctor turn his head to replace the equipment. A hand swept in front of Sibert's eyes. There was something metallic in it. It made a queer, hollow sound when it hit the doctor's head.

"Wake up, Eddy! You've got to wake up!"

The coolness came against his face again, soothing his fever. He stirred. A groan escaped him.

"You've got to get up, Eddy. We have to find another place to hide."

He worked his eyes open. Barbara's face was above him, her eyes wide and concerned, her face haggard.

She wiped his face again with a damp cloth. "Try, Eddy!" she urged. "We can't stay here much longer."

I'll die, he thought. *That's what the doctor said.* Then he remembered Locke, and what he was fighting for.

He tried to get up. After a few seconds of futile struggle, he slumped back, moaning. The second time, Barbara helped him. She slipped an arm under him and lifted him. He sat up and the dark basement reeled, spun crazily around him.

A little later he was standing, although he couldn't remember how he got to his feet. His legs were miles away. He told them to move, but they were stubborn. He had to lift each one carefully and as carefully put it down. Only Barbara beside him kept him upright.

Against the dark old octopus that was an ancient, gas-fueled furnace, the doctor was propped, his chin against his chest. "Dead?" Sibert asked. His voice sounded thin.

"Don't talk. He's drugged, that's all. They'll be looking for him soon. He was just leaving the hospital when I made him come with me. Nobody saw us, but they'll begin to wonder when he doesn't show up for duty. I let you rest as long as I could, but now we've got to leave."

Somehow they reached the rickety steps that led upward toward brightness. Beside him, holding him up, Barbara sobbed suddenly. "Eddy, Eddy! What are we going to do?"

Sibert called for strength, silently, and straightened

his shoulders and scarcely leaned on her at all. "Come on, Bobs," he said, "we can't give up now."

"All right, Eddy." Her voice was stronger, firmer. "It's you they'll kill, isn't it, Eddy? Not me?"

"How do you—know?"

"You were out of your head. You were trying to tell me things."

"Yeah." Painfully they climbed the shaky steps. The old wooden boards sagged dangerously as their weight came down upon them. "They'll kill me, all right. Not you. Anybody but you."

As they came out into the sunshine pitilessly revealing an aridity of cracked concrete heaped with refuse— ashes, old boards, tin cans, bottles, boxes—Sibert felt a sort of giddy strength. It came and went, like a low pulse, leaving blank spots.

Suddenly they were past the clutter and into an alley. It held the sleek, molded beauty of a two-year-old Cadillac Turbojet 500. As he sagged against the polished side, Barbara slid the door open.

"Where'd you get it?" he asked weakly.

"Stole it."

"It's no good. Too bright. They'll pick us up."

"I don't think so. Anyway, there's no time to change. Get in the back. Curl up on the floor."

The plastic surface of the car felt wonderfully cool against his hot body. He tried to think of an alternative, but his brain wouldn't work. He let Barbara help him into the car. He sagged gratefully to the floor. His chest felt sticky and hot; he was bleeding again.

There were suitcases in the backseat. Barbara stacked them around him carefully until he was completely hidden.

A single spot of sunlight filtered through. He watched it mindlessly as the car started and then moved away with the powerful acceleration of the 500-horsepower turbine. As the car moved, the spot of light jiggled and swayed. . . . Sibert slept.

When he woke, the car was stopped and a harsh voice was saying, close to his ear, "Sorry, miss. My orders are to stop all cars leaving the city. We're looking for a wounded man. He's got someone with him."

They didn't know about Barbara, then, Sibert thought, *or how badly he was injured. They were far behind.*

Cold reason crept in. Optimism was foolish. They were powerful enough to command the aid of the police; discovery was only a few feet away. And they would know a great deal more as soon as the doctor recovered consciousness. It would have been wiser to kill him.

"Then I can't help you." Barbara's voice was brittle and bell clear. "Wounded men are not my specialty. I like them like you, Officer—strong and able. But," she added carelessly, "you can look if you want to."

The policeman chuckled. "Don't tempt me. You're not hiding him under your skirt, I bet. And there's not much else in this buggy but engine. What'll she do on a straightaway?"

"I've had her up to two hundred myself," Barbara said casually. "Two-fifty is supposed to be tops."

"I don't believe it." There was awe in his voice.

"Watch this!"

The car took off like a rocket. In a few seconds the tires began to hum. Sibert felt the car lighten as air rushing past the stubby, winglike stabilizer fins gave them lift. The acceleration continued long past the time he was sure it would stop.

Was it going to be that easy? he thought.

The acceleration slowed. They cruised along, wheels whining. It made a kind of lullaby that sang Sibert back to sleep.

He woke with a start that hurt his chest. The car had stopped again, and the whine was gone.

For the second time he thought: *I'm going to die.* The doctor had said so. With a clarity he had not known since the bullet had hit him, he thought: *Missus Gentry's bullet went through a lung. I'm bleeding to death inside. Every movement makes it more certain.*

He felt a petulant anger at Barbara, who held his life so lightly, who cared so little if he lived or died, who made him stagger blindly in search of a hiding place, dying on his feet.

Prompt medical attention could have saved him. That's what the doctor had implied.

She had given him blood, true. But what was one pint of blood when the thick, red life fluid was leaking from him so persistently, so inevitably. Even the blood of an immortal.

Futile anger rose higher. *Damn her!* he thought. *I am dying, and she will live forever.*

Dying was a strange thing, much like birth, filled with long drowsings and gray, half-conscious awakenings. Each time the grayness lifted for a moment, Sibert was surprised that he was still alive. The remnants of life drifted away in a long doze, until at last he came finally, completely, to full, cool wakefulness.

Gray light drifted through a dusty windowpane and lay across the many-colored squares of the heavy comforter that pressed down on him. *I'm going to live,* he thought.

He turned his head. Barbara was asleep in a heavy chair beside his bed. Its old upholstery was ripped and torn; stuffing had pushed through, gray and ugly.

Barbara's face was haggard with fatigue and unattractive. Her clothing was wrinkled and dirty. Sibert disliked looking at her. He would have looked away, but her eyes opened, and he smiled.

"You're better," she said huskily. Her hand touched his forehead. "The fever's gone. You're going to get well."

"I think you're right," he said weakly. "Thanks to you. How long?"

She understood. "It's been a week. Go back to sleep now."

He nodded and closed his eyes and fell into a deep, dark, refreshing pool. The next time he woke, there was food, a rich chicken broth that went down smoothly and warmly, and gave strength—strength for more talk.

"Where are we?" he asked.

"An old dirt farm. Abandoned ten years or more, I imagine."

She had found time to wash and change her clothing

for a dress she must have discovered in a closet; it was old, but at least it was clean. "Hydroponics probably drove the farmer out of business. This road's pretty deserted. I don't think anyone saw me drive in. I hid the car in the barn. There are chickens nesting there. Who were those people you shot?"

"Later," he said. "First—do you remember your father?"

She shook her head puzzledly. "I didn't have a father. Not a real father. Does that matter?"

"Not to me. Didn't your mother tell you something about him?"

"Not much. She died when I was ten."

"Then why did you insist that the doctor use your blood for the transfusion?"

Barbara studied the old wooden floor for a moment. When she looked back at Sibert, her light brown eyes were steady. "One thing my mother told me—she made me promise never to tell anyone. It seemed terribly important."

Sibert smiled gently. "You don't have to tell me."

"I want to," she said quickly. "That's what love is, isn't it—wanting to share everything, to keep nothing back?" She smiled shyly. "It was my legacy, my mother said— what my father had given me. His blood. There was a kind of magic to it that would keep me young, that would never let me grow old. If I gave it to anyone, it would help them grow well again or young again. But if I ever told anyone or let anyone take a sample of my blood—the magic might go away."

Sibert's smile broadened.

"You're laughing at me," she said, withdrawing. "You're thinking that it was only a little girl's make-believe, or that my mother was crazy."

"No, no."

"Maybe it was make-believe," she said softly, her eyes distant. "Maybe it was only to keep a plain little girl from crying because she was not beautiful, because no one wanted to play with her. Maybe it was meant to convince her that she was really a princess in disguise, that under the ugly duckling was a beautiful swan. I believed it then. And when you were dying I believed in it again. I wanted to believe that I had this power to save you, that the magic was real."

"Your mother was right," Sibert said sleepily. "You are a princess, a swan. The magic is real. Next time . . ."

Next time there was the white meat of chicken for Sibert to eat, with broth that had egg drops cooked in it. He sat up for a little. There was only a twinge of pain in his chest and a muscular ache in his shoulder.

He tired quickly and sank back to his pillow after a few minutes. "Your mother was right," he repeated. "Not in any fairy-tale sense. In a real, practical way, you have new blood, whose immunity factors—the gamma globulins—can repel cellular degeneration, as if death itself were a disease."

He told her the story of Marshall Cartwright, the fabulous creature who had gone secretly about the country to father an immortal race, like some latterday Johnny Appleseed. He told her about the Institute and the men who had founded it, and its purpose. He told her that he had been an unwitting part of it until he had found, by accident, what all the rest had been looking for.

"How did you find me?" she asked, her face pale.

"I was going through some old medical records—doctor's notes, case histories, that sort of thing. One of them was for a maternity case: Janice McFarland, unmarried. She had given birth to a daughter, Barbara. She needed blood; she was dying. The attending physician was a Dr. Russell Pearce. He must have known your father."

"Why?"

"I found this note stuck to the back of one of the lab reports: 'Baby fine but mother dying. Contact Cartwright. Only chance.'"

"That seems like such a small thing."

"When I forced the information out of Locke, I knew I was right. It all fitted together."

"You had traced me before, then," she said, her voice distant.

"Yes," he said quietly, "but a funny thing happened: I fell in love with the girl I was searching for."

Her face changed. "Oh, thank God!" she said prayerfully. "For a little while I was afraid—"

"That I was a vampire, interested only in your blood?" Sibert shook his head chidingly. "Bobs! Bobs!"

"I'm sorry." She squeezed his hand in heartfelt repentance. "Then you came back for me," she prompted.

"Les—that's the only name I knew him by—was waiting for me, watching from his first-floor apartment. And Missus Gentry was watching him, probably without knowing what his job was."

"Then he was going to shoot you because you wouldn't tell him my name," Barbara said quickly.

"No, not that. He knew I wouldn't tell. The shooting was to silence me quickly. As soon as I came directly back to the apartment building, they were sure they could find you. But I shot first. Missus Gentry shot me and was killed when I fired back. You know the rest."

"The rest?" Slowly she smiled; her radiance seemed to brighten the room. "The rest will make up for all we have suffered. It will be so beautiful, Eddy—so lovely it seems impossible and unreal. If what you say is true, I'll never die, and I will keep you young, and we will be together forever."

"If it were only that simple!" He sighed.

"Why shouldn't it be?"

"The power of wealth and the fear of death are a terrible combination. After fifty years of disappointment, the Institute smells blood. It will never leave the scent until it finds you—and eliminates me."

"Then what can we do?"

"I keep thinking: What kind of man was your father? And I think: He must have made some provision for protecting you, some hiding place, some help. As soon as I can travel, we'll begin a search of our own."

The electric Ford chugged along the highway at less than eighty miles per hour. It was a dusty, rain-spattered ten-year-old, a farmer's car. When it came up beside the old man plodding along the highway, it hesitated and stopped.

Unhurried, the old man with grizzled hair and beard marched forward until he reached the car. Behind the wheel was a middle-aged farmer. The old man nodded curtly as he got in. When the door slid shut behind him, he leaned against it, his head bent sullenly over his hands.

"Don't recognize the face," the farmer said cheerfully. "New around here, or just passing through?"

"Passing through," the old man said in a cracked voice.

"Lots of people on the road these days," the farmer said, shaking his head soberly. "Old fellows like you, some of them. Hydroponics done 'em in, and now this new fisheries stuff, farming the sea, they say—why, a few more years and a man won't hardly be able to pay his medical bills with what he can grub out of the dirt. Where'd you say you was from?"

"Didn't say."

The farmer shrugged and turned his full attention to the road.

Ten minutes later the Ford passed the same spot. It was going in the opposite direction. On a crossover, it turned left and pulled to a stop. The farmer had disappeared. The old man was driving.

A young woman, her hair so blond it was almost colorless, stepped from behind a clump of trees and ran quickly to the car. Before she had settled herself, the car began to move. As she turned toward the old man, the speedometer stood at 120.

"Why did you change plans?" Barbara asked. "You

told me to wait an hour, hitch a ride, and we would meet in Joplin."

"That was the smart way," Sibert said, "but I couldn't do it. I couldn't let you get that far away from me."

He glanced at his face in the visor mirror and nodded. The beard and the shoe-blacking had changed his appearance drastically. The illness had left his face drawn and hollow. He looked old. With his training, he walked old and talked old. He almost felt old.

Barbara's frown faded in spite of herself. "What did you do with the farmer?"

Sibert glanced at her quickly. With even less effort, she had been changed more. It was amazing what the old peroxide had done for her. The blondness changed her whole face. The contrast with her dark eyes was striking. Sibert felt his pulse stir.

"I knocked him out and left him behind some bushes. He'll be all right. He'll come to and get help, like the doctor."

"If we were going together, we might as well have taken the Cadillac."

"They've connected it with us by now, and that car could be spotted by a helicopter ten miles away. At this stage of the search, the area is blocked off in sectors. As long as we stayed still, we were safe until they started nets through. But as soon as we move we start attracting attention, setting off alarms, coming under surveillance."

Barbara looked down at her hands, clasped in her lap. "I don't like this business—shooting and stealing and slugging. . . ."

"Bobs!" Sibert said sharply. "Look at me!" Her eyes swung over; he fixed them with his gaze. "You think I like it? But it's something we can't escape. It's the times we live in. It's you. You attract violence. You're the princess, remember, and you're heir to the greatest fortune on earth—life eternal. Wherever you go, men will fight for you, lie for you, kill for you."

"I never asked for that."

"You got it as a gift at conception—life. Just as the rest of us inherited death as our portion. There's nothing you can do, nothing anyone can do."

Then there was silence.

As they approached Joplin, Sibert slowed the car. "Much as I dislike it, now our only chance is to split up. They'll be looking for two people together, and they may know by now to look for a man and a woman. Get out here. Catch a taxi to the airport and get a ticket on the first plane to Washington—"

"Why Washington?" she asked quickly.

"No time to explain now. Trust me. I'll try to be on the same plane. Don't recognize me or speak to me. Whether I'm on the plane or not, take a room in Washington at the airport motel under the same name you use for the ticket—Maria Cassata, say. With your dark eyes, you can pass for one of those blond Italians from the north. If I don't show up within twenty-four hours, forget me. You'll be on your own."

Silently she climbed out of the car, and it moved away. Sibert didn't look back.

*   *   *

The old man hobbled down the jetway toward the impatient transport as fast as his ancient arteries would let him go. As soon as he had climbed aboard, the jet taxied toward the end of the runway. Two minutes later it was in the air.

Settled in his seat, Sibert glanced around with doddering curiosity. When he saw Barbara toward the back, he suppressed a sigh of relief. Her eyes met his without changing expression and returned to the paper she was reading.

For the rest of the trip, Sibert didn't look back—she couldn't get off.

Although he had spotted nobody at the Joplin airport, he was certain that watchers had been there. When he tottered off the plane at Washington, he was equally unsuccessful in identifying any Institute men.

He settled himself with a sigh in a battered plastic waiting-room chair and watched the ebb and flow of the human tides until he could keep himself still no longer. Nearly an hour had passed and he had not seen anyone who lingered, who had not passed toward the ticket machines or the exit doors.

He got into the next motel transport when it was about to leave, and let it take him to the motel lobby. There he got the number of Maria Cassata's room from the front-desk computer, made his way up in the elevator and down the hall, and announced himself quietly to the monitor square on the door. Silently Barbara let him in. As soon as the door closed behind him, he straightened his bent back and caught her in his arms. "We made it," he said gleefully.

She was stiff and unresponsive. "Did we?"

"Of course we did. What's the matter with you?"

She pushed him away and picked up a newspaper from the table beside her. It was a Joplin paper. The headline read:

LOCAL MAN MURDERED BESIDE OLD TOLLWAY

"You lied to me," she said without inflection.

He nodded slowly, watching her face, gauging the depth of her disillusionment.

"Why did you kill him?"

"Do you think I wanted to kill him? A nice old guy like that?" Sibert grimaced. "It was the only safe way. I told you how it would be. I couldn't take the chance he'd raise an alarm before we got away."

"Yes, you told me."

"Bobs, I did it for you."

"Did you?" She closed her eyes and opened them wearily. "Well, maybe you did. But now you've got to tell me the truth—you've got to stop lying to me—why did we come to Washington?"

Sibert shrugged. "A wild guess, a hunch, an intuition. I tried to put myself in Cartwright's place. He couldn't have his kids watched; he couldn't even keep in touch with them or let them know what they really were. Anything unusual would show up in the Institute's files or computers, would bring down the full resources of the Institute's search upon the very persons Cartwright was trying to shield."

"What has that got to do with Washington?"

"Cartwright's problem, then, was identical with the Institute's problem: to locate his kids, who may be scattered all over the United States, or even the world by now. He had to establish his headquarters where he could keep track of nationwide phenomena: that meant Washington. But he had no organization; the very act of organizing would alert the Institute. He had few people he could trust—one person maybe, surely no more than two. Where could he place one man to do what must be done? There's only one place where one man could be effective: inside the Institute itself. As long as the Institute doesn't locate any one of Cartwright's children, the kids are reasonably safe. But if the Institute finds one of them—then Cartwright's agent can act."

Barbara nodded slowly. "It sounds logical. What are you going to do?"

"Get in touch with the agent—whoever he is. I'm going to smoke him out, and you're the smokescreen. I'll report to the Institute as I promised, and I'll offer to sell you—for a price. The agent will hear about it; he must be in a position where he'll hear things. And he'll get in touch with me.

"Meanwhile, as soon as I leave here, check out. Get a room somewhere else—in a private home, if possible. Use another name. No, don't tell me what it is. What I don't know, Locke can't force out of me. When I want to get in touch with you, I'll put a personal on the Net. I'll address it to Leon, for Ponce de León. That will be our signal."

"Why all the precautions?"

Sibert smiled grimly. "From now on, you're my insurance. As long as you're free, they won't dare kill me."

As soon as the taxi sagged to a stop in front of the block-square building, Sibert was seized. From the car behind, four men poured out, guns in their hands. Four more came through the building's entrance.

They went over him thoroughly, swiftly, and found the tiny automatic. They took him directly to Locke's office through a subterranean passage Sibert had never suspected.

Only Sanders, the file clerk, and Liz, Locke's secretary, were in the outer office as they passed through. They did not look at him; it was as if he did not exist.

Locke was unchanged, but the office was different. One corner was hidden behind an impenetrable barrier of blazing light. Wordlessly Locke waved his men out of the room.

Sibert straightened his shoulders and smoothed down his rumpled coat. He peered futilely into the hidden corner.

"Who's there?" he asked.

"To you it doesn't matter," Locke said cheerfully. He looked at Sibert steadily. He smiled slowly. "So, the prodigal returns, bearded, weary, but more than welcome, eh? Aged considerably, too. Shall we kill the fatted calf?"

"Depends on whom you're calling the fatted calf."

Locke's face sobered. "What brought you back?"

"Money."

"What for?"

"Cartwright's kid."

"Have you got any proof it's Cartwright's kid?"

"As you must know," Sibert said, unbuttoning his shirt, "I was shot a little over two weeks ago." He spread his shirt open. The scar in his chest was only a pink dimple. "Enough?"

Locke raised his old, hungry eyes to Sibert's face. "What do you want?"

"Security: money and a guarantee I'll stay alive to get the transfusions when I need them."

"The money is easy. How do you propose to get the other?"

"I want the Cartwright story, the whole thing," Sibert said evenly; "documents, affidavits, complete. I want it put where nobody can touch it. I want it fixed so that on the day I don't verify that I'm alive, it gets released to every news outlet in the United States."

Locke nodded over it, considering. "You'd feel safe, then, wouldn't you? Anyone would. Then we'd have to keep you alive, no matter who had to die. It would make us all very uncomfortable, but we'd have no choice. If you had Cartwright's kid."

"I have."

"You had," Locke corrected gently. He touched the arm of his chair. "Bring in the girl."

Three men brought her into the office. Her blond head was erect; her dark eyes swept the room. Locke nodded. The men left. As the door closed, out of the hidden corner of the room rolled a self-powered wheelchair. Huddled in it was the oldest man Sibert had ever seen. The man was completely bald. His face and head were a wrinkled mass of gray flesh discolored with liver spots. Out of it, faded eyes stared fixedly like marbles dropped into decaying fungus. Saliva drooled uncontrollably from the lax mouth.

The eyes stared at Barbara. In spite of her self-control, she shrank back a little.

"Not yet, Mister Tate," Locke crooned, as if he were speaking to a small child. "She'll need a complete physical examination before we can let her give more blood. She's given a liter recently, and her health comes first. The children, you know."

Barbara looked at her future: Mr. Tate. She shuddered. When she looked at Sibert, her face was dead and white. "Why did you do it?" she asked.

"You've got it all wrong, Bobs—" he began desperately.

"No," she said without inflection, "I've finally got it all right. I couldn't let myself wonder, before, why you should fall in love with someone as plain as I am. I was still the princess in disguise; I wouldn't let myself doubt. Now I've got it straightened out."

"No, Bobs!" Sibert protested hoarsely. "I was following the plan—"

"*Your* plan, maybe. You changed the ending a little. You were going to sell me, really. I should never have believed that absurd story you told me at the motel. I should have known you could never believe it yourself.

You're too ruthless to understand a human impulse. You've killed three people already—"

"Bobs, I swear this wasn't part of it!"

"Oh, I believe that. You were clever, but not clever enough. They win. And you lose everything. I'm sorry for you, Eddy. I loved you. You could have had immortality. But you threw it away."

Sibert's face worked ungovernably as he looked away, unable to endure the cold knowledge in her eyes. When he looked toward her again, the three men were once more beside her. They led Barbara toward the door; she did not look back.

"Put her in the apartment below," Locke said. "You know the one—it's been ready for long enough. Man every guard station; she must be watched every second. She'll try suicide. The man who lets her succeed will take a year dying."

Then she was gone. Locke turned back to Sibert. He smiled. "You can't beat the organization; you should have known that. No one can." He paused. "You told me once that you weren't a very good actor, Sibert. You were right; we picked you up at Joplin. As soon as you left the motel, we grabbed the girl. My only problem now is what to do with you."

"I've got protection," Sibert said quickly.

"That letter you wrote before you were shot?" Locke shook his head pityingly. "It was routine to check the mailbox after your escape."

The lips of the thing in the wheelchair moved; a thready whisper escaped into the room. Locke nodded.

"Mister Tate says there is no problem: You must die. You saw his face. You must die, of course. The question is: How? We'd like to hand you over for murder, but you know too much.

"For now, we'll put you away. You'll have time to consider your sin. It's an old one—Adam and Eve succumbed to it, too. And it's the unforgivable one: too much knowledge."

The cell somewhere in the interminable levels beneath the building was bare except for the plastic bunk. Sibert sat motionless on the bunk, unable to sleep, unable to stop thinking. Somewhere he had gone wrong. And yet— he couldn't pin down any moment when he could have acted otherwise. He had to look out for himself; no one else would. He had to make the only possible deal that would give him immortality and freedom from violent death.

You can't fight organization. He and Barbara could never have escaped permanently and hidden forever. One day they would have been found, and then—the end for him—and for her, her destiny, however arrived at. She was too rare a thing ever to be a person, too valuable to be more than a possession. She was something to be used.

Yes, Barbara had loved him; many women had loved him. But only because he had learned them, and played upon them, had wooed them skillfully and with eternal patience. Where had he gone wrong?

The bolt whispered in the solid steel door, the only

exit from the cell. Silently Sibert was on his feet, his body tense, prepared for anything. The door swung toward him.

"Liz!"

She stood in the doorway, her eyes fixed on his face. He was beside her in two strides.

"I thought you were—Liz!" he said brokenly. "Am I glad to see you!"

In her hand was a handgun. She held it out. He wrapped his hand around it and around her hand. She pulled her hand free.

"Liz!" he said. "I don't know what to—"

"Don't say it!" she said. "You've used me, just as you've used every other person you ever knew. You're a cold-blooded snake and a killer. But I couldn't let them kill you. From now on it's up to you. Don't ever let me see you again; I may kill you myself."

She turned and walked away swiftly. She didn't look back.

"Liz!" Sibert called after her in a whisper. "Where's the girl?"

Then she looked back at him, pointed a finger straight up, and was gone.

Cautiously Sibert followed her along the dark corridor. By the time he reached a ramp leading up, even her footsteps were gone. Sibert eased up one ramp. The corridor above was empty. He climbed a second ramp, puzzled by the silence.

In the second corridor a man was crumpled on the cold concrete floor. Sibert bent over him. He was breathing heavily; there wasn't a mark on his face or head.

Violently the corridor began to clang!

Sibert straightened instantly and ran. A few paces along the corridor, beside a window looking into a room within, a second man was stretched on the floor. Sibert didn't pause.

At the first ramp he sprinted up again—directly into the midst of a handful of guards descending. They twisted the gun out of his hands. After a moment's discussion, two of them took him to Locke.

The office was thunder and lightning. Scenes flickered across one wall, revealing room after room of chaos and shouts of madly running men and women. Locke, spinning from desk to wall to phone, barked orders into the air. In the corner Mr. Tate huddled in his chair, his parchment eyelids closed over sunken eyes.

With a final vicious gesture, Locke gripped his chair arm, and the wall went dark. With the lightning went the thunder. In the silence he groaned. "She's gone."

"Gone?" Sibert echoed.

"Where is she?" Locke snapped. "How did you do it?"

"What makes you think I did it?"

"Somehow you got out of your cell. Somehow you knocked out five guards and got the girl away. Why you stayed behind I don't know, but you'd better start answering questions now."

Slowly Sibert shook his head. "It's hard to find the hen that lays the golden eggs," he said softly, "but it's even harder to keep her."

"Take him to the interrogation room," Locke ordered.

The guards gripped his arms tighter. The thing in the corner rolled forward; its mouth opened.

"Wait!" Locke said. The guards hesitated. "Mister Tate is right. You're a stubborn man, Sibert, and you're our only link to the girl. We'll work with you. If necessary we'll pay your price. Meanwhile you'll be watched. You'll have no chance to escape. One thing I want to know: who helped you?"

"Isn't there someone else missing?" Sibert asked quietly.

"Sanders," Locke growled. "It couldn't be Sanders. He's been here twenty years."

"Well?" Sibert said, shrugging. He would save Liz; she might come in handy once more. He had lost Barbara, but he had won a reprieve. It would last as long as the patience of men who are dying, day by day, and cannot face the night.

They would not catch Barbara now. Not the girl who had snatched a mortally wounded man from among them and hidden him away and nursed him back to health, who had only been caught because that man had delivered her into their hands.

She was wiser now. She would trust no one. It was a lesson immortals should learn early.

Sometime soon, Sibert thought, he would have a chance for escape; he must be ready for it. He would play their game and wait and watch, and before they learned that he'd had nothing to do with Barbara's escape, his chance would come.

Afterward would not be pleasant. For as long as his furtive life should last, he would be a fugitive from powerful fear-driven men, and he would be driven himself to a fruitless search for a lost princess disguised as an ordinary mortal—who held a priceless gift he had thrown away.

But he would not think of that now. His mouth twisted at the irony of the way things had worked out: The implausible story he had told Barbara had been true.

Sanders! For twenty long years that colorless, nearly anonymous man had shuffled through dusty papers and waited for an opportunity that might never come. Twenty years! And Cartwright had disappeared twenty years ago. The coincidence was too striking to be accidental.

He could not blame himself. Who would have dreamed that a man who might live forever would risk eternity for a child he had never seen?

PART III

ELIXIR

The mouse lay dead upon the stainless-steel table, its dark, empty eyes staring out blindly at a world that for it and its siblings had been set about by bars into which nectar and ambrosia had fallen from the heavens and a hand had descended from time to time to lift and stroke and inject foreign substances. But in what significant way did that differ from the experience of the men and women who used it in their experiments?

The laboratory was shiny and sterile and neat, windowless and isolated. It was not the movie laboratory of test tubes and smoking retorts and laddering electricity. This was a biological laboratory in a modern hospital, and it was fashioned from glass and stainless steel. Here and there pieces of equipment rested on scrubbed tables: microscopes and autoclaves and centrifuges, refrigerators and petri dishes and computers, all carefully cleaned each morning and evening with antiseptic solutions. Ultraviolet fluorescent bulbs added their invisible radiation, and the single entrance was an airlock with negative pressure.

In the midst of the latest symbols of contemporary science, Dr. Russell Pearce looked like an anomaly—aging, contaminated with various kinds of microorganisms, rumpled, and dejected. His latest effort to synthesize the *elixir vitae* had failed. At first the synthetic blood protein had seemed promising; some of the mice to whom test substances had been administered had grown more active and the ones who sickened or aged were discovered to have received double-blind placebos. But now the proof of failure lay in front of him, a mouse dead of senescence, whose numbered tag matched a number assigned to those that had received what Pearce had hoped would be the elixir. The mouse was, in fact, the last of the group that had been administered the latest cure-all, the miracle fluid that would heal the sick, restore the elderly, and extend the life span indefinitely.

Pearce sighed, entered the results in his computer, and stared at the inscrutable screen as blindly as the mouse in front of him. It was a long road he had started down fifty years before, when an unemployed wanderer had sold 500 ccs of his blood and that magic red fluid had rejuvenated an aging billionaire. But the restoration was only temporary, lasting as long as the gamma globulins had conferred their immunities, thirty to forty days. For fifty years now Pearce had been searching for the secret to immortality, just as, he was sure, aging men of wealth and power had been searching for Marshall Cartwright and his children.

The executive vice chancellor's office occupied a prime corner location of the Medical Center. Windows on both sides admitted the autumn sunlight and a view to the south and west toward the green suburbs, not north and east toward the carcinogenic inner city. The room looked like a seventeenth-century English library with pale wood shelves and a massive desk, and, in fact, had been purchased in entirety from a British estate, dismantled, and rebuilt in this upstart midwestern city. It was the tribute youthful vigor pays to decadent tradition.

The vice chancellor seemed young and inexperienced, obviously uncomfortable talking to Pearce and what had to be communicated to him, but Pearce waited with the patience of his years. Then she swung her chair away from the windows and said, "How long have you been working at this Ponce de León project?"

"Fifty years," Pearce said.

"Isn't that a bit long to pursue a will-o'-the-wisp?"

"It's one of the two basic dreams of humanity: unlimited wealth and immortality."

"Even Ponce de León finally gave up."

"He was killed by Indians before he had the chance."

"The transmutation of base metals into gold and the concoction of the elixir of life," she said. Her smooth forehead furrowed. "But the alchemists abandoned their futile quests when the physical sciences proved their impossibility."

"Not exactly," Pearce said. "The alchemists transmuted themselves into chemists and physicists, and they learned that you can change base metals into gold, but it costs too much. And some of the alchemists became biologists, and they learned that the lifespan can be extended, but unless you reduce the birthrate, you get overpopulation, pollution, starvation, and disease."

"You have an interest in the history of medicine, as

well," she said. Clearly there was something on her mind other than simply getting acquainted with the faculty. "I understand now why you're the senior geriatrician on the staff." She looked down at the folder open on her desk. "Indeed, the senior physician at the Medical Center."

Pearce smiled ruefully. "The trick of being senior is to outlast everybody else. I used to be a young geriatrician. Now I'm a subject for my own specialty."

"That's why it's so difficult to tell you what I've got to say." Color rose in her cheeks. "You're a legend. You've done so much for this hospital, both in the classroom and the hospital."

Pearce waited, although it was clear what she had on her mind. He wasn't going to make it any easier.

She looked embarrassed. "The funds for your research have not been renewed."

"The National Research Institute has decided to discontinue its funding?"

She nodded. "What is the National Research Institute, by the way? It's new to me."

"In spite of the 'National' in its name, it is a private philanthropy that sponsors research into the causes and treatments for aging. I don't know much more than that. They came to me, many years ago, and my only contact with them has been my annual report and request for renewal. The Institute has always seemed eager to receive the report, and up to now to renew the grant."

"No longer, apparently. We received the termination letter today."

Pearce looked thoughtful. "And the last experiment ended in failure yesterday. That's odd."

"What's odd?"

"The coincidence. It's been my experience that most coincidences are not coincidences at all."

"And most so-called conspiracies turn out to be coincidences," she said.

Pearce laughed. "True, and no doubt this is one of them."

"In any case, the termination came at the customary time, in response to our application."

"What reason did they give?"

"No reason. They just didn't renew. Maybe you can get results in the few months that are left on the grant. Or maybe you can persuade the Institute to renew."

Pearce smiled. "After fifty years? Well, I can understand their impatience. Thanks, anyway, Vice Chancellor."

"Please call me Julia," she said. "And you forgot a third basic dream of humanity."

"And what is that?"

"Love," she said and color rose in her cheeks. She colored beautifully. It was a trait that might yet interfere with her administrative duties.

"The alchemists left that to the magicians," Pearce said. "Maybe because it wasn't basic. Or maybe they thought they could buy love with unlimited wealth."

"Or the promise of immortality," she added.

He got up to leave, but she stopped him at the door.

"Fifty years," she said. "You must be—"

"Ninety," he said.

"You don't look more than fifty," she said. "If I didn't know better, I might suspect that you have found the elixir and kept it to yourself."

"Good genes," he said, "and the power of positive thinking."

And then, as the solid wooden door closed behind him, he stood in the hall, with its special hospital odor that spoke to him of the practice of medicine more than the stethoscope and the scalpel themselves, and wondered what he was going to do now.

He was late for his hospital rounds, but the summons from Julia Hudson had been urgent. Now he wondered about the hurry to inform him of termination and why it had come through the executive vice chancellor, in person, rather than through customary channels. Maybe, after all these years, the regents were trying to get him to resign, which might explain why Hudson hadn't offered to finance his research out of the Center's own funds. Or maybe Hudson had wanted to break the bad news in person, to soften the blow, and he was being paranoid again.

But that was soon driven from his mind by the patients waiting for him in room after room of the hospital wing devoted to geriatrics. As the population had aged, the wing had grown until now it occupied an area as large as that of the next two specialties combined.

His group of senior medical students had preceded him, but his resident physician and research assistant,

Tom Barnett, was perfectly capable of supervising them and of replacing him, as, Pearce was sure, Barnett hoped someday to do. One problem with longevity, particularly longevity in career or profession, was the difficulty of the young in getting on: The road ahead was clogged with slow or stalled vehicles. Death was evolution's way of improving the species, and if death is delayed, the basic processes of life are frustrated.

As one of the roadblocks on the highway of progress, Pearce felt a bit ashamed of the way he clung to his practice and his research. But he had never married, his work gave meaning to life, and he didn't feel ninety years old. In fact, inside he felt about the same age as when he had stared down at a rejuvenated Leroy Weaver. He was as good as any physician on the staff, he knew—indeed, with the accumulated clinical experience of more than fifty years, he felt he was a good deal better. And his skills in the laboratory were superior to what they had been when he was forty and had been driven there by the miracle of Marshall Cartwright.

Now as he went from room to room and bed to bed, taking a hand here, feeling a brow there, checking a chart, speaking a cheerful greeting, asking an interested question by name, saying goodbye with feeling, he noted the ages of his patients. There were fewer sixty- or seventy-year-olds among them than there once had been when he was first starting his practice. Now most were in their eighties or nineties and a number of them into their hundreds.

People were living longer, but the diseases and systemic failures they avoided in earlier life left them prey to the degenerative diseases and cancers of old age. You avoid heart failure, and you live long enough to have a cancer metastasize from your prostate; you keep your kidneys and liver working properly, and your brain finally succumbs to stroke or Alzheimer's disease. And the costs of treating the diseases of old age were far greater than the quick and easy deaths of youth or middle years. Even if one included the Acquired Immune Deficiency Syndrome related diseases. Small wonder the social costs of medical care had soared until today only those were treated who could afford to pay, and the rest were left to their traditional resources: nostrums and faith healers and the few clinics that hospitals such as this one kept open to the public. Mostly to the old to use as clinical material for finding cures to the diseases of old age. Someday, Pearce thought, the few who could afford the best of care would become totally dependent upon it, and medicine would turn for its source of vaccines and antibodies and even antibiotics to those who had been denied the benefits of modern medicine.

Pearce could foresee a time when medicine would become a kind of contemporary religion where the common people came to worship, and physicians, indistinguishable from witch doctors shaking their rattles over their patients to drive out demons, would become the priests of a new mythology. Their altar would be an operating table, and their communion, a vitamin tablet and an oral antibiotic.

Pearce caught up with his group of students before

the end of rounds. The group had grown larger over the years, to match the growth in the geriatrics wing. Geriatrics was a growth industry, and medical students alert to the latest trends invested their time and hopes in an appropriate specialty. Pearce wondered if it had been different when he had made his own choice so many years before, but it was so long ago that his younger self was like a stranger and he could not remember.

He waited at the back of the group, unnoticed, while Barnett had each of them, in turn, prod the patient, poor Mr. Sam Aikens with his chronic nephritis, and jabbed at the physicians-to-be with hard questions, as if trying to trick them into a faulty answer that would allow him to display his erudition and wit, and demonstrate to everyone the necessity of study and of being right. It was one way of teaching, and he had been subjected to that in his medical school days, as well as the three-days-on and three-days-off ordeal of residency, but it wasn't his way. A ready answer was not always a right answer, and being quick was often inferior to being thorough.

Mr. Aikens was a charity case. Barnett would have treated a paying customer more gently.

Barnett was quick, but his quickness had produced no better results in the elixir synthesis than Pearce's thoroughness. Of course, he thought ruefully, there is little discrimination between failures.

"I'll take over, Doctor Barnett," he said, making his way to the front of the group. He felt the students' relief and sensed the reluctance with which Barnett surrendered his place. He would have to do something for Barnett, he told himself, as he told the students about Mr. Aikens and his life and his family situation, and asked the patient to describe his symptoms. He asked each of them, in turn, to hold Mr. Aikens's wrist and feel his pulse, a function measured better by instruments and recorded on a panel behind the patient's bed, along with other vital signs. And he asked them to feel Mr. Aikens's back gently, to sense his pain, and to try to get inside Mr. Aikens's illness.

"All these devices," he said, sweeping his hand around the room, "are wonderful, but they cannot replace the physician's inner sense and a caring—one might almost say, a curing—touch."

The students reacted differently as they were dismissed for the day, some of them relieved to discover that the practice of medicine had not yet been mechanized, others, uneasy in human relationships, resentful that this old doctor was asking them to do more than memorize the names of the body parts and the various ailments to which they were prone. But Barnett was gone before Pearce could tell him about the outcome of the grant application. When he got back to his office, he opened the piece of paper that Mr. Aikens had slipped into his hand when Pearce had held it.

"I need you," the note read. "Come to 3416 East 10th tonight and ask for Marilyn. Destroy this note. We're both in danger."

The address was in an area that once had been middle class but had been sliding down the income slope ever since. The neighborhood was poor, but the people within it were not yet hopeless. It lay outside the inner city, but the inner city was metastasizing toward it, and Pearce had been forced to cross oncological arms after leaving the comparative safety of the interstate. He had kept the bulletproof windows of his armored car rolled up and a prayer on his lips to Hephaestus, the god of craftsmen, that his engine had been well and truly made.

The house stood among narrow, two-story residences on narrow lots. Once, no doubt, they had been single-family homes, but now, Pearce suspected, they were carved up into single rooms for multiple families. The computer map had got him this far, but Pearce could not have deduced which house was his destination had he not been able to determine from an old street sign that this was Tenth Street and from an intact house number that he was in the 3400 block. The house just to the west had a *4* and a *1* hanging awry beside it from the edge of the front porch roof, and the one in front of Pearce, a *6*. Behind it, in the dusk, loomed the blank wall of a structure built of concrete blocks, either a small factory or a large garage. Beside the house was a lot piled with old iron pipes and littered with rusting construction equipment, and the remains of a small drilling derrick.

What once had been a small front yard had been paved for parking, but the only other vehicle was a rusted hulk from which the wheels had been removed. Pearce would have preferred to pull his car around to the back and out of sight, but the lot was too narrow for a driveway and he had to trust his vehicle to luck and its own defenses.

He stepped out cautiously, his black bag in his hand, wondering why he was responding to this anonymous cry for help. It might well be a trap. Physicians had been abducted before by gangs desperate for medical treatment, or for their instruments and drugs. But seldom had a plan been laid to lure a physician into danger, and he did not think Aikens would join any such attempt.

He moved carefully up squeaking wooden stairs, shining a light onto a porch with boards missing like a ghetto-dweller's teeth. The front door was unlocked, and when Pearce pushed it open, he noticed that the frame had been splintered, not once but many times, until, no doubt, the residents had surrendered to the inevitable.

The hall was dark. Above, Pearce's light revealed an empty socket; if a bulb had been available, and the electricity had not been cut off long ago, it would have been stolen. Stairs led up from the hall to a landing and a door and then turned to ascend toward a mysterious second floor. To his right was an archway, perhaps to the building's one-time living room, but the arch had been closed by plywood covered with graffiti. The plywood had been painted and repainted in a futile effort to maintain a minimal level of self-respect, but the graffiti showed through like palimpsests of earlier civilizations.

In the middle of the plywood was a hinged panel that served as a door. No name or number on it—anyone who had reason to be there knew who lived within, and anyone else had no good reason to be there. Except himself, he thought, and knocked.

"Come in," a woman's voice said.

He pushed open the panel to find himself blinded by a flashlight. He had a feeling there was a weapon behind it. "Marilyn?" he asked.

The light went out. "You're Doctor Pearce?"

"Yes." Several moments passed before his eyesight returned.

"I'm Marilyn Van Cleve, and I need your help."

He could see now. An oil lamp on an old card table illuminated a woman seated beside it in a large, shabby recliner. She had a flashlight in her lap and an old-fashioned revolver on the table beside the lamp. She was an attractive woman with brown hair cut short and large brown eyes that looked at him warily but unafraid. Her most attractive feature, however, was her health; in the midst of a sea of sickness, she glowed with a well being that made her seem lit from within.

At first glance Pearce thought perhaps she was in her early twenties, but then he looked again at her eyes; they had seen a great deal of human joy and sadness and suffering.

"What kind of help?" he asked.

"You'd better come in and lock the door. It won't hold anybody out, but it would give me time to get my defenses ready," she said calmly.

"Who are you expecting?" he asked.

"You and whoever may be following you."

"No one is following me," Pearce said impatiently. "I ask you once more, what kind of help?"

"I'm pregnant," she said. She stood up. She was a sturdy woman of medium height, and she was, indeed, pregnant, perhaps eight months along or more, Pearce guessed.

He half-turned toward the door. "I'm not an obstetrician. I have delivered only one baby in the last sixty years. What you need is a midwife."

"This is going to be a difficult delivery. I'm going to need more help than a midwife can provide."

"How do you know?"

"I know," she said.

"Then you belong in a hospital. Even if you can't afford it, there is a clinic for indigents. Medical students need the practice."

"They'd draw blood," she said simply.

"They'd do some routine tests, typing in case of the need for transfusions, checking for drugs, diseases, anemia—but that's all to the good."

"I can't," she said. "That's why I need you."

He shook his head wearily. "It's been a long day. If you can't use a midwife and you can't go to the hospital, then I can't be of any help to you."

"Don't you understand?" she asked. "I'm a Cartwright."

Pearce's mind slowed, waiting for the implications of Van Cleve's statement to seep through the walls he had built around the image of Marshall Cartwright. After fifty years of searching, he had found his Holy Grail. But she was also in terrible danger—and so was he.

"Clearly you can't go to a hospital," he said. "Even if I were to admit you myself, I couldn't deliver your baby without attracting attention, and attention could be fatal. But why do you think the delivery will be difficult?"

"Cartwright women mature late. I'm fifty years old—"

"The first generation," he said. Cartwright had wasted no time putting into action Pearce's admonition to be fruitful and multiply.

She nodded. "But menopause may have no meaning for us. That remains to be seen. Our organs are tough, however, and the mouth of the uterus may not expand sufficiently to allow the baby to be born. Although I never get sick and injuries heal quickly, and the baby will be the same, it can strangle or suffocate. A Caeserian may be necessary."

Pearce looked around the room. It was not dirty. It had been swept, perhaps even scrubbed, but grime was embedded in the painted walls and the wooden floor and the ancient furniture so deeply that mere soap and water could never reach it. "Not exactly the most sanitary of conditions."

"Not here," she said. "The time is not yet right."

"How far along are you?"

"Nine months." She held up a hand. "But Cartwright babies take a week longer. I got that from my mother. She died when I was only five years old. She never really got over the trauma of my birth. But she told me about my father—a wandering man, she called him, who loved her, she said, but could not stop to take care of her, or me. So I've been on my own since then, and I've done all right, in spite of the knowledge that I had to hide who I was, that people were searching for me. But then—" with a hint of bitterness—"women have always had to hide their superiority from men."

"What about your husband?"

"Him?" She laughed. "He wasn't what you would call a husband, but then I've never had good judgment where men were concerned. My mistake was allowing him to get me pregnant. He disappeared as soon as he found out."

"You never told him about your—special ability?"

"To keep him young forever?" She smiled ruefully; even in rue her smile transformed her face into something approaching what Pearce would call beauty. "You think any man is worth keeping under those terms? Or maybe the habit of concealment ran too deep." She shook her head. "No, I would never tell anybody."

"And you've existed like this?" He waved his hand at the room, implying in that gesture the house, the neighborhood and the neighbors, and all the dirt, disease, degradation, and deprivation that involved.

"It's not what you think," she said. "There are good people here, maybe more than among the medically privileged. But I haven't always been here, even though it is the best place to hide, here where anonymity is a way of life. Sometimes I've allowed myself to rise into the middle class, but I can't remain anywhere very long or the chances of suspicion, or even detection, become too great.

"The difficult part is knowing that I can help people who are sick or injured, and realizing that I can't. The moment I let my sympathies take over, the stories will start, the scent will be picked up, and the chase will begin. Do you realize—?" She broke off, unable to continue.

Pearce nodded slowly. "I've seen patients that I might be able to save if I used all the medical resources at my command, but I couldn't because the antibiotics were scarce or prohibitively expensive, or because they would not stretch to all who needed them. Deciding who is to live and who is to die—that's called triage."

"It's even worse when you realize that you, yourself, are the fountain of youth."

"And how did you get my name?"

"That's part of the legend, too, part of my inheritance, like a fairy godmother I could call upon in extremity. 'There's Doctor Pearce,' my mother said. 'He's the only one you can trust, but don't call upon him unless you're really in trouble.'" She laughed again, putting her hands on her swollen belly. "I guess that's what I am—a woman in trouble."

He nodded. "It's happened once before, and I tried to help then. I'll help you, of course. But"—he hesitated—"could I take a sample of your blood? I've been trying to synthesize the Cartwright difference ever since I ran across your father, but the original samples ran out long ago and I've had to proceed on guesswork. A sample from you might give me the clue I need."

"Do you think that's wise?"

"To synthesize the elixir?"

She nodded.

"I've thought about it. Knowledge can be used for

good or ill, but on the whole more knowledge is better than less. I'll work it out, and then I'll decide what to do with it."

"If the world lets you," she said. "But I can't very well ask your help and then deny your fee." And as he got out his syringe and his bottle of alcohol and sponge, she added, "And what's even more important, you can have the placenta and blood-filled umbilical cord when the baby is born."

He stopped in the midst of inserting the syringe. Of course. Aside from the genes themselves, the placenta and the cord were nourishing, maybe defining the baby. Who knew what magic they might contain?

"But you must promise me not to trust anybody," she said.

"I have assistants," he said.

"Nobody."

He nodded and went about his task. When he was done and the sample was stored in the refrigerated section of his black bag, she said, "I'm going to leave by the back way." She picked up her flashlight and her revolver. "Your pursuers will be here any moment."

She was more paranoid than he. "When do you want me to return?"

She hesitated at a door set into another plywood wall in an archway at the back of the room. "I won't be here. I'll get word to you where and when. Be careful, Doctor Pearce. The world is more treacherous than even you suspect." And she was gone.

*　　　*　　　*

The world had turned dark by the time Pearce emerged from the house. Night belonged to the citizens, hiding their blemishes, concealing their movements, masking their intentions. Pearce played his light around the porch, throughout the paved yard, and around his car. Everything seemed as empty and untouched as when he had arrived, but a feeling of danger jangled at his nerves. He shrugged his shoulders and essayed a chuckle. Van Cleve had infected him with her paranoia.

And then, as he picked his way down the stairs and moved toward his car, something monstrous loomed up behind him, and he turned to splash his light upon a ragged, hulking, unshaven creature with a club in its hand raised to strike. It was so nightmarish, so traditional in its attitude, that he almost laughed.

He didn't get the chance. A voice from the street shouted, "Stay where you are! Don't move!" But as Pearce turned toward the voice, the figure behind him twisted away. A laser beam hissed through the night, and a voice cried out, but when he turned back the creature was gone.

"Who's there?" he called out, although he thought he had recognized the voice.

"Doctor Pearce," a voice said as it moved toward him. "Are you all right?"

When a figure came into the light, Pearce saw who it was. "Tom," he said. "What are you doing here?" He thought briefly of Van Cleve's confidence that he was being followed before he dismissed it. "Not that I'm not glad you showed up."

"I happened to be passing the monitoring station as I was leaving," Tom Barnett said, "and your telltale showed your car in this dangerous part of town. I thought maybe you'd been hijacked or kidnapped, so I reported to the police and thought I'd better start immediately. But what are you doing here?"

That was it, of course. The computerized map system automatically reported its location. No one needed to follow him. Even if he had thought of that and had believed the note's warning of danger, how could he have made his way here on foot, and how could he have known it was wise to do so?

"I'm one of the few remaining physicians who still make house calls," Pearce said lightly. "A habit from the old days I find hard to break." He thought quickly: Trust nobody, Van Cleve had insisted. "I got a message—someone just pushed it into my hand." Might as well stick as closely to the truth as possible, he thought, and electronic messages left trails that could be checked. "I thought it was somebody I ought to know, but by the time I got here I knew there was something wrong."

"You've got to stop this, Russ," Barnett said. His voice was husky with concern. "You're getting up in years, and you're too valuable, and there may be people out to get you."

"Who could be out to get me?" Pearce scoffed. "But you're right: These are dangerous times. You said the police have been called? We'd better cancel that alarm before we have to answer a lot of questions, and get back to the hospital compound before my attacker returns with his friends."

"You lead the way, and I'll follow behind," Barnett said.

Pearce nodded and swung his bag with its priceless contents into the front seat beside him, where it wouldn't be far from him, and pulled his car into the street where his headlights splashed across Barnett's car. It was newer and more heavily armored than his, and Pearce wondered how Barnett could afford it on a resident's salary. Perhaps he had inherited money or had his funds supplemented by his family, or a patron protecting his avenue of supply.

They retraced Pearce's route, but this time with the comfort of convoy and Barnett's laser gun. As Pearce drove, he was swept by a wave of weariness. The day had been long and filled with energy-consuming events, and he felt every one of his ninety years. A great sense of relief washed over him when he pulled through the Medical Center's guarded gates and into the living compound where nothing but an all-out attack by a fully equipped military unit could threaten him.

And yet, as he said good night to Barnett and thanked him once more for saving him from robbery or even death, he could not help but wonder why the police had never arrived.

Early morning hospital corridors echo footsteps like late night sidewalks, and Pearce pushed away his uneasy feeling of being followed as he made his way to the laboratory with his tube of irreplaceable fluid still locked in his black bag. His sleep had been more than usually disturbed by the awakenings of the elderly, the swirling memories, the bladder pressures, the terminal insomnia, and at last he had surrendered to his impatience to be up and about his work. Soon the corridors would be thronging with breakfast wagons and hospital gurneys headed for morning tests and surgeries, nurses bustling about their innumerable tasks, and the hospital once more engaged in its epic struggle between sickness and good health, between death and life. But he reached the laboratory in the bowels of the basement without seeing more than a couple of night-shift nurses yawning at their stations.

Pearce poured half the blood sample into a tube that he sealed and returned to his black bag. The other half he poured into a density gradient tube, diluted it with cesium chloride, and inserted it into the ultracentrifuge. He set the dial at 100 and turned it on. After a few minutes he turned off the machine and removed the test tube. He held the tube in the ultraviolet light case. DNA molecules were the heaviest part of the blood, and the bottom of the tube was the darkest. He poured the top ninety percent of the fluid into another tube that he put into his black bag.

He should turn this process over to a laboratory that specialized in these procedures, he knew, but he could trust none of them. That wasn't Van Cleve's paranoia; it was simple realism. The price of liberty might be eternal vigilance, but the price of immortality was eternal suspicion.

Tom Barnett came into the laboratory while he was

cleaning and sterilizing the tubes, and Pearce told him the grant renewal application had been rejected. "We're out of business, Tom," he said. "You might as well use your remaining assistantship working on something that will have a payoff."

"What about you?" Barnett asked.

"I'm going to keep tinkering," Pearce said. "They'll probably reclaim the space, and the live subjects probably are too expensive, but maybe I can hang on to the equipment. No use starting a new line of research at my age."

"I'd like to help," Barnett said, "even if I can't be paid."

"I couldn't allow that. You've got a career ahead of you. Go on with you," Pearce said roughly. "Get about it. I'll give you glowing references as a clinician and a researcher." Barnett left reluctantly, and Pearce returned to his labors.

He removed from the refrigerator a flat silica gel in a sterile plastic wrapping, placed it between two electrical contacts that passed a current across the gel, and carefully poured what was left in the density gradient tube over the gel. A few minutes later he put the gel under the ultraviolet light and with a sterile, sharp-bladed knife scraped from the top of it the darkest rungs of the ladder. He put them into a receptor tube and removed the gel remnants through electrophoresis. What he had left, if he was lucky, was DNA.

He put the rest of the gel into his black bag for later analysis of the remaining blood fractions, but for now he was going to focus on DNA. Whatever special properties were possessed by the Cartwright blood had to be traceable to the DNA and, what was even more important, reproduceable.

Pearce put his DNA sample into an aluminum box stuffed with test tubes. He added some primer, polymerase, and nucleotides. The PCR machine would do the rest, applying heat to the DNA, breaking the bonds that hold the strands of the double helix together. When the temperature was reduced, the primers would attach themselves to either end of the strip. Polymerase, the magical substance, would trigger the formation of new DNA strands from the nucleotides. Then the process would begin over again, with the PCR machine raising the temperature to separate the strands of the DNA molecules that now had doubled in number.

It was like a chain reaction, each raising and lowering of the temperature creating twice as many strands of DNA as had existed before. The process was exponential. That was why it was called a polymerase chain reaction. Within a few hours Pearce would have a billion copies, and a supply of DNA that he could separate into fragments with enzymes and then test each fragment on a separate sample of tissue cells.

The process had just begun, but at least it had begun. He felt a curious sense of elation that he had not felt for more years than he could remember. It made him feel youthful again. He never felt truly old. He always felt forty inside, that age at which his internal calendar had stopped when the most important event of his life had happened, but his body was less flexible, his muscles didn't recover as quickly from exertion, and he felt pains where once had been nothing but silky articulation. And yet he had the feeling that aging was a state of mind. If there was such a thing as psychosomatic illness, why couldn't there be such a thing as psychosomatic wellness? It would bear thinking about.

He had been so busy with his tasks that he was startled to turn around and find someone in the laboratory with him. It was the executive vice chancellor, Julia Hudson, and she was looking at him with an intensity that first startled and then alarmed him.

"How long have you been standing there?" Pearce asked.

"Only a minute or two. Part of my tour of the Center, you know," she said, answering a question he had not yet asked. "And I wanted to see the Project in action." Her voice capitalized the Project, as if to concede it the importance that he himself would place on it. But he felt as if she were looking at the space occupied by the laboratory and the equipment it housed as assets to be used for better purposes.

"This is where it happens," he said. "Or doesn't happen. The search for the *elixir vitae,* the rejuvenation factor."

"I hate to see you wasting your time searching for a substance that doesn't exist."

"And the Center's funds?"

She nodded acknowledgment. "That's part of my job, to weigh priorities against resources. The issue is immortality, and nobody lives forever."

"Except the Cartwrights."

"That's mythology, like Santa Claus and the Easter Bunny."

"I have good reason to believe it isn't," Pearce said. "In fact I once was in possession of some of that magical Cartwright blood."

She looked surprised, perhaps even astonished. She was an attractive woman, Pearce had time to think—and even to surprise himself with the thought—with dark lustrous hair, blue eyes, a shapely face, and lips that many young men must have longed to stop with theirs.

"So that's why you have been so persistent," she said. "You're the doctor who treated Leroy Weaver."

"All that has been expunged from the record and is best forgotten," Pearce said. "You can imagine what my life would be like, and how much work I would get done, if it were general knowledge."

"And your research, then—"

"Has been an effort to replicate the properties of Marshall Cartwright's blood. I've always thought the rejuvenating factor must be associated with the gamma globulins, and I have been analyzing Cartwright's DNA ever since, but I had so little to start with, and what I had was diluted and mixed with Weaver's blood and the blood of my laboratory animals, and possibly corrupted, and DNA research then was relatively primitive and undiscriminating—"

"Then it is a will-o'-the-wisp."

"The will-o'-the-wisp isn't an illusion, you know. It's

swamp gas, methane, spontaneously ignited. It can be found and identified. This will-o'-the-wisp exists, and it, too, can be found and identified, and maybe synthesized."

Her eyes were alive now with the zeal of the quest. "If only a Cartwright would reveal himself, allow himself to be studied. The synthesis could be accomplished in a matter of a few years."

"Now you believe," Pearce said. "But what you propose is impossible. How long do you think a Cartwright would last in a world increasingly obsessed with the fear of dying?"

"But if the *elixir vitae* were synthesized, the pressure would be off, the Cartwrights no longer would be the Holy Grail—"

"If—if—so many *ifs*. The only one certain is that if they don't reveal themselves, they may survive and so may the human species. And therefore my research blunders on."

Her gaze moved around the laboratory, with its gleaming surfaces and functional shapes, with an expression that resembled wistfulness. "I would like to help."

"How?" he asked.

She raised a hand in supplication. "In person, I mean. Research is so neat, so definitive—so much better than the equivocal, messy business of administration. I always loved the laboratory, and I wish I could get back to it. Maybe I could steal a few minutes a day, just to lend a hand?"

"Of course," he said, not committing himself to anything. It was a bit of a coincidence, he thought, that she had showed up just as he was working on the Van Cleve sample. "Any time."

"Have you thought," she asked, "that the rejuvenation factor might be related to the stem cells?"

He paused to reflect. "That's a good idea. I'll think about it. One thing I have begun to suspect over the years is that the phenomenon is more complex than I thought. The Cartwright mutation may combine several improvements, and the stem cells might be one of them."

"Meanwhile," she said, "I'll see that you keep your laboratory and your equipment, even when the grant runs out. And minimal biological supplies if we can camouflage them as clinical. No salaries, I'm afraid," she added apologetically.

"I'll be grateful for whatever you can do," he said and was musing about stem cells as she was turning toward the door. As soon as she was gone he changed the code on the entry panel and added the security that he had never before thought was necessary, his palm print.

The next few days he could steal only an hour or two away from his hospital rounds and teaching duties to check the results in the laboratory. He had nurtured human cell cultures and treated each with a different fragment of DNA that he had separated with enzymes. He had locked them into a machine that periodically washed away the waste by-products and added fresh nourishment.

Each time he entered the laboratory, however, he had the feeling that someone had been there in his absence. Everything was as he had left it, nothing ever was out of place, but he could not shake the conviction that, in spite of his precautions, someone had been in the room while he was gone, checking on the progress of his research. It was like the prickly sensation one gets at the back of the neck that says you are being watched even though you can't ever catch anybody watching, as intangible and as inarguable.

Before he could take any additional precautions, or even think of any additional precautions he could take, he was summoned by Marilyn Van Cleve. Sam Aikens had died, and Pearce was wondering who Van Cleve could use as a conduit. It happened at his free clinic attached to the Center's walls. It had an external entrance so that the security of the hospital compound would not be breached or its purity compromised. He was examining a wiry old man in dirty working clothes that once had been dark blue. The old man was coughing from emphysema, and Pearce smiled sadly at the package of cigarettes protruding from the old man's shirt pocket even though he could not smoke while within the Center's walls. Pearce heard unusual sounds from within the old man's sunken chest. He frowned and moved his stethoscope to another spot to listen more intently. On the third try he realized the sounds were words: The old man had learned the trick of esophageal speech, when cancerous vocal cords had to be removed. Perhaps, he thought, the diagnosis was not emphysema but cancer. The old man had even learned how to whisper into his chest cavity.

It was then Pearce realized what the words were saying: "Marilyn needs you. I'll be waiting across from the main gate at sunset. Come by foot." And then, as soon as the examination was completed and the free sample of a bronchial inhaler was handed over, the old man rose from the examination table and left the room.

Pearce got through the rest of the day mechanically, unable to concentrate on the task at hand because of the possibilities that lay in front of him, half dread and apprehension, half anticipation. Finally, as the sun edged gold around a dark cloud on the horizon, he put his black bag and a second small bag into the front seat of his car and drove through the main gate, nodding to the guards as he passed through.

He pulled the car out of sight behind the ruins opposite the gate and looked around for the old man who whispered from his chest. The ruins of what seemed to be ancient restaurants and taverns for bored medical students were deserted. Pearce waited impatiently, not wanting to leave the safety of the car, not sure this wasn't a trap or a diversion.

After ten or fifteen anxious minutes, something tapped on his window. Pearce turned, startled, but it was the old man. When Pearce rolled the window down, the old man forced words into speech like hoarse whispers, "I said 'no car.'"

"How do you think I was going to leave the compound? On foot?" Pearce said. "Wouldn't that attract suspicion?"

The old man shrugged, coughing. Pearce got out of

the car with his bags, feeling a shiver of—what? Anticipation? Apprehension? He didn't know which. Maybe
both. Behind the remains of what was once a concrete-
block trash enclosure stood an antique motorcycle.
Pearce hadn't seen anything like it for a quarter of a century. It seemed as big as a small horse, but it was old—
dented and rusty and only the letters *Ha* and, widely separated, *son* appeared on the forward section. Pearce
noted with a shiver of horror that the machine operated,
if indeed it still worked, on gasoline with all its fumes
and carcinogens.

The old man coughed and threw his leg over the saddle. He motioned for Pearce to put his bags in the containers fastened on each side of the rear wheel and to
take the jump seat behind him.

"If you think I'm going to join you on this—this appa-
ratus," Pearce said, "you're out of your mind."

The old man motioned again, impatiently, and nodded
at the top floors of the Center compound visible over the
tops of the ruins. Pearce looked longingly at where his
car was hidden, but he remembered the computerized
map and telltales, and shrugged, stowed away his bags,
and got behind the old man.

The old man kicked the machine into life. He was
stronger than he had seemed in the clinic. Pearce
thought of him as the old man, but he probably was two
or three decades younger than Pearce himself. As the engine roared like a wounded animal, unmuted by a muf-
fler, Pearce wondered what he was doing here in the
gathering dark, committing himself to strangers on a

quixotic mission that might end in disaster for everybody.

Then the motorcycle lurched into motion, its roar modulating into a husky snarl, and Pearce had no more time for reflections on his folly. Instead he hung on to the old man's emaciated waist as wind and dust tugged at his clothes and hair and beat into his face. The night was chilly, and the cold ate through his clothing and down to the bone. Now that they were traveling, the old man wasn't coughing as much, as if the strength of the machine he rode seeped up into his body through some kind of sympathetic magic.

The old man avoided all but short stretches of the trafficways and their patrols. Instead the motorcycle weaved through unlighted side streets, avoiding potholes and wreckage as if by instinct, skidding around corners, going over sidewalks and through yards to avoid barricades behind which lurked dangers that Pearce did not want to consider.

The experience was far different from traveling the same distance by car. After his terror subsided to a constant fear punctuated by panic, Pearce began to feel the inner city as a place where people lived rather than a jungle to be flown over or passed through. Like a medieval leech drawing blood from a patient dying of anemia, the suburbs had drained wealth from the inner city, and what the suburbs had started the Medical Centers had completed, taking block after block of housing for their expansion, pricing their snake oils and nostrums beyond the reach of the people in whose midst they lived and thrived. And yet the citizens endured. In spite of everything, they endured.

That was the strength of the people, he thought. They endured and they survived, and after all those who elevated themselves above their fellows had decayed from their excesses and destroyed themselves, the people remained. Pearce saw them now, looking out their windows into the uncertain night, standing on their porches to stare at the unaccustomed noise, in hovels falling apart around them, and realized their strength.

Their lives were short and disease ridden—no better than the animals of the fields or the forests—which is why the Medical Centers remained in their midst, harvesting their antibodies and their antigens, their gamma globulins and their vaccines, even their organs. But they survived. They nourished each other between casual killings, they dreamed, they loved, they raised families, they got old too soon, and they died, often among friends, as opposed to the sterile dyings in the Medical Centers, no matter how long postponed, ignored by everyone except those paid to administer the medical last rites.

By then they had nearly reached their destination as they crossed the divided thoroughfare of the Paseo and slowed on what Pearce glimpsed on a sagging street sign as INDEPE . . . VEN . . . The motorcycle veered off the poorly illuminated, four-lane street into a darker drive behind a dark building that hulked against the late evening sky like an abandoned warehouse. The old man who had ferried him here like some latter-day Charon cut off the engine and waited a moment in the sudden silence, testing the night for danger. Then, as if deciding for the moment that movement was safe, he removed the bags from the containers, handed them to Pearce, and motioned Pearce to follow.

As they entered a dark door Pearce noticed a sign above it, still intact. It was like an omen: CHILDREN'S MERCY HOSPITAL, it read.

The building had been taken over by the homeless. The old hospital, once the new one had been built, had been used for a few years as offices for social welfare, then as an orphanage, and finally boarded up and forgotten. The poor had not forgotten. They had pried open doors and windows and made the building a warren for their fertility. Children played in the halls, barely lit by an occasional oil lantern, or stuck their heads out of doors to inspect the strangers passing by. Some came to tug at Pearce's clothing or the bags in his hands until the old man shooed them aside. Sometimes an adult made an appearance, an unshaved face to glare at them or a curious woman with a toddler tugging at her leg.

Children's mercy, Pearce thought. He hoped they got it, but he knew that this was a world that had little mercy except for those it favored, and they lived outside the inner city and had few children.

On the second floor was a room that Pearce recognized. He had never been there, but the layout was unmistakable. It was an operating room, no matter what uses had intervened. Glareless lights once had turned this room into day. Dials and gauges had lined the walls.

Bottles of oxygen and anesthetic had been nearby. Tables and autoclaves for instruments. A T-bar for infusions. And a stainless steel operating table in the center.

Now it was lit by candles. It held only battered, old furniture pushed against the walls and in the middle a narrow bed. On the bed, propped up with ragged pillows, was Marilyn Van Cleve. She had her eyes closed but turned as Pearce entered with the old man and gave them a half-smile that turned into a grimace as a contraction seized her body. "You came," she whispered.

"I said I would," he answered.

"Not everybody keeps promises."

"I've always kept mine. When did the contractions start? How far apart are they?"

"Almost twenty-four hours ago," she said, panting. "They were ten minutes apart twelve hours ago, about an hour ago they were five minutes apart, and now they're down to two. I—just—can't—squeeze—him—out. I think it's time to help him get born."

Pearce nodded. "Get some boiling water," he told the old man who waited by the door.

"Too long," she said.

"At least," he said, "get me some soap and water to wash my hands."

While he waited for the old man, he folded back Van Cleve's long dress to just beneath her breasts and placed his hands on her belly to feel the contractions. "It's been a long time," he said. "I hope it hasn't been too long. And these operating conditions—they're beyond contamination."

"You can't hurt a Cartwright," she said.

"You'd better be right."

When the old man returned with a bucket of dirty water and a thin bar of soap, streaked with dark veins, Pearce shrugged and washed as thoroughly as he could. "I need more light," he said, and the old man brought two kerosene lamps that he placed on either side of the bed at Van Cleve's hips.

From the second bag Pearce removed a large plastic bag and from his black bag a bottle of alcohol with which he swabbed his hands and Van Cleve's belly before wiping it a second time with iodine. He pulled on a pair of clear plastic gloves that shrank to fit his hands and picked up an instrument that looked like a fat stainless-steel pen.

"I could give you a shot for the pain," he said, "but I'm not an anesthesiologist, and I don't know the effect on the baby."

"Go ahead," she said. "Knowing that injuries aren't fatal helps control the pain." And she did not make a sound as the laser made a vertical cut through her belly and into the womb.

He worked quickly, as if he knew what he was doing, and when the cutting was done reached his hands into her body and lifted out the baby, trailing its umbilical cord. The baby began to cry, loudly.

He looked up at Van Cleve. She was still conscious, though clearly in pain. "You have a son," he said. "I'm no expert, but he looks as big and healthy as any baby I've seen. I'd say ten or eleven pounds. No wonder you had trouble."

She laughed. "Give him to me." She held out her arms.

"Just a moment." He tied off the cord close to the baby's navel and again a few centimeters away before he cut it. "I need a blanket or a sheet or something," he said.

"Never mind that," she said.

He placed the screaming baby in her arms. Its body left reddish smears on her gown, but she didn't notice. Instead she looked down at the small face that immediately quieted and began looking up at her and then around the room.

Pearce breathed deeply. Obstetricians were at the right end, the satisfying end, of the life process. Maybe he had made a mistake going into geriatrics.

He removed the placenta from the womb, along with the trailing umbilical cord to which it was attached at one end, and dropped them into the plastic bag. He adjusted the switch on his laser scalpel and sealed the cuts in Van Cleve's uterus and belly. They closed neatly, and he hoped there was no infection. But Cartwrights had to be resistant to almost every microorganism, and he thought, as he worked, that he could detect signs of healing even before the laser touched the wounds. He bandaged the incision and pulled down her gown as far as it would go.

Finished, he pressed the cuff of the gloves on each hand, and they peeled away. Once more he washed his hands in the bucket before returning his instruments and bottles to his black bag. Into the other bag he put the bag holding the umbilical cord and placenta. Stem cells, he said to himself. When he was finished, he looked up at Van Cleve once more. She had placed the baby to her breast; it was trying to suckle.

"Thank you, Doctor," she said. "Mother was right."

"I wish I could do something more," he said. "It isn't going to be easy for you, with recent surgery and a new baby. But from now on I bring only danger of discovery."

"Don't worry about me. I'll be able to move on in a day, and for now I'm among good people." She looked over at the doorway, where men and women had crowded to see what was going on. "When you don't have anything, you can let yourself care about others, because no one can use your kindness against you."

As Pearce watched, three men pushed their way through the throng into the room. One had a small, ragged blanket that he placed over the baby, the second, a shabby baby carrier that he put at Van Cleve's side, and the third, a shriveled orange that he gave to Van Cleve's free hand.

Pearce had the old man stop a block from his car. All the way he could feel the old man's body racked with coughs, worse now in the night air and without the adrenaline of the original wild trip. But the old man had brushed aside any suggestions for treatment and offers of help, and Pearce trudged wearily toward the car as the old man roared away.

He had triggered the front door of the car when he was twenty paces away, but as he was stooping to get in, he felt his arms grabbed from behind.

"Easy," a man's voice said.

A light was splashed in Pearce's eyes.

He struggled, futilely. The arms holding him were strong. "I'm Doctor Pearce. This is my car."

"That's what they all say."

"Russell," Julia Hudson said. "We were worried when we found your car abandoned."

"Julia," Pearce said. "Tell this thug I'm who I say I am."

"Let him go," Hudson said. The hand released him and the light turned toward her. She was standing at the front of the car looking young and concerned. "The guard noticed your car identifier not moving, thought you might be in trouble, and notified me. What happened? We thought you were kidnapped, or worse."

Pearce had had lots of time on the ride back to think of an explanation if his car had been found. "I had a house call nearby, and when my car malfunctioned I decided to walk."

"A house call?" Hudson said incredulously.

"Difficult as that may sound," Pearce said, "I do make house calls. Ask Tom Barnett."

"Oh, I believe you," Hudson said. "It's just that I can't understand it, and I can't let you continue. It's too dangerous."

Pearce shrugged. "Can we go now?" He put his bags in the backseat of the car. "I've got some laboratory work yet to do."

Hudson got into the other front seat. "Take my car back," she said to the guard. She turned to Pearce. "I'd like to see how you're doing."

"It's pretty late," he said.

"I'm used to working late," she said, and he could think of no other excuses.

As they made their way through the night-stilled corridors toward the laboratory, he thought that surely she must be able to smell the blood on him or the odor of harsh soap or disinfectant, but she gave no sign. "I've been thinking about your suggestion," he said, "about the stem cells. An improvement in them must be involved in the Cartwright mutation."

She nodded. "They would produce more red blood cells, more platelets, more white cells for the Cartwrights themselves, and when transfused, for the ailing or aging recipient."

"Of course," he said. "I don't know why I never thought of that."

"Sometimes the original workers are too close to the problem to consider alternatives," she said. "And you might think about the primordial chordamesoderm."

"PC?"

"It causes formation of all the organs in the body before it turns off after the embryo has developed. But what if it were capable of being turned on again, by some feedback mechanism, to repair a damaged organ or stimulate the development of a new one—a new liver, a new kidney, a new heart, even new arteries—from surrounding tissue?"

They had reached the laboratory, and he put his hand casually on the palm plate as he punched in the code. He didn't want Hudson to know that he was taking extra precautions. He raised the lid on his cell experiment and showed her his samples. "What I'm checking for is whether some portion of the DNA sample I'm working with might delay or eliminate apoptosis."

"Apoptosis?" she said. "It's been a long time since medical school."

"Not as long as it has been for me," he said. They both laughed and their eyes met. Pearce had the peculiar sensation that he was attracted to a woman who was young enough to be his granddaughter, perhaps even his great-granddaughter. And not only that, she might be one of those sent to watch him. He went on hastily. "But I have the advantage of studying up for my research.

"Apoptosis is the unexplained phenomenon by which cells die. Given sufficient substrate and their by-products washed away, cells will survive approximately forty-five cycles, so it may not be a matter simply of inadequate circulation leading to insufficient food or a buildup of waste or free radicals. It may be a built-in termination, a death sentence that must be canceled."

"And has anything happened here?" she asked, looking back at the experiment in the machine before them.

He closed the lid. "Too soon to tell," he said. "In any case, it's probably just a practice run for the rare possibility that I might come into some authentic Cartwright blood."

She put a hand on his arm. "Take care of yourself, Russell," she said.

"Russ," he said. "You, too."

After she had gone, he went back to the experiment.

He thought he could tell that all but two of the cultures had already started to die. Two. One of them might be an illusion, but two might mean that more than one segment of Van Cleve's DNA was involved.

He returned to his apartment with his second bag and hung the placenta by clamps from a shelf of the refrigerator. He cut the umbilical cord just above the place he had tied it off so that both drained into a stainless-steel pan. For the first time in years, he went to bed happy.

He awoke to panic. Alarm bells rang and somewhere a siren screamed. Pearce rolled over and checked the time—5:38—and fumbled into his pants and shirt and white hospital jacket. He stuck his feet sockless into shoes and moved toward the door before he remembered the priceless treasure in his refrigerator and the experiment progressing in his laboratory, and it all seemed too much of a coincidence.

He slowed his pace and opened the door normally. Residents were running up and down the corridor in various states of undress, shouting questions and getting no answers. Tom Barnett was waiting outside the door.

"Quick, Russ," he said, "let's get out of here!"

Pearce turned to double-lock the door before he turned back to Barnett. "What are you doing here, Tom?"

"Concern for you, Russ."

"You live on the other side of the compound."

"I was up early and heard the alarm. I thought you might sleep through it."

"Old men sleep lightly, Tom," Pearce said. "Let's go."

"What about the laboratory?" Barnett asked.

Pearce shrugged. "It will have to take care of itself."

As they turned toward the distant exit, Julia Hudson was coming toward them, relief on her face. "Doctor Barnett, isn't it? Russ, I was worried." She was fully dressed but without makeup. Even so, Pearce thought she was a remarkably attractive woman.

"Up early, too?" he asked.

"Paperwork," she said wryly, and then, "I'm not much of a sleeper."

As they moved toward the exit to the outside, following the other residents, who now had decided that their lives were more important then their belongings, Pearce asked Hudson, "What's the alarm?"

"Fire," she said. "Two. One in the basement. One in a janitor's closet on the top floor. Like the compound, the hospital is being evacuated as a precaution."

"Two fires? That sounds like arson."

They emerged into the open air of the parking lot. It was filled not only with residents but with nurses and interns tending patients in wheelchairs and gurneys.

"That's what I think."

"One in the basement?"

"Near your laboratory. But don't worry. It's under control."

"Why would someone want to burn a hospital?" Barnett asked.

"Why, indeed?" Pearce said.

"A disgruntled employee?" Hudson suggested.

"An unhappy patient?" Barnett added.

"Or one who's mentally disturbed?"

"Or someone denied care?" Pearce said ironically. "Two at the same time?"

The distance between the fires rendered improbable the thesis that one person might have set both, and the possibility of two unrelated people acting simultaneously was even more unlikely. They all saw that.

"Not only arson," Pearce said, "but conspiracy. But why? Maybe as a warning that the hospital is vulnerable. Maybe as a ploy to empty the buildings so that rooms can be searched, perhaps valuables stolen."

"We'd better get back inside," Hudson said.

Pearce glanced around the disheveled parking lot and its disheveled inhabitants. "I think you're right."

But before he could get back to his apartment door, he was stopped by a large male nurse. Pearce couldn't remember seeing him around the hospital, but something about him seemed vaguely familiar. "Doctor Pearce, there's an emergency in your wing."

Pearce waited for Barnett to volunteer to take care of it, but Barnett said nothing. "I'll follow you," Pearce said, and had time only to notice, as he passed his apartment on the way to the elevator, that the door seemed untouched.

The nurse preceded him, glancing back occasionally to see if Pearce was following. He wore green scrubs that left his biceps bulging incongruously below the short sleeves. When they arrived at one of the private rooms, the nurse stepped aside and stood with his back to the door as Pearce entered.

A man in a wheelchair sat on the far side of the room, looking out at the smoggy inner city. He turned as Pearce entered. He looked bulky and malformed under his robe. Pearce looked at his face. The man was old, perhaps well past the century mark, and his face, that once might have been round and full, was little more than skin stretched over the prominent bones of his face. But now that the subcutaneous fat had been skimmed away by time, the strength of the man was revealed in the set of the jaw and the fierceness of the eyes. Among the wrinkles around his eyes were the faint reminders of old scars; a long one ran down his right cheek to the point of the jaw. His nose had been broken once or twice.

"You don't remember me, Doctor Pearce?" the man said.

Something stirred in Pearce's mind, a vision of a sign on a glass door panel, a man in a cocoa-colored tropical suit, and later the same face bearded and battered. "Locke," Pearce said. "Jason Locke, the private investigator I hired to find Marshall Cartwright."

"The private eye you hired to make sure that Marshall Cartwright could not be found," Locke said.

"And after all these years have you come to report success?" Pearce asked. "Have you found him?" The combination of Locke's age and determination made Pearce shiver inside, but he wasn't going to let Locke know.

"No," Locke said, "and I've been looking ever since. I'm the executive director of the National Research Institute."

"Ah," Pearce said, as pieces fell into place.

"The organization that has been funding your research for the past fifty years, but, as you have deduced, its principal mission is to find Marshall Cartwright and his children. I didn't know the story until after Leroy Weaver's death, when his doctor, a man named Easter, and his private secretary, a man named Jansen, offered me the chance to work for them. It was my idea to recruit other people of wealth and declining years, and to organize the Institute along its present lines. Easter and Jansen are long gone, but the search continues."

"You switched sides easily," Pearce said.

"I was never on anybody's side. You hired me for your purposes, and I allowed myself to be hired by Jansen and Easter for mine. Besides, we're all in the Ponce de León business."

"And has your search been successful?"

"No more than yours. We came close once," Locke said, almost wistfully. "Had her in our hands. But she was spirited away, perhaps by Cartwright himself."

"But you keep on."

"Just as you do. People die easily, but hope dies hard. And old people hope until the end. Death has come to billions of people in the fifty years the Institute has been functioning, and to dozens of the Institute's board of directors, but their estates revert to the Institute and the search goes on. Actually, as time passes, the possibilities for success increase."

"How so?" Pearce asked. "I'd think the trail would have gone cold long since."

Locke laid his right hand out palm up, as if to reveal a gem of truth. "The more Cartwrights there are, the more difficulties they have keeping hidden and the more chances we have to identify one. Sooner or later they will begin to pop up like corks in the ocean."

Pearce remembered a woman and a baby in an abandoned operating room. "What brings you here?"

"You," Locke said.

The bluntness took Pearce aback. "Me?"

"Your reputation as a geriatrician is international," Locke said. "Even without the urban myth of Leroy Weaver's rejuvenation, you would be renowned as one of the magicians of senescence. I thought it was time for a checkup."

"What seems to be the problem?"

"Old age," Locke said. "I may look good for my years, outside of the nerve damage that keeps me in this wheelchair. I've had growth hormones and fish oil, vitamins and health foods. My arteries have been Roto-Rooted, and I've had a heart and lung transplant and two new kidneys. But I feel old."

"Apoptosis," Pearce said.

"What's that?"

"The cells themselves age and die after about forty-five divisions. Almost as if they have a counting mechanism."

"Except for the Cartwrights."

"And cancer cells. You want to be young again, like Leroy Weaver," Pearce said. "But that happened only once. You are old. I'm old. It's not a bad thing to be."

Locke's expression wore a steely rejection. "That was all right when there was no alternative. But now there's a chance for immortality, and only a helpless fool would settle for anything less."

"I guess that's what I am, then," Pearce said.

"No, you're the most powerful man around," Locke said, "and that's why we decided to renew your grant."

"We?"

Locke smiled. "Me, then. I decided to renew your grant."

"And why did you turn down the renewal in the first place?"

Locke studied Pearce as if gauging how open to be. "I wanted to see how you'd react."

"You wanted me to make a personal appeal?"

"Maybe."

"Be spurred to greater effort?"

"If that were possible. Time passes swiftly. Some of us are getting nervous."

"And why did you set the fires this morning?"

Silence grew deep in the room before Locke said, "You know about that?"

"I don't believe in coincidences. It was a mistake to set two."

Locke spread his hands helplessly. "Subordinates make mistakes. They don't make them twice."

"But what were you after?"

"Proof. Evidence. Anything." Locke bent his head forward to prop his chin on his fingers.

"Proof of what?"

"Of your Cartwright connections. Of your success with the *elixir vitae*."

"What makes you think that I could make connections where you could not?"

"They might contact you; they wouldn't trust me."

"There's no reason for them to contact me. In fact, there is every reason they shouldn't, just as they shouldn't contact each other. All they need is freedom and the opportunity to be fruitful and multiply and make the species immortal; sentimentality is their enemy."

"I'm not interested in the immortality of the species, nor is any of my board of directors. The world ends when we do."

Pearce went on as if he could eliminate Locke and his board of directors by ignoring them. "And they don't know anything about you. I didn't."

"There's a mythology that encompasses us both."

"As for the *elixir vitae*," Pearce said, "it is more complicated than I thought, not only the gamma globulins but the stem cells and maybe primordial chordamesoderm. But why would you think I had been successful?"

"There's your appearance, for one thing," Locke said. "You're not much younger than I am, but you could pass for fifty, say—no more than sixty anyway."

Pearce looked at Locke. "You're the second person who has told me that. I'm beginning to believe it myself. But it's all due to choosing long-lived parents, clean living, and a positive attitude."

Locke shrugged. "There's intuition as well: When you've been in the 'needle in a haystack' business as long as I have, you get a sense for these things."

"You also get paranoid," Pearce said.

Now it was Locke's turn to look at Pearce.

Pearce turned toward the door and saw the outline of the big male nurse against the corridor wall. In that moment it transformed itself into the image of a large shadowy figure looming over him out of the darkness, holding a club. He remembered a laser that lit up the night, and he understood. The nurse was not a nurse but a bodyguard, and he performed other services as well, perhaps even setting fires.

Pearce turned back to Locke. "No doubt you hoped I would hurry to my laboratory to rescue my samples," he said, "but I'm afraid there's nothing there to rescue. Or to search my apartment for notes. But I don't keep them there, as Tom Barnett no doubt told you."

"Who?" Locke asked.

"But I'll accept you as a patient, if you're still serious about that, because I'm a physician and that's what I do. And I will accept your grant to perform my research, if you're still serious about that, because I need it and the work is important."

Locke stood up, revealing what had been malformed about his figure. Through the part in the gown Pearce could see a metal framework that supported Locke's body from his shoulders to his ankles and no doubt turned Locke's nerve impulses into movement. Locke moved toward Pearce. Pearce kept himself from recoiling as Locke grasped his wrist in fingers like steel. No nerve damage here, or perhaps the external skeleton dived into Locke's hands to become bone and sinew. Herod had turned himself into Frankenstein's monster.

"I will fund your research," Locke said, "because I think you may be the only one who can do it. I believe you have Cartwright connections because that's what I would do if I were in your place. And when you have the elixir, you will turn it over to me."

"I will publish the results like any scientist."

"You will submit them," Locke said. "They will not be published."

"You're overconfident."

"Just realistic. I know my powers. And I know what would happen to the world if the elixir became public knowledge. There would be murders, riots, wars—and later on there would be the insoluble problems of over-population or a dropping birthrate and stagnation. But you will do the research because you are the kind of person you are, and you will give it to me because I am the kind of person I am."

Pearce pried Locke's hand from his wrist, one finger at a time. "I'm not your creature," he said. "But we understand each other. I will synthesize the elixir with the hope of getting it free from you somehow and getting it to the people who can use it more wisely than you or I. And if I fail at that and it becomes yours to do with as you wish, I won't despair. It will take the pressure off the Cartwrights, and gradually, no matter what you do, the secret will leak out and it will become the property of all humanity."

Pearce turned and walked through the door past the threatening bodyguard and through the familiar corridors and down the elevators until he found himself once more in the clean, cool purity of his laboratory, his refuge from the aggravations and petty concerns of the outside world. Now he knew that his apprehensions about someone's presence while he was gone had been mere paranoia. If Locke had known he had samples of Cartwright blood, he would never have let him go without confiscating them.

Someone buzzed at the door for admission, and Pearce went to the intercom.

"It's me, Julia," a voice said. "Are you all right?"

Pearce went into the airlock to admit her, hoping she was alone but knowing that it didn't matter: He could not exclude the world. She was alone, and she took hold of his arm in reassurance as she entered. "Sure," he said.

"So much has happened."

"My grant has been renewed," Pearce said. "It seems the executive director of the National Research Institute has checked in as a patient." Did he detect a flicker of awareness? "But I think it's time Tom Barnett moved on. He's capable enough to handle his own operation. Do you think you can find him another position?"

They had moved into the laboratory and stood in front of his experiment in apoptosis. "I'll do better than that," Hudson said. "I'll recommend him to a friend in Chicago, who's looking for a senior geriatrician."

"I'll need a new assistant," Pearce said. "Would you like to apply?"

She looked at him as if he had made a declaration of love. "I'd have to give up what little free time I have, like reading and maybe some social obligations, but I can't think of anything I'd rather do."

"I was hoping you'd give up administration," he said.

"Not yet," she said. "Maybe in a couple of years."

"I want you to see this," he said, opening the lid of his experiment. All the cell cultures were dead except for two.

"Success already?" she said.

"It's a beginning," he said, and put his arm around her shoulder. But it was more than a beginning. It was the beginning of the end. The long search was almost over, and he knew he would discover what the alchemists had searched for all their lives: the secret of immortality. But he would not give it to the world until Locke was dead; no doubt he would be replaced by someone just as determined and just as ruthless, but he would not have Locke's combination of qualities or experience.

Julia put her arm around his waist, and they stood looking down at the immortal cells. He felt like the hero of an interplanetary romance.

And yet he knew that it would take a long time before he was confident that Julia herself was not one of Locke's agents, as Barnett had turned out to be. He could love her, and he would have to trust her, but he might never be sure.

Maybe that was the human condition.

PART IV

MEDIC

He woke to pain. It was a sharp, stabbing sensation in the pit of his stomach. It pulled his knees up toward his chest and contorted his gaunt, yellowed face with an involuntary grimace that creased the skin along familiar lines, like parchment folded and refolded.

The pain stabbed again. He grunted; his body jerked. Slowly it ebbed, flood waters retreating, leaving its detritus of tormented nerve endings like a reminder of return. "Coke!" shouted the man on the twenty-ninth floor.

The word echoed around the big room, bounced off the tall ceiling and the wood-paneled walls. There was no answer. "Coke!" he screamed. "COKE!"

Footsteps pattered distantly, clapped against marble floors, muffled themselves in carpeting. They stopped beside the broad, silken bed. "Yes, Boss?" Even the voice cringed. Cringing made the man even shorter. The little eyes wavering on the monkey face refused to focus.

The sick man writhed on the bed. "The medicine!"

Coke snatched up the brown bottle from the gray metal nightstand and shook out three pills into a trembling hand. One of them dropped on the floor and he retrieved it. He held them out, and the sick man grabbed them greedily, popped them into his mouth. Into his hand Coke put a glass of water he had poured from a silver pitcher. The sick man drank, his Adam's apple jerking convulsively.

In a few minutes the sick man was sitting up. He hugged his knees to his chest and breathed in exhausted pantings. "I'm sick, Coke," he moaned. "I've got to have a doctor. I'm going to die, Coke." Terror was in his voice. "Call the doctor!"

"I can't," Coke squeaked. "Don't you remember?"

The sick man frowned as if he were trying to understand, and then his face writhed and his left hand swung out viciously. It caught Coke across the mouth and hurled him into the corner. He crouched there, one hand pressed to his bleeding lips, watching the sick man with a rodent's wary eyes.

"Be here!" the sick man snarled. "Don't make me call you!" He forgot Coke. His head dropped. He hammered futilely against the bed with a knotted fist. "Damn!" he moaned.

In that position he sat, as if graven, for minutes. Coke huddled in the corner, unmoving, watchful. At last the sick man straightened, threw back the heavy comforter, and stood up. He walked painfully to the curtained windows. As he walked he whimpered. "I'm sick. I'm going to die."

He tugged on a thick, velvet cord; the curtains whispered apart. Sunlight flooded into the room, spilled over the sick man; it turned his scarlet pajamas into flame, his face into dough. "It's a terrible thing," said the sick man, "when a dying man can't get a doctor. I need the elixir, Coke. I need treatment for this pain. I can't stand it any longer."

Coke watched; his eyes never left the tall, thin man who stood in the sunlight and stared blindly out over the city. Coke took his hand away from his mouth; the back was smeared and red, and blood welled through three cuts in the lips.

"Get me a doctor, Coke," the sick man said. "I don't care how you do it. Just get him."

Coke pulled his feet under him and scuttled out of the room. The sick man stared out of the window, not hearing.

From here the ruins were not so apparent. The city looked almost as it had fifty years ago. But if a man looked closely, he could see the holes in the roofs, the places where the porcelain false fronts had fallen and the brick behind them had crumbled and toppled into the streets.

Twelfth Street was blocked completely. Mounds of rubble made many other streets impassable. The hand of Time is not as swift as that of man, but it is inexorable.

The distant, arrowing sweep of I-35 drew the eye like movement, bright through the drabness of decay. The Kansas Medical Center was out of sight behind the rising ground to the south, but the complex, walled entity on Missouri's Hospital Hill was brilliant in the sunlight. It was an island rising out of a stinking sea, an enclave of life within the dying city.

The sick man stared out the window at the first tendrils of smog thrusting up the streets from the river, climbing toward the twenty-block-square fortress on Hospital Hill. But they would never get that far.

"Damn them!" the sick man whimpered. "Damn them!"

Flowers peered out the slit-windows of the one-man ambulance into the sooty night. The misting rain now was mixed with smog. The weather was a live thing against which the fog lamp struggled helplessly. It shifted constantly, there was no place to grab it, and the amber beam retreated in defeat, let itself be rolled back.

Ever since Flowers had left the trafficway with its lights and its occasional patrols, he had been lost and uneasy. Even the trafficway wasn't safe anymore. A twenty-millimeter shell caroming from the ambulance's armored roof made a fearful din.

Where had the police been then?

The maps that listed Truman Road as "passable" were out of date. This had to be Truman Road; it was too wide to be anything else. But he had only a vague notion how far east he had come. On either side of the street was darkness; possibly it was a shade denser on the right.

Unless that was a strip razed by wind, fire, or dynamite, it was a park. He visualized the city map. It was either the Parade or the Grove.

Something exploded under the front wheel. The ambulance leaped, shuddering, into the air. It came down hard. Before the shocks absorbed it, the chauffeur lost control and the ambulance slewed toward the left.

Flowers grabbed the emergency wheel and took over from the chauffeur, turning the ambulance in the direction of the skid. Like the muffled wail of a parturient woman came the sound of screaming tires.

Lights loomed up unexpectedly, dim-red lanterns in the

night, almost invisible in the swirling smog. They would have been waist high to a man standing in the street. That meant there was something supporting them.

Flowers twisted the wheel sharply to the right this time, clutched his seat with taut legs as the ambulance took the curb, fought the crazy tilt as it lit in mud and skidded again. It was a park, all right. He raced through it, fighting desperately for control, dodging trees and bent telephone poles with their tangles of old webs, until he jogged the ambulance back into the street. He was blocks past the beginning of madness. He pulled up.

In the ambulance, balanced at the side of the road, Flowers sat and sweated. He rubbed the back of a hand across his forehead and fought the twitching nerves across his shoulders. *Damn the city!* he thought savagely. *Damn the street department! Damn the resident who would send out a medic on a night like this.*

But it was nobody's fault.

The night traveler went at his own risk. There weren't enough of them to waste scarce taxes on street repairs, and it was no trick to avoid the holes, ruts, and uprooted slabs of concrete by daylight.

He thought back over the near accident. That hadn't felt so much like a hole. It had felt more like a landmine. And those lanterns could have been sitting on a barricade that sheltered a band of hijackers.

Flowers shivered and stepped on the accelerator and wished fervently that he were back at the Center, working out his shift in the antiseptic, bulletproof comfort of the emergency ward.

The chauffeur seemed to have settled down again. As Flowers eased the ambulance back into the middle of the road, he relaxed his grip on the wheel.

The smog shifted, and he saw the light. It glimmered far down the street like something lost in the night.

Flowers turned off all illumination and coasted past the café. Inside was a waiter behind a long counter, and a single customer. Flowers swung the ambulance around the corner into a puddle of darkness.

Before he opened the door, he broke open a fresh filter packet and slipped the filters into his nostrils, taking time to see that they were a good fit. He slid the needle gun out of the holster on the ambulance door. The magazine was full. He set the ambulance controls for automatic defense and stepped into the night.

He sniffed the air tentatively. It wasn't conditioned, not by a wild stretch of imagination, but the odor wasn't unbearable. A few minutes shouldn't reduce his life expectancy appreciably. The smog swirled around him, clutching, trying to insinuate its deadly tendrils down into his lungs. Boyd was right: *We swim in a sea of carcinogens.*

There were two ways to deal with the problem. You could climb out of the sea, or you could filter out the carcinogens. But while you were about the first, the ideal solution, you had to do your best for those who had to live in the sea.

The rain had almost stopped, but Flowers pulled his coat tight at the collar. He had left his black bag in the ambulance, but even a flash of his white jacket could be dangerous here. He could run into hijackers or Antivivs, or just an ordinary citizen with a grudge.

Flowers passed quickly in front of the broad, patched window, through the pool of yellow light, his cropped, bare head bent. His hand rested on the right-hand coat pocket where he could feel the comfortable shape of the needle gun.

The street number was long gone from above the door. Flowers pushed his way through the airlock and into the brightness.

The waiter was a thick-necked urban with a battered nose and a scar starting at his hairline and seaming the left side of his face down to his neck. He wore a filthy white jacket in obvious imitation of a doctor's uniform.

The man puffed carelessly on a cigarette that was almost lost between his fingers. Flowers's brief thrill of horror turned to disgust. The urbans weren't content merely to live in the sea; they had to add their own carcinogens.

Flowers diagnosed the thin, weasel-faced customer automatically: *Thyroid. Hypertension.* He gave the man five years. The customer eyed Flowers slyly as he spooned something out of a bowl into his crooked mouth.

"What's for you?" asked the waiter eagerly. "Got a new health-food menu. Got a new tonic fresh from the lab— all the known vitamins, plus trace minerals, iron, and a new secret ingredient in an oral suspension of medicinal alcohol. You wanta see the lab sheets, analysis, testimonials?"

"No," Flowers began, "what I—"

"Augmented fruit juice?" the waiter continued doggedly. "Vegetables? Got a drink contains the liquified whole vegetable, eighteen different kinds. One glassful gives you your weekly requirements of eleven vitamins, eight minerals and—"

"All I want to—"

"Say now," said the waiter, his voice dropping conspiratorially, "I got some stuff under the counter—straight Kentucky bourbon, no vitamins, no minerals, just plain rotgut."

"All I want to know is the address here," Flowers said.

The waiter looked at him blankly. Suspicion was like a wall between them.

Finally he jerked a thumb back the way Flowers had come. "That way," he said, "that's Benton."

"Thanks," Flowers said coldly. He turned toward the door, danger at the back of his neck, prickling. He went out into the night.

"Pssst!" Something hissed behind him.

Flowers jerked and looked back. The hiss came from Thyroid, his weasel face screwed up ingratiatingly. Flowers stopped. The man sneaked close. "Where are you going? I can maybe tell you."

Flowers hesitated. "Tenth," he said. "Thirty-four hundred block." What possible harm?

"Two blocks east, turn left. It's straight north," the man whispered huskily. Flowers muttered his thanks and turned away. He had just noticed that the man had no filters in his nose and felt embarrassed. "Look!" the man said quickly. "Want some penicillin?"

Flowers stood rooted for a moment, too surprised to act. Then his right hand went casually into his pocket to grab the pistol butt while his left hand pressed two studs on his belt buckle. Faintly, listening for it, he heard the ambulance motor rev up. "What did you say?" he asked.

"Penicillin," the shover repeated urgently. "Hot stuff. Straight from the lab, and the price is right."

"How much?"

"A buck per hundred thousand. Look!" He stuck out a grimy hand; the yellow restaurant light filtered over it, over the metal-capped ampule that nestled in the palm. "Here's three hundred thousand units all ready to go to work. Suppose you get an infection tonight. It can lay you away for good. With this little ampule here, you catch it yourself. Three bucks, okay? Save a day's work, and you got your money back."

Flowers looked curiously at the 10 cc. ampule. Any penicillin in it was cut heavily. A dollar per hundred thousand units was less than wholesale.

The shover rolled the ampule across his palm in a gesture meant to be irresistible. "Three bucks, and I throw in a syringe. You can't beat that. Well"—he pulled his hand back as if he were going to thrust it into his pocket and walk away—"it's your life. End up in a hospital."

Flowers stepped backward into the darkness, closer to the ambulance, and listened for the beat of rotors. The night was silent. "There's worse places," he said.

"Name one," the shover challenged, and edged closer. "Tell you what. I'll make it two-fifty. How about it now—two-fifty, eh? Two-fifty and the hypo?"

Finally the price dropped to two bucks. By then the shover was close. Too close, Flowers thought. He backed away. The shover grabbed at the coat to hold him. The coat fell open.

Flowers damned the fool who had failed to magnetize the closure properly. The shover staggered back from the white jacket and looked wildly around for help that was unavailable.

Flowers pulled out the pistol. "That's far enough," he said firmly.

The shover came back immediately, like a ball on a string. "Look, say. I mean there's no reason we can't do business. I give you the penicillin, you forget we ever met, eh?"

"How much have you got?"

The shover looked as if he wanted to lie but didn't dare. "Ten million. Take it. Take it all."

"Keep your hands out of your pockets." Ten million. A hundred bucks. That was a load for a shover of his caliber. "Where did you get it?"

The man shrugged helplessly. "You know how it is. Somebody passes it to me, and how do I know where it comes from? Stolen maybe. Diverted at the factory. Like that."

"Bone?"

The shover looked startled. He glanced apprehensively into the shadows. "What do you think? Come on, medic, give me a break. You wouldn't really shoot me, would you? A medic and all?"

"Sure I would," Flowers said evenly. "Who'd care?"

The light came on like a detergent spray, cleansing the darkness. Flowers heard the rotors overhead and blinked blindly.

"Don't move," said the bull voice. "You're under arrest."

The shover dashed for the darkness. Flowers aimed carefully. The needle caught him in the back of the neck, just below the basi-occipital bone. He took one more step and crumpled, half in darkness. The police sergeant listened to Flowers's description of events with unconcealed impatience. "You shouldn'ta shot him," he said. "What's the man done, he should get shot?"

"Shoving," Flowers began firmly, counting on his fingers with the muzzle of the needle gun. "Bribery. Adulterating, too, if you'll analyze that ampule." It was in the middle of the broken sidewalk, miraculously whole. The sergeant stooped for it reluctantly.

"That's no proof," he said sourly. "You think we got nothing better to do than answer false alarms? I ought to run you in for disturbing the peace and false arrest." He glanced again at the ambulance, speculatively, and back to the needle gun.

"Proof?" Flowers echoed, scowling darkly. "What do you need? There's a man with ten million units of penicillin. There's my testimony. There's this." He pressed the Playback button on his belt buckle.

The voice was rich and cultured. "Contraindications are known ilotycin sensitivity and—"

Flowers hit the stud hastily and reeled off a few feet of tape before he started it again.

"Penicillin," said the shover's husky whisper. "Hot stuff. Straight from the lab, and the price is right. . . ."

When it was finished, Flowers erased the tag end of Dr. Curry's lecture on internal medicine and added his own affidavit, "I, Benjamin Flowers, seventh-year medic, do hereby swear by Aesculapius and Hippocrates that . . ."

The officer's reluctant confirmation made it legal, and Flowers dropped the bobbin-sized spool into the officer's meaty hand. "That should be plenty. There's your prisoner."

The shover was on his hands and knees, weaving his head back and forth like a sleepy elephant. Flowers put one foot on his back and shoved him over. "I'm going to follow up on this case," he said. "I want to see this man get the full penalty. I've got your badge number. I wouldn't let him escape or lose any of the evidence."

The sergeant's voice dropped to a whine. "You don't have to get tough. I'll do my job. You should understand, though—a man's got to live. These is hard times. Why, that man's probably trying to meet payments on a medical contract! Look at it from our angle. If we was to run in every shover in town, we'd have 'em stacked eight deep in the city jail. How'd we feed 'em? How'd we keep 'em there if they didn't want to stay?"

"That's your problem, Sergeant. It's rats like that who are chewing away the foundations of medical treatment. If drugs and antibiotics circulate without supervision, the life span will plummet to seventy or lower. We have enough trouble with antibiotic sensitivity and resistant bacteria strains without this."

Flowers looked down again at the shover. He was sitting up, bewildered. He rubbed the back of his neck and pulled his hand away to stare at it. "I ain't dead," he said.

"My business is saving life, not taking it," Flowers said harshly.

The shover looked up at the voice and snarled. "You! You lousy body snatcher! Quack! You ain't gonna get away with this! John Bone'll take care of you, butcher!"

"Here, now!" the sergeant broke in sharply, hauling the shover to his feet. "That's enough out of you."

But his hands were surprisingly gentle. Flowers's lips twisted wryly.

Over the muffled throb of the helicopter's rotors, the shover shouted at him, "You and your kind—you're responsible for all this!"

The searchlight swept along the front of the porch roof and picked out two numbers hanging rusty and askew. Luckily they were the last two.

The house stood beside a vacant lot crammed with disintegrating pipe and machinery and the decaying derrick of a gas-drilling outfit. At one time the yard had been paved; now it was little better than powdery gravel as Flowers drove up to the front steps.

He turned off the lights and sat in the darkness staring up at the place. There were two stories and an attic. A dilapidated porch reached across the front. The windows stared dark and blind into the night.

Had the resident made a mistake? It would be typical.

Then he saw a dim flicker behind the west second-floor window.

Carefully, Flowers climbed the rotten wooden steps. The light built into the black bag splashed against the old door. Flowers knocked. There was no answer. The only sound was the comforting vibration of the ambulance motor.

He tried the antique brass handle. The door swung open. He pulled out the needle gun and entered cautiously. To the right an archway had been boarded off with worm-eaten plywood. Ahead was a flight of stairs.

As he climbed noiselessly, the light gleamed from hand-turned spindles, polished by generations of small hands. When he could afford a place of his own in the country, he told himself, he would have something in it like that—old, haunted by a thousand memories of the past. If he found some really good examples of early woodwork in this hovel, he could buy the place or have it condemned by the public health department.

At the top of the stairs were six doors. Flowers turned right. The door he tried was locked. It rattled under his hand.

He listened uneasily to the noises of the house. It creaked and squeaked and stirred as if it had acquired a life of its own over the centuries. His shoulders twitched.

The door opened.

The light from the black bag spilled over the girl like quicksilver. She stared into it, unblinking. Flowers stared back. She was perhaps five feet five. Her dark hair would have been very long, he thought, if it had been allowed to fall free, but it was braided and wound around her head like a coronet.

Her face was delicate and slender, the skin very white, the features regular. Her dress was yellow, flowing, belted in to a small waist; it was impractical and unflattering and completely unlike the straight, narrow fashions women were wearing these days. But there was something suggestive about the hint of figure beneath the cloth and the bare, white feet. His pulse climbed ten beats per minute.

Only then did he notice that she was blind. Her corneas were opaque, darkening the pale blue of her eyes.

"Are you the medic?" Her voice was low and gentle.

"Yes."

"Come in before you arouse our roomers. They might be dangerous."

As the girl bolted the door behind him, Flowers surveyed the room, which was reasonably spacious. Once it had been a bedroom; now it was a one-room apartment containing two chairs, a gas burner, an upended crate serving as a table for a smoking kerosene lamp, and a cot made of wood and canvas.

On the cot was a middle-aged man, sixtyish, his eyelids closed, his breathing noisy in the bare room.

"Philip Shoemaker?" Flowers asked.

"Yes," the girl said.

He noticed her eyes again. In the sun they would be the color of wild hyacinth.

"Daughter?"

"No relation."

"What are you doing here?"

"He's sick," she said simply.

Flowers studied her face. Its peace and calmness told him nothing.

As he sat down on the chair beside the cot, he unlocked his black bag. Quickly, without wasted motion, he brought out a handful of instruments, trailing their wires. One small pickup went over the old man's heart; another was fastened to his wrist; a third, to the palm. He wrapped a sphygmomanometer band around the bicep and watched it grow taut, slipped a mouthpiece between pale lips, fitted something like a skullcap to the head. . . .

When he was finished, Shoemaker was a fly caught in a web, transmitting feeble impulses to the spider lurking in the bag. This spider, though, was linked to the ambulance below by intangible lines, and together they would pour life back into the fly, not suck it away.

It took one minute and twenty-three seconds. During the next second, Flowers noticed the adhesive tape on the patient's forearm. He frowned and tore it loose. Beneath was a compress dark with blood and a small, welling slit in the median-basilic vein.

"Who's been here since this man fell ill?"

"Me," the girl said clearly. One hand was resting gently on the box that held the lamp.

Beneath the head of the cot was a quart jar. In it was a pint of blood, clotting now but still warm. Flowers put it down slowly. "Why did you perform a phlebotomy on this man?"

"There was no other way to save his life," she said gently.

"This isn't the Dark Ages," Flowers said. "You might have killed him."

"Study your lessons better, Medic," she told him softly. "In some cases bloodletting is effective when nothing else will work—in cerebral hemorrhage, for instance. It lowers the blood pressure temporarily and gives the blood in the ruptured vessel a chance to clot."

Involuntarily Flowers glanced into the bag. From the bottom, the diagnosis fluoresced at him. It was cerebral hemorrhage, all right, and the prognosis was hopeful. The hemorrhage had stopped.

He took a compress out of a pocket in the bag, pulled the tab, and watched the wrapper disintegrate. He pressed it firmly over the cut. It clung to the skin as he took his hand away. "There are laws against practicing medicine without a license," he said slowly. "I'll have to report this."

"Should I have let him die?"

"There are doctors to treat him."

"He called one. It took you an hour and a half to get here. If I had waited, he'd have died."

"I came as fast as I could. It's no joke to find a place like this at night."

"I'm not criticizing." She put her hand back until she felt the chair behind her and sank down into it, lightly, gracefully, and folded her white hands in her lap. "You asked me why I bled him. I told you."

Flowers was silent. The girl's logic was impeccable, but she was wrong all the same. There weren't any reasonable excuses for breaking the law. The practice of medicine had to be the monopoly of men who were carefully, exactingly trained for it and indoctrinated in the ancient ethics. No one else could be permitted to tamper with the most sacred thing in the world.

"You were lucky," he said. "You might have guessed wrong."

"There are no degrees to death."

She rose and walked toward him confidently, put a hand on his shoulder, and leaned past him to touch Shoemaker's forehead. "No," she said, and her voice was firm with an odd certainty. "He'll get well now. He's a good man. We mustn't let him die."

The girl's nearness was a warm fragrance, stirring, provocative. Flowers felt his blood pressure mount. *Why not?* he thought; *she's only an urban*. But he couldn't, and it wasn't just a medic's honor or even, perhaps, that she was blind.

He didn't move, but she drew away, took back her hand, as if she sensed the emotions fermenting inside him.

"I've got to get him to the hospital," Flowers said. "Besides the hemorrhage, there'll be infection."

"I scrubbed the arm with soap and then with alcohol," she said. "I sterilized the knife in the lamp flame and scorched the bandage over the lamp chimney."

Her fingers looked blistered. "You *were* lucky," he said coldly. "Next time someone will die."

She turned her face toward his voice. Flowers found the movement strangely appealing. "What can you do when they need you?"

It was too much like a physician's response to the world's plea for help. A doctor had the right to respond to the plea; she didn't. He turned brusquely back to Shoemaker and began stripping away the instruments and stowing them in his bag. "I'll have to carry him down to the ambulance. Can you carry the bag for me to light the way?"

"You mustn't take him. He hasn't kept up payments on his contract. You know what they'll do."

Flowers stopped in the act of snapping the bag shut. "If he's a defaulter . . ." he began, his voice trembling on the verge of fury.

"What would you do," she asked quietly, "if you were dying and alone? Wouldn't you call for help? Any help? Would you stop to weigh legalities? He had a contract once, and the payments ruined him, cost him his home in the country, drove him here to the sustenance life. But when he was sick, he turned to his old faith, as a dying Catholic calls for his priest."

Flowers recoiled from the comparison. "And he deprived several people of vital, lawful attention. The chances are he traded his life for that of someone else. That's why the laws were passed. Those who pay for medical treatment shouldn't be penalized by those who can't—or won't, which is usually the case. If Shoemaker can't pay, he ought to be repossessed." He stooped toward the old man.

She pulled him back with surprising strength and slipped between them, bent backward, one arm thrown back protectively toward Shoemaker. Her eyes were cloudy embers in the lamplight. "Surely you've got enough blood, enough organs. They'll kill him."

"There's never enough," Flowers said. "And there's research, after that." He put an impatient hand on her shoulder to push her aside. Under the dress material, the flesh felt warm and soft. "You must be an Antiviv."

"I am, but that's only part of it. I'm asking for him, because he's worth saving. Are you so inflexible, so perfect, that you can't—forget?"

He stopped pushing, looked down at his hand for a moment, and let it drop. He refused to fight with the girl for the man's body.

"All right," he said.

He picked up the black bag with a snap that locked it shut and started toward the door.

"Wait!" she said.

He looked back at her as she moved toward him blindly, her hand outstretched until her fingers touched the arm of his coat. "I want to thank you," she said gently. "I thought there wasn't any mercy left in the medical profession."

For a moment his viscera felt cold, anesthetized, and then the icy feeling melted in a surge of anger. "Don't misunderstand me," he said brutally, shrugging her hand away. "I'm going to turn in his name to the Agency. I'm going to report you, too. That's my duty."

Her hand fell to her side in a gesture of apology, for her own mistake and perhaps also for humanity itself. "We do what we must."

She moved forward past him, unbolted the door, and

turned toward him, her back against the door. "I don't think you're as hard as you pretend to be."

That stopped him. He wasn't hard. He resented the implication that he was, that medics in general were incapable of understanding, were devoid of sympathy.

Those who must live in the midst of sickness and death, upon whose skill and judgment rest health and life and their concomitant, happiness, can't be touched by the drama, the poignancy, the human values of every situation. It would be unendurable.

"There's an old man downstairs who needs help," she said hesitantly. "Would you see him?"

"Out of the question," he answered sharply.

Her head lifted for a moment. That was pride, he thought. Then she nodded. "I'm sorry," she said softly.

The light was dangerous, she said, and offered to lead him. Her hand was warm and firm and confident. Three-quarters of the way down there was a landing, where the stairs turned left. A door opened in the darkness to the right of the landing.

Flowers tore his hand loose and stuck it into his coat pocket onto the solid reassurance of the needle gun.

Glimmering whitely in the dark rectangle of the door was a ghost of a face. "Leah?" it said. It was a girl's voice. "I thought it was you. Give me your hand. Let me hold it for a moment. I thought I would never get through the night. . . ."

"There now," said Leah. She put out a hand toward the face. "You're going to be all right. Don't let yourself believe anything else."

Flowers snapped on the light of the black bag. It hit the girl in the doorway like a blow; she recoiled, moaning, her arm over her eyes.

Flowers turned the light off—he had seen enough. The girl, in her thin, mended nightdress, was a bundle of bones wrapped tautly in pale skin. Except for two feverish spots of color in her cheeks, her face was dead-white.

She was dying of tuberculosis.

Tuberculosis. The white plague. It had made a new assault on humanity a century ago, when the old bacilli had developed immunity to the drugs that had once threatened to wipe it out. But today! Why do they do it!

"Go up and stay with Phil," Leah said. "He needs you. He's had a stroke, but he's better now."

"All right, Leah," the girl said. Her voice seemed stronger, more confident. She slipped past them silently and climbed the stairs.

"What's the matter with them?" Flowers's voice was strained and puzzled. "Tuberculosis is no problem. We have narrow-band antibiotics that can cure it easily. Why do they let themselves die?"

She stopped in front of the worm-eaten plywood partition and raised her face toward him. "Because it's cheaper. It's all they can afford."

"Cheaper to die?" Flowers exclaimed incredulously. "What kind of economy is that?"

"The only kind of economy they know. The only kind the hospitals will let them practice. You've made good health too expensive. A few months of bed rest," she said wearily, "a hundred grams of neo-dihydrostreptomycin, a thousand grams of PAS, perhaps some collapsed-lung therapy, some rib resections. That girl has never seen more than fifty dollars all at once. If she lived to be a hundred she couldn't save half the money necessary for the treatment. She's got children to support. She can't stop working for a day, much less for months—"

"There are clinical contracts," Flowers said impatiently.

"They don't cover the kind of treatment she needs," Leah said wistfully. A door opened behind her. "Good night, Medic." Then she was gone.

At the door he turned back impetuously, words pouring to his lips: *If there isn't enough to go around, who are you going to treat—the indigent or the prosperous, the wasters or the savers, the bottomless pits or those who can finance the future, more medicine, more health for everyone?*

But the words died on his lips. The panel in the partition had come ajar. In the room behind it was a battered old aluminum chaise lounge—Twentieth Century Modern. An old man was propped upright in it, so straight and still that Flowers thought for a moment the man was dead. He was a very old man. Flowers thought that he had never seen a man as old, although geriatrics was one of the Medical Center's leading specialties. His hair was pure white and thick; his face was seamed, like old leather, the flesh sagging away from the strong facial bones.

Beside the chair Leah had sunk to her knees. She had

one of the bony hands in hers, pressed to her cheek, her eyelids closed over their clouded corneas.

Flowers found himself standing in the doorway, the panel swinging noiselessly away from him. There was something familiar about that old face, something he couldn't place, pin down. As he was thinking about it, he noticed with a shock that the old man's eyes had opened. It was like a return from the dead. The old eyes had life in them, faded brown though they were, and the wrinkled old skin seemed to smooth and grow firm. The body warmed and grew strong as the face smiled gently.

"Come in, Medic," the old man whispered.

Leah's face came up, her sightless eyes open; she turned toward him. She smiled, too. It was a warming thing, like sunlight.

"You came back to help," Leah said.

Flowers shook his head slowly and then remembered that she couldn't see. "There's nothing I can do."

"There's nothing anyone can do," the old man whispered. "Even without your gadgets, Medic, you know what's wrong with me. You can't mend a whole body, not with all your skill and all your fancy instruments. The body wears out. With most of us it happens part by part. With a few it goes all at once.

"You could give me a new heart from some unfortunate defaulter, but my arteries would still be thickened with arteriosclerosis. And if, somehow, you replaced those without killing me, I would still have a fibrotic liver, scarred lungs, senile ductless glands, probably a few carcinomas. And even if you gave me a new body, you still couldn't help me, because down deep, where your knives can't reach and your instruments can't measure, is the me that is old beyond repair."

When Leah turned her face back toward Flowers, he was shocked to see tears trickling from the blind eyes. "Can't you do something?" Her voice broke. "Aren't you good for anything?"

"Leah!" Even the old man's whisper was reproof.

"It leaves a permanent recording in the ambulance library," Flowers explained reasonably. "I can't afford that; neither can you."

She pressed her forehead fiercely against the back of the old man's hand. "I can't stand it, Russ. I can't bear to lose you."

"Tears are wasted on a man who has outlived his generation," Russ said, "and almost his own era." He smiled at Flowers; it was almost a benediction. "I'm one hundred and twenty-five years old." He drew his hand gently from Leah's firm young hands and folded his across his lap. They lay there as if they no longer belonged to him. "That's a long time."

Leah stood up angrily. "There must be something you can do—with all your magnificent knowledge, all the expensive gadgets we bought you!"

"There's the elixir," he said thoughtlessly.

Russ smiled again, reminiscently perhaps. "Ah, yes—the elixir. I had almost forgotten. *Elixir vitae.*"

"Would it help?" Leah demanded.

"No," Flowers said firmly.

He had said too much already. Laymen weren't

equipped for medical information; it confused them; it blurred the medical picture. What patients needed more than anything else was not an understanding of their conditions but implicit faith in their doctors. When every treatment is familiar, none is effective. It is better for medicine to be magical than to be commonplace.

Besides, the elixir was still only a laboratory phenomenon. Perhaps it would never be more than that. The stuff was a synthesis of a rare blood protein—a gamma globulin—which had been discovered in the bloodstreams of no more than a handful of persons in the whole world. This protein, this immunity factor, seemed to pass on its immunity as if death itself were a disease. . . .

"A tremendously complicated process," he said. "Prohibitively expensive." He turned accusingly toward Russ. "I can't understand why you didn't have new corneas grafted onto her eyes."

"I couldn't take the sight of anyone else," Leah said softly, reproachfully.

"There's accidental deaths," Flowers pointed out.

"How can the recipient be sure?"

"Don't you want her to see?" Flowers demanded of Russ.

"If wanting were enough," the old man whispered, "she would have had my eyes many years ago. But there's the expense, my boy. It all comes back to that."

"Stupidity!" Flowers turned to leave.

"Wait, boy," Russ whispered. "Come here a moment."

Flowers turned and walked to the old man's chair; he

looked down at Leah and back to Russ. The old man held out his hand, palm up. Automatically Flowers put out his hand to meet it, let his hand rest upon it. As the hands met, Flowers felt a curious sensation, almost electrical, as if something had stimulated a nerve into sending a message up his arm to his brain and carrying an answer back.

Russ's hand dropped back limply. He lowered his head wearily against the back of the chaise lounge, his eyes closed. "A good man, Leah, troubled but sincere. We might do worse."

"No," Leah said firmly, "he must not come here again. It wouldn't be wise."

"Don't worry about that," Flowers said. He wouldn't be back; he hadn't felt like this since he was a little boy listening to his father tell him about medicine.

"Some empty time," Russ said distantly, "you might think of this, a conclusion I reached many years ago: *There can be too many doctors and not enough healers.*"

Leah rose gracefully from the floor. "I'll see you to the door."

Her unconscious use of the phrase brought pity chokingly into Flowers's throat. It was a tragedy because she was beautiful—he thought of her now as beautiful—and peacefully beautiful inside. Reporting her was going to be painful.

He wondered how his hand had felt to her: hot, sweaty, nervous? How had he seemed to her?

He paused at the outside door. "I'm sorry I couldn't help your grandfather."

"He's not my grandfather—he's my father. I was born the year he was one hundred. He wasn't old then. He was middle-aged, everyone thought. It's only these last few months he's grown old. I think it's a surrender we make when we grow very tired."

"How do you live—with him sick, and—"

"And me blind? People are generous."

"Why?"

"They're grateful, I suppose. For the times when we can help them. I collect old remedies from grandmothers and make them up; I brew ptisans; I'm a midwife when I'm needed; I sit up with the sick, help those I can, and bury those I can't. You can report this, too, if you wish."

"I see," Flowers said, turning away and swinging back, irresolute. "Your father—I've seen him somewhere. What's his name?"

"He lost it more than fifty years ago. Here in the city, people call him *healer*." She held out her hand toward him. Flowers took it reluctantly. This was the end of it. The hand was warm; his hand remembered the warmth. It would be a good hand to hold if you were sick.

"Goodbye, Medic," she said. "I like you. You're human. So few of them are. But don't come back. It wouldn't be good for any of us."

Flowers cleared his throat noisily. "I said I wouldn't," he said; even to him it sounded petulant and childish. "Goodbye."

She stood in the doorway as he turned, shifted the bag into his right hand, and picked his way down the porch stairs. It was a good bag, and it felt solid in his hand. It was on semipermanent loan from the Center. Against its black side were two words imprinted in gold: BENJ. FLOWERS. Someday there would be two more letters added: M.D.

A few months more and he would have earned them; he would buy the bag, make a down payment on his library, pass the state examination. He would have a license from the state to practice medicine upon the bodies of its citizens. He would be a doctor.

For the first time since he could remember, the prospect didn't excite him.

A man was lying almost under the front wheel of the ambulance. Beside him, on the broken pavement, was a crowbar. Flowers rolled the man over. His eyes were closed, but he was breathing easily. He had got too close and the supersonics had knocked him out.

He should call the police about this, too, but he felt too tired for another battle with the police.

He pulled the body out of the path of the wheels and opened the ambulance door. There was a whisper of movement behind him.

"Medic!" Leah screamed. Her voice was distant and frightened.

Flowers started to turn, but it was too late. The night came down and covered him.

He opened his eyes to darkness, and the thought was instantaneous: *This is what it is to be blind. This is what Leah knows always.*

His head throbbed. There was an egg-sized lump on

the back of it, where someone had hit him. The hair was matted with dried blood. He winced as his fingers explored the depth of the cut, but it wasn't too bad. He decided that there was no concussion.

He didn't feel blind. Probably there was no light.

He had a faded, uncertain memory—as of something lost in childhood mists—of a wild ride through city streets; of a heavy door that swung upward, clanging; of an entrance into a place cavernous, musty, echoing; of being carried—on what? the ambulance stretcher?—up a short flight of stairs, through something awkward, up more steps, down dark halls, and being lowered to the floor.

Someone had said something. "He's coming around. Shall I tap him again?"

"Never mind. Just roll him out until we need him. He won't go anywhere."

Thump! Blackness again.

Concrete was under him, cold and hard. He got to his feet, feeling shaky, aching all over, not just his head. He took a cautious step forward, and another, holding one hand straight out in front, fingers extended, the other arm curled protectively over his face.

At the fifth step his fingers touched a vertical surface. Concrete again. A wall. He turned and moved along the wall to a corner and along a second wall that was shorter and had a door in it. The door was solid metal; it had a handle, but the handle wouldn't turn. The other walls were unbroken. When he had finished the circuit, he had a mental picture of a windowless room about fifteen feet long by nine feet wide.

He sat down and rested.

Somebody had booby-trapped him, knocked him out, brought him to this concrete box, locked him in.

It could have been only one person. The man he had pulled from under the wheel. He had crept in close to the ambulance, so slowly that the detectors hadn't reacted. When Flowers had come, they had clicked off, and the man had been released to club him. A crowbar might make a wound like that.

If he was a hijacker, if he had wanted the drugs and the instruments, why had he bothered to bring along the medic?

Flowers went through his pockets—futilely. The coat and the jacket underneath were empty. They had taken the needle gun.

He would hide behind the door, he decided. When it opened—he could tell from the hinges on this side that it opened inward—he would be behind it. He had fists. He was big enough; maybe he was strong enough. He would have a good chance of taking the hijackers by surprise.

Meanwhile, he sat in the dark silence, remembering the dream he had wakened from. It had seemed to him that he was a little boy again, and his father was talking to him in the grown-up fashion he had affected with his son. It had always embarrassed Flowers, even when he was very young.

"Ben," his father said, "there may be more important

things than medicine, but you can't be sure of any of them." He put his hand on the boy's shoulder. It was heavy and Ben wanted to shrug it off, but he didn't dare.

"It's different with medicine. You deal with life, and life is always important. You'll feel it every day, because every day you'll have a personal fight with death, you'll beat him back a foot, surrender a few inches, and come back to the battle. Because life is sacred, Ben. No matter how mean it is or crippled, it's sacred. That's what we bow down to, Ben. It's the only thing worth worshipping."

"I know, Dad," Flowers said, his voice high and a little frantic. "I want to be a doctor. I want to—"

"Then bow down, boy. Bow down!"

But why should he think of Leah's father? Why should the memory of something that had probably never happened make him think of Russ?

Was it what the dying man had said: "Some empty time . . ."

What time could be emptier than this?

Too many doctors and not enough healers! That's what the old man had said. Absurd. It was like so many meaningless phrases that seem portentous because of their vagueness. It reminded him of arguments with other medics.

In the darkness the hospital incense seemed to drift to him—anesthetic and alcohol. The good smells. The reverent smells. Anyone who criticized medicine just didn't know what he was talking about.

He remembered standing by the dormitory's bullet-proof window, staring out at the block of houses being razed to make room for the two new wings, geriatrics and the premature section of obstetrics. It seemed to him that the twin processes of destruction and construction never stopped. Somewhere on the Center's periphery there were always new wings growing over the old ruins.

How many square blocks did the Center's walls enclose? Forty? Forty-five? He had forgotten.

He must have said it aloud, because Charley Brand answered from his desk. "Sixty and three-fourths." Brand was a strange person, an accretion of miscellaneous information waiting to be mined, a memory bank awaiting only the proper question. But he lacked something; he was cold and mechanical; he couldn't synthesize.

"Why?" asked Hal Mock.

"No reason," Flowers said, vaguely irritated. "I went on a call a few days ago—into the city."

"'Thus conscience doth make cowards of us all,'" Brand quoted, not looking up from the desk where he flipped the frames in the viewer, one every second. Mechanical, mechanical.

"What does that mean?" Flowers snapped.

"Sometimes," Mock mused, "I wish something would happen to a few medics in our class. Like getting sick—not seriously, you understand—or breaking a leg. The school can only graduate so many, you know. It has a quota. But we're all so healthy, so careful. It's disgusting." He brooded over it. "Think of it. Seven years of torture, grinding my brains to a sharp point, and the prize depends on the right answers to a few stupid questions. It makes me sick to think about it."

Brand shifted uneasily and changed the subject. "What are you going to specialize in, Ben? After you graduate."

"I don't know," Flowers said. "I haven't thought about it."

"I have," said Brand. "Psychiatry."

"Why be a head-shrinker?" Mock asked scornfully.

"Simple economics," Brand said. "The incidence of mental disease in this country is sixty-five point three percent. Almost two out of every three persons needs the services of a psychiatrist during his lifetime. On top of that are the neuroses and the stress diseases like stomach cramps, rheumatoid arthritis, asthma, duodenal ulcers, hypertension, heart disease, ulcerative colitis. And life doesn't get any simpler. You can't beat those figures."

"How about geriatrics?" Mock asked slyly. "The incidence of senescence is one hundred percent. That's the well that never runs dry."

"Until they bring out the elixir in quantity!"

"They'll never do that," Mock said shrewdly. "They know which side—"

Flowers listened intently in the darkness. Was that a noise on the other side of the door? A rattling, clanging sort of noise?

He sprang to his feet, but the noise—if it had been a noise—wasn't repeated. There was no use taking chances. He felt his way into the corner, behind the door, and leaned against the wall, waiting.

"There's more to medicine than money," he repeated softly.

"Sure," Mock said, "but economic facts are basic. Ignore them and you can't do an acceptable job at your profession. Look at the income tax rate: It starts at fifty percent. On one hundred thousand a year, it's eighty percent. How are you going to pay for your bag, your instruments, your library? You can't practice medicine without them. How are you going to pay your dues in the county medical society, in the AMA, special assessments . . . ?"

"Why are the income taxes so high?" Flowers demanded. "Why are instruments so expensive? Why are a hundred million people without adequate medical facilities, condemned to a lingering death in a sea of carcinogens, unable to afford what the orators call 'the finest flower of medicine'?"

"It's the cost of living," Mock said, curling his lip. "Whatever you want, you have to pay for. Haven't you figured it out?"

"No," Flowers said savagely. "What do you mean?"

Mock glanced cautiously behind him. "I'm not that foolish," he said slyly. "You never know who might be listening. Some medic might have left his recorder turned on inside his desk on the off chance of catching somebody with his ethics down. I'll say this, though: *We can be too healthy!*"

"Nuts!" Flowers muttered in the darkness of the concrete cell. He let himself sink down the wall until he reached the floor.

They were all wrong, Mock and Russ and Leah and the rest of them who hinted at dark things. In another age they would have been burned at the stake. He had seen Dr. Cassner refute them brilliantly in a beautiful three-hour display of microsurgical virtuosity.

It began as an ordinary arterial resection and transplant. The overhead shadowless light was searching and cold on the draped body of the old man. The assistant surgeons and nurses worked together with the exquisite precision that is the result of years of training and experience.

The air conditioners murmured persistently, but sweat beaded Cassner's broad forehead and trickled down beneath his mask before the nurse could mop it away with sterile cotton. But Cassner's hands never stopped. They were things in motion, disembodied, alive. His fingers manipulated the delicate controls of the surgical machine with a sureness, a dexterity unmatched in this part of the country, perhaps anywhere. Genius is incomparable.

Flowers watched with a hypnotized fascination that made time meaningless. The scalpels sliced through the skin with unerring precision, laying bare the swollen old arteries; deft metal fingers tied them off, snipped them in two, accepted a lyophilized transplant, and grafted the healthy young artery to the stump of the old; the suture machine moved swiftly after, dusting the exposed area with antibiotics, clamping together the edges of the incision, sealing them with a quick, flattening movement. . . .

Cassner's eyes flickered from the patient on the operating table to the physiological monitor on the wall behind it, absorbing at a single glance the composite picture of the patient's condition: blood pressure, heartbeat, cardiography, oxygen content, respiration. . . .

The microsurgeon saw the danger first. The operation was, comparatively, a speedy thing, but there were disadvantages. The area involved was large, and even the chlorpromazine-promethazine-Dolosal cocktail and the chilling could not nullify the shock entirely. And the heart was old.

It was impossible to transfer the instruments to the new area swiftly enough. Cassner took the scalpel in his own fingers and opened up the chest cavity with a long, sure stroke. "Heart machine," he said in his quick, high voice to no one in particular.

It was pumping within thirty seconds, its tubes tied to the aorta and the left atrium. Two minutes later a new heart was in the old chest; Cassner grafted the arteries and veins to it. Ten minutes after the monitor had signaled the heart stoppage, Cassner pulled out the old heart and held it, a dead thing of worn-out muscle. He motioned wearily for his first assistant to inject the digitalis and shock the new heart into action.

As the chest cavity was closed, the new heart began squeezing powerfully, forcing the blood through the healthy new arteries.

Cassner would have had a good excuse for turning the more routine job over to the assistant, but he completed the arterial job before he turned away toward the dressing room. . . . That's what the scoffers forgot, Flowers thought—what a man got for his money: the skill, the drugs, the instruments. Twenty years earlier, without modern medicine, the man on the operating table would have died.

That man wasn't too healthy. If he were any less healthy, he'd be dead. Now he was good for five to ten years more.

"That's nothing," Mock said. "I saw Smith-Johnson save a five-month fetus and I had to wonder: Why?"

Flowers looked scornful. He knew why: It was because life was sacred, any life, all life. That's what a doctor bowed down to.

"Sometimes in the night," Mock said distantly, "I can hear their voices wailing, muffled by the incubators, all the premies that were too weak to live, that nature wanted to be rid of, and we saved—for blindness and disease and perpetual care. Oh, Cassner's good, but I wonder: How much did the operation cost?"

"How should I know?"

"Why don't you find out?"

Flowers shivered in the darkness, although the room was hot, and pushed his hands into his pockets. He touched his belt buckle.

He started, and wondered why he hadn't thought of it before. He pushed the alarm button hastily.

It was a chance, and any chance was worth trying. He supposed that the hijackers had turned off the ambulance motor when they parked it.

Flowers sank back against the wall, remembering how he had gone to the business office. They had taken down his name, but they had shown him the statement. The old man had put down a $200,000 deposit. The business office had figured it pretty shrewdly. The total bill was only a few hundred less.

He glanced down the Debit column with its four- and five-digit numbers:

Operating Room: $40,000

Well, why not? The heart machine alone had cost $5,000,000, and that microsurgery had been the marvel of the Middle West when it had been constructed and equipped. Someone had to pay for it.

After that was the room fee, anesthesia, laboratory fees, X-ray, tissue exam, EKG-EEG-BMR fee, drugs and dressings, and, most prominently, the prices for new organs and arteries:

New Arteries (1 set): $30,000

New Heart (1): $50,000

Some poor devil of a defaulter had paid his bill.

Flowers sat in the concrete cell and told himself that a medic shouldn't have to weigh questions of relative value. So the operation had cost the old man $30,000 to $40,000 for each year of life it promised him. It was worth it—from the old man's viewpoint. Was there another viewpoint? Was someone else footing the bill?

Society, maybe. Was it worth it to society? Maybe not. The old man was a consumer now, eating up and using up what he had been smart enough or strong enough or ruthless enough to have produced when he was younger.

So maybe it wasn't worth it to society.

That was a brutal, inhuman viewpoint. That was the reason nobody wanted society to be the judge of what was worthwhile. Medicine had been fighting that possibility for centuries; on that point the AMA was immovable. A man had an inalienable right to the doctor of his choice and the medical treatment he could afford.

Of course, of course. It illustrated the danger of looking at the problem all backward, as Hal Mock might. The knowledge was there; the skill was there; the equipment was there. If it wasn't used, it would be an outrageous waste.

But maybe, he thought sharply, the mistake came earlier, in developing the knowledge, the skill, and the equipment in the first place. That was when society footed the bill.

Society puts a price on everything. In every era there are limited quantities of intelligence, energy, and what people collectively inherit from the thought and labor of the past, capital. Society's value system determines how these assets are distributed among a thousand different enterprises.

It was like a budget: so much for food, so much for shelter, so much for clothing, education, research, entertainment; so much for the doctor.

What was more valuable than good health? Nothing, said society. Without it, all is worthless.

What did Mock mean when he said we can be too healthy?

Was there an optimum beyond which medicine consumed more than it produced in benefits? And was there a point past that at which medicine became a monster, devouring the society that produced it?

Maybe the cost of living could be too high. Maybe a society could be too healthy, like a hypochondriac, spending itself into bankruptcy in a vain effort to cure small or fancied ills.

"Charley," he asked Brand one day, "what percentage of the national income went into medicine last year?"

"Therapy, education, research, production, or construction?"

"Everything."

"Let's see—fifteen point six, ten point one, twelve point nine, five point two, eight point seven—that's—what does that add up to?"

"Fifty-two point five," said Flowers.

In the darkness of the concrete room, he repeated the figure to himself. "Nonsense," he muttered.

It was a relief from thought to discover that the recorder was running. He had only to press the playback stud to discover the identities of his captors.

He pressed the stud and listened, engrossed, to the voices of Leah and Russ and himself. . . . But before the tape reached Leah's frightened cry, the door swung open and a blinding light dazzled his eyes.

He stabbed the recorder into silence and cursed silently. He had lost his chance.

"Who are you?" he demanded.

"Police officers," said a harsh voice. "Didn't you send out an alarm?"

"Get that light out of my eyes," Flowers said suspiciously. "Let me see you."

"Sure."

The light turned away, splashed against dark trousers, lighter tunics, glittered on badges, exposed faces, caps.

One of the two officers looked familiar; surely that

was the sergeant to whom he had turned over the shover.

"Well, Medic," the sergeant said, "we meet again, eh? Come on, we'd better get out of here."

"Certainly, but where's the ambulance? Did you find it? Did you catch the hijackers? Did you—"

"Hold it." The sergeant chuckled. "We ain't got time for everything now. The hijackers might come back, eh, Dan?"

"You bet," said Dan.

They went down long marble corridors, echoing with their footsteps, opening before them as the flashlight moved forward into the darkness. They reached a wide hall. On each side were three sets of heavy brass doors, one set standing open. Behind it was an elevator. Flowers followed the officers into the car. The sergeant pushed a button. They started up with a jerk. The elevator creaked and rattled and wheezed until Flowers wondered whether it would ever make it. That was the sound he had heard in the concrete room, he thought. He leaned back wearily against the ornate brasswork of the wall and thought, *I'm lucky*.

In his moment of safety he found time to wonder about Leah. Was the blind girl all right? Surely she hadn't been hurt. And her father—what was familiar about his face?

It reminded him of a picture, of the time he had wandered through the hall of past presidents in the courthouse headquarters of the county medical society. There were dozens of the portraits, all done in dark oils, all with their solemn faces and their stern eyes that seemed to watch him as he passed, as if to say, "We received the great Aesculapian tradition intact, unblemished; we hand it down to you, unchanged. Live up to it if you can."

It was a pretty grim business, Flowers thought, this presidency of the county medical society. No occasion for laughter.

No, that was wrong. One of them had worn a ghost of a smile, the vague possibility around the painted lips that they once had smiled, that they did not take this matter quite as seriously as the painter.

He had bent over, curiously, to read the name on the tarnished brass plate fastened to the bottom of the frame, but he had forgotten it. He bent again, in imagination, trying to read the memory engraved on his brain. He visualized it, getting closer, clearer. He read the name:

DR. RUSSELL PEARCE
President, 1972–1983

Russell Pearce—of course, how could he forget? Discoverer of *elixir vitae*, developer of the synthesis which bore his name, dying now of senescence in a rotting house in the middle of the city.

Dr. Russell Pearce—Russ—Leah's father.

The door opened in front of them. Hesitantly Flowers stepped out into the hall. It was almost identical with the one below.

To the left were tall windows opening on a graying night. "Where are we?" Flowers asked fretfully.

"City Hall," said the sergeant. "Come on."

"What am I doing in City Hall? I'm not going anywhere until you answer my questions."

"Hear that, Dan? He ain't going anywhere. Ain't that the truth? Go tell Coke we're here."

The other officer, big and sullen-faced, slipped through a pair of glass doors at the other end of the hall. The sergeant grinned and ostentatiously adjusted a pistol in the holster at his side.

That one, Flowers thought with a shudder, wouldn't be loaded with anesthetic slivers. "You've got no right to keep me here against my will."

"Who's keeping you here against your will?" the sergeant asked, surprised. "You want to leave? Go. Of course, you gotta be careful about little accidents on the way, like tripping on the stairs. It's a long way down."

This degradation of the police power of the city paralyzed Flower's will.

The wizened little man who came back with Dan peered at Flowers speculatively. "He's just a medic," he said petulantly, his bruised mouth curving down in disappointment.

"You expect us to be choosy?" the sergeant complained.

"Well," Coke said timidly, "I hope it's all right. Follow me." He motioned to Flowers.

The medic compressed his lips defiantly. "No!"

The sergeant's hand moved in a blur of speed. It hit Flowers's face, palm open, with a solid, meaty sound. The room reeled; Flowers's knees buckled. Anger burst over him redly, and he straightened, his arms ready for battle.

Dan stepped forward, grinning, and kicked him in the groin.

The pain blurred everything as Flowers lay curled on the floor, trying to get his breath. Gradually the pain ebbed, and his muscles relaxed enough to let his legs fall away from his belly. Flowers forced himself to his knees on the cold marble floor and struggled up. He found the sergeant's arm around him, helping him stand.

"There now," the officer said casually, "we're going to be sensible, aren't we?"

Flowers gritted his teeth and did not groan. He let himself be led through swinging glass doors into a large room bisected by a long, darkly polished counter. Against the right wall was a bench. On the bench was a thin, weasel-faced man.

The weasel face smirked at Flowers. *Thyroid,* Flowers thought dazedly. The shover. Free. Laughing. While he was held by the police, in agony.

By the time they reached the heavy walnut door in the right wall, Flowers could walk without crippling pain. "Where are we going?" he got out between clenched teeth.

"The Boss needs a doctor," Coke said, trotting past him to open the door. Beyond was darkness. "It's about time he should wake up."

The Boss? "Who's he?"

The gray little man stared at him incredulously. "John Bone!"

"Coke!" screamed a voice thinned with pain. "Coke! Where are you?"

"Here, Boss!" Coke said in a frightened voice. "Here with a medic!"

He scurried across the room to draw curtains away from tall windows. The smog-smeared light crept across the floor, onto the wide bed with its tumbled covers. A man was sitting upright among them. He was cadaverously thin, his face a blade, his arms and legs mere sticks.

"A medic!" he screamed. "Who wants a medic? I'm dying. I need a doctor!"

"This is all we could get," Coke said as if he had been born cringing.

"Oh, all right," Bone said. "He'll have to do." He swung his feet over the edge of the bed and fitted them into baby-blue mules. "Come on, Medic. Treat me!"

"Where's your contract?" Flowers asked.

"Contract!" Bone screamed. "Who's got a contract? If I had a contract, do you think I'd be hijacking medics?"

"No contract, no treatment."

The hand hit him on the back of the neck like a club. Flowers sagged and almost fell. Distantly he heard his own voice saying, "That won't do any good."

When the blackness went away, he was sitting in a chair near the bed. He turned his head painfully. The policemen were standing behind him, one on each side. In the doorway the shover was lurking, watching eagerly. Coke was in front of him. Pacing back and forth between the chair and the window was Bone, his mules clacking against the marble floor and then clumping on the thick carpeting.

"I want treatment, Medic! Can't you see I'm dying?"

"We're all dying," Flowers said.

Bone stopped and stared fiercely at Flowers. "Sure. But some of us can put it off longer if we're smart. I'm smart. I want treatment. I can pay. Why shouldn't I have treatment? Why should I be discriminated against? You think nobody ever got treatment who wasn't entitled to it?"

"The only thing I know is that there are ethical standards and I'm bound to them. What difference does it make?" Flowers said defiantly. "You don't need a doctor; you need a psychiatrist. The only disease you've got is hypochondria. Everybody knows that."

Bone turned to stare at Flowers with dark unreadable eyes. "So," he said softly. "A hypochondriac, am I? I am not dying, eh? Who is to say? These pains in my belly, they are imaginary? My head is sick? Well, maybe. Come here. I want to show you something."

Flowers didn't move quickly enough. A rough hand shoved him out of the chair, propelled him across the room. He stopped beside Bone in front of one of the tall windows. The dawn had come in earnest, and the city lay beneath them, gilded by the sun, the signs of decay hidden.

"Look!" Bone said, encompassing the city within the sweep of his arm. "My city! I am the last of a dying breed, the political boss. After me, the deluge. There will be no more city. It will fall apart. Isn't that a sad thing?"

Flowers looked at the city, knowing its ruins, and thought it would be a very good thing if it were all destroyed by fire or flood, wiped off the earth just as medicine had wiped out smallpox, diphtheria, malaria, and a hundred other infectious diseases—only in a different way, of course.

"The City," Bone mused. "It is a strange thing. It has a life of its own, a personality, emotions. I woo her. I rage at her, I beat her. But underneath it all there is love. She is dying, and there is no medicine to save her." There were real tears in Bone's eyes.

"I can't help her," Bone said softly, beating his fist gently against the paneled wall beside the window. "I can only weep. What has killed her? That cancer there upon the hill! The doctors have killed her. Medicine has killed her."

Flowers looked where the skeletal finger pointed, toward the hill rising like an island of sunlight out of a sea of night. The reddish, slanting rays gleamed on the stout walls and sky-reaching towers of Hospital Hill.

"You killed it," Bone said, "with your talk of carcinogens and urban perils. 'Get out of the city!' you said, and wealth left, moved into the country, built its automatic factories, and left us bloodless, cancer eating at our veins. And inside, the hospitals grew, gobbling block after block, taking a quarter of the city off the tax rolls and then a third. Medicine killed her."

"All medicine did was present the facts and let the public act upon them as it saw fit," Flowers said stiffly.

Bone beat at his forehead with the side of a fist. "You're right, you're right. We did it ourselves. I wanted you to see that. We gave ourselves into the hands of the physicians, saying, 'Save us! Make us live!' And you did not ask, 'How live? Why?'

"'Take these pills,' you said, and we swallowed them. 'You need X rays,' you said, 'and radioactive iodine and antibiotics and specifics for this and that,' and we took them with our tonics and our vitamins." His voice dropped into a chant. "Give us this day our daily vitamins. . . . 'With microsurgery we can give you another year of life,' you said; 'with blood banks, another six months; with organ and artery banks, a month, a week.' We forced them on you because we were afraid to die. What do you call this morbid fear of disease and death? Give it a name: hypochondria!

"Call me a hypochondriac," Bone went on, "and you are only saying that I am a product of my environment. More intimately than you, than anyone, I am connected to my city. We are dying together, society and I, and we will die crying out to you, 'Save us! Save us or we die!'"

"I can't do anything," Flowers insisted. "Can't you understand that?"

Bone took it with surprising calm as he turned his dark eyes toward Flowers. "Oh, you will," he said, offhandedly. "You think now that you won't, but there will come a time when the flesh conquers, when it screams that it can endure no more, when the nerves will grow weary of pain and the will agonized with waiting, and you will treat me."

He studied Flowers casually, from head slowly toward the feet. His eyes grew bright. Flowers thought he would not look, but he couldn't resist. He glanced down. His jacket had come open. Below its immaculate whiteness was the button-and-spool of the belt buckle. Bone reached curiously toward the buckle. Before Flowers's tension could achieve action, his arms were caught from behind, pinned back.

"A spool," Bone said, "and something on it." With an experienced finger, he punched the button for Rewind and then Playback. As the voices came disembodied into the room, he leaned back against the paneled wall, listening with a thin, speculative smile on his pale lips. When it ended, his smile broadened lazily. "Pick up the girl and the old man. I think they might be useful."

Flowers understood him instantly. "Don't be foolish," he said. "They mean nothing to me. I don't care what happens to them."

"Then why protest?" Bone asked blandly. He turned his eyes toward the police officers. "Keep him close. In the broken elevator, there's an idea."

A minute later big brass doors clanged behind Flowers, and he was in darkness again.

But this was darkness with a difference. This was night gingerly supported above a pit of nothingness. It gave him a prickling, swelling feeling of terror. . . .

He found himself trembling in front of the doors, hammering against them with futile, aching fists, screaming. . . .

He forced himself to sit down in a corner of the car. He forced himself to forget that it was a car, hanging broken over a void. There was no escape.

He remembered punching the old buttons of the control panel. In his frenzy he had torn off a fingernail trying to pry the door open.

He found the black bag that, like the faithful physician he hoped to become, he had never relinquished and flipped on the light. He rummaged for a bandage, pressed it across the finger where the nail had been.

Then he sat in the dark. It was uncomfortable; he didn't like it. But it was better to sit in darkness with the knowledge of light available if it was needed than to be without any chance of light at all.

Two hours later the doors swung open, and Leah was thrust between them. His watch told him the time; otherwise he would not have believed that a day had not passed.

The girl staggered as the doors closed and Flowers was as blind as she. He sprang to his feet, though, caught her before she fell, and held her tightly. She fought against him, twisting in his arms, lashing out wildly with her arms and feet.

"It's me," Flowers said repeatedly, "the medic." When she stopped struggling, Flowers started to release her, but she stiffened, clutched at his arm, and held herself, trembling against him.

Holding her was a curious sensation for Flowers. Putting his arms around her was a comforting thing, not professional, skillful, or impersonal like his medical skill. This was clumsy; it offered part of himself.

"Where are we?" she whispered.

"A broken elevator car in City Hall," he said huskily. "John Bone."

"What does Bone want?" she asked. Her voice was almost steady; it made him feel stronger, abler, listening to it.

"Treatment."

"And you won't." It was a statement. "You're consistent, anyway. I reported your kidnapping to Medical Center. Maybe they'll help."

Hope flamed up, but reality put it out. Center would have no way of locating him, and they wouldn't tear apart the city for one minor medic. He was on his own.

"Did Bone get your father, too?"

"No," Leah said evenly. "The Agency got him. They saw Russ when they came about the kidnapping. One of them recognized him. They took him in."

"That's fantastic!" Flowers exclaimed incredulously. "But where did they take him?"

"The Experimental Ward."

"Not Doctor Pearce!"

"You remember now who he was. So did they. They used his old, reciprocal contract as an excuse because the terminating date was set arbitrarily at one hundred. Doctors didn't used to live that long. I guess they still don't."

"But he's famous!"

"That's why they want him; he knows too much, and too many people remember him. They're afraid the Antivivisection Party will get hold of him and use him against the Profession in some way. They've been looking for him thirty years now—ever since he walked out of the hospital and went into the city and never came out."

"I remember now," Flowers said. "It was like Ambrose Bierce, they said. He was lecturing to a class—on hematology, I think—and he stopped in the middle of a sentence, and he said, 'Gentlemen, we have gone too far; it is time to retrace our steps and discover where we went astray.' Then he walked out of the classroom and out of the hospital, and no one ever saw him again. No one ever knew what he meant."

"Those days are forgotten. He never talks—talked about them. I thought the hiding was over. I thought they had finally given him up. . . . Why does John Bone want me?"

"He hopes he can force me to treat him—by—"

"Threatening me? Did you laugh at him?"

"No. No, I didn't do that."

"Why not?"

"Maybe I didn't think fast enough."

Slowly Leah pulled her hand away, and they sat silently in the darkness. Flowers's thoughts were painful; he could scarcely bear to consider them.

"I'm going to look at your eyes," he said suddenly.

He got out his ophthalmoscope and leaned toward the girl, focusing the spot of light on the clouded cornea. She sat still, let him pull up her eyelids, pull down the soft skin of her cheek. He nodded slowly to himself and put the instrument away.

"Is there any hope, Doctor?" she asked.

He lied. "No," he said.

It was unethical; it gave him a queer, dizzy feeling, as if he had thrown mud at the hospital wall, but it was mixed with a strange feeling of elation. It was mercy. Of course she could see—if she had an operation costing several thousand dollars more than she would ever have. It was mercy to kill that hope quickly and finally.

Maybe it wasn't ethical, but he'd just begun to realize there were times when a doctor must treat the patient and not the disease. In spite of what the professors said. Each patient was an individual with his own problems and his own treatment, and only part of both were medical.

"I don't understand," he said abruptly, "why the people let John Bone continue here with his corruption and his graft and his violence."

"That is only one side, and a side few people see. To most of them he is the patron—or, in longer translation, the one who does things for us. What are you going to do about him?"

"Treat him," Flowers said quietly. "There's no point in being quixotic about this."

"But, Medic—" she began.

"Ben," he said. "Ben Flowers. I don't want to talk about it. Someone might be listening."

After that there was more silence than talking, but it was a warm sort of silence, warmer perhaps than speech, and her hand came creeping back into his.

When the policeman opened the door, it was night again. Flowers had only a glimpse of the hall before they were hustled in to see Bone in the dark-paneled room. The political boss had a warm red robe wrapped around his body, but he still looked chilled.

Bone watched Flowers's eyes studying the room, and he said, "This used to be the city manager's office. The mayor's office is on the other side. I use that one for business, this one for pleasure, although there isn't much business anymore—or pleasure, either, for that matter. So this is the girl. Blind. I should have known that. Well, Medic, what is it to be?"

Flowers shrugged. "I'll treat you, of course."

Bone rubbed his thin hands together with a dry, sandpaper sound. "Good, good." Suddenly he stopped and smiled. "But how can I be sure that you will treat me properly? Maybe we should show the medic what my lack of treatment will mean to the girl?"

"That isn't necessary," Flowers said quickly. "I'm not a fool. You're filming this. After I treat you, you'll use it as blackmail to get future treatment. If you aren't satisfied, you can turn it over to the county society. Besides,"—his voice deepened suddenly, surprisingly— "touch the girl, and I won't lift a finger to save your life!"

The light in Bone's eyes might have been admiration. "I like you, Medic," he said. "Throw in with me. We'd make a pair."

"No, thanks," Flowers said scornfully.

"Think it over. Let me know if you change your mind," Bone said. "But let's get down to business." His voice was eager.

"Have the ambulance motor started," Flowers said.

Bone nodded at the sergeant. "Do it!"

They waited, the four of them, stiff with a watchful

uncertainty. When the depths of the bag glowed dimly, Flowers began fastening the instruments to Bone's emaciated body. *Where's Coke?* he wondered.

He read the diagnosis, removed the instruments, and slowly stowed them away. Thoughtfully he explored the pockets of the bag.

"What is it?" Bone asked anxiously. "Tell me what's wrong!"

Flowers's face was sober. "It's nothing to be concerned about," he said, trying to hide his concern, but failing. "You need a tonic. You're taking vitamins already, I'm sure. Double the dose." He pulled out a bottle of pink pills. "Here's some barbiturate-amphetamine pills to put you to sleep at night and wake you up in the morning. And here's some extra ones." He handed Bone a second bottle; in it the pills were round, flat, and green. "Take one of these three times a day."

Bone frowned cautiously. "What's in them?"

"Nothing that can hurt you." Flowers shook out a couple into his hand, tossed them into his mouth, swallowed. "See?"

Bone nodded, satisfied. "Okay. Take the two of them back," he said to the policeman.

"Wait a minute," Flowers objected. "Aren't you going to turn us loose?"

"Where'd you get that idea?" Bone chuckled. "I like having a medic around. Gives me a feeling of security."

Flowers sighed, accepting it. "Well, I guess there's nothing I can do." He bent to pick up the bag and noticed the expression of disappointment that flickered across Leah's face. His hand strayed past Bone's neck. "Here," Flowers said to the officer watching them suspiciously, "I suppose you'll want to keep this."

The policeman stepped forward to accept the bag and moved back with it in his hand. With the hand that held the gun, he reached down to scratch the back of his other hand.

Slowly Bone collapsed behind Flowers. It made a rustling sound. The policeman tried to lift the gun, but it was too heavy. It pulled him down. As he fell, he half turned.

"What's happened?" Leah asked, startled. "What are those noises?"

Flowers caught up her hand and scooped up the black bag in one swift motion. "I knocked out Bone with supersonics and the cop with a hypodermic of neo-curare. Come on."

As they went through the glass doors into the hall, he wondered again: *Where's Coke?* There were probably stairs, but he couldn't run down them leading a blind girl. He thumbed the elevator call button and waited in a frenzy of impatience. Leah held his hand firmly, confidently.

"Don't worry. You'll get us out."

Cool certainty flooded over him. His shoulders straightened.

"What medicine did you give him?" she asked.

Flowers chuckled. "Sugar pills. Placebo. Imaginary medicine for an imaginary illness."

When the elevator doors opened, the sergeant was behind them. He stared at them, surprised, and his hand dropped to his gun.

Flowers stepped forward confidently. "Bone said to let us loose."

"That don't sound like Bone," the sergeant growled. He tugged his gun loose. "Let's go check."

Flowers shrugged, released Leah's hand so that he could shift the bag into that one, and swung around so that the bag bumped into the sergeant's leg. The sergeant brushed the spot casually, took two steps and fell, heavily.

As Flowers and Leah stepped out of the elevator into the basement hall, the lights went out. *Coke*, Flowers thought, and groaned.

"What's the matter?" Leah asked, alarmed.

"The lights went out."

"I could help if I knew what you were trying to do."

"Find the ambulance. It should be somewhere in the basement."

"They must have brought me in that way," Leah said thoughtfully. "There was a door that clanged, some steps, another door, some more steps, and then a straight stretch to the elevator. Come on."

Flowers held back for a moment and let her pull him into the darkness. "There are steps," she said. They walked down carefully. Flowers found the handle of the door and held it open. A moment later they were going down more steps.

"This way," Leah said confidently.

Within seconds they were beside the ambulance, climbing through the door, switching on the light. Flowers swung the responsive vehicle around with a feeling of elation approaching giddiness. Even the sight of the closed garage door didn't bother him. He eased the ambulance as close as possible, swung out, touched the door gingerly, and tugged at the handle. It rose with well-oiled ease.

After that it was nothing. Flowers headed north for I-35, to avoid ambush and shake off pursuers. On the road he could outdistance anything. After a few minutes they hit Southwest Trafficway. Flowers turned the driving over to the chauffeur, and swung around to look at Leah. She was sitting on the cot.

"Look!" he began. "I—" He stopped.

"Don't you know what to do with me?" she asked gently.

"Well, I—I guess that's right. I can't leave you alone out here, and if I take you to your home, Bone might pick you up again. There are rules against taking anybody but a patient into the Center—" He took a deep breath. "The hell with the rules. Listen! You're a patient. For—an eye operation, replacement of opaque corneas. You've been transferred from the Neosho County Hospital—that's just outside Chanute, Kansas, in case they ask questions—and you don't know why your records haven't got here yet. Understood?"

"Won't that mean trouble for you?" she asked.

"Nothing I can't get out of. If anyone sees us together—why, I was fooled, too, that's all. No argument now. It'll give us an extra day to decide what to do with you."

"Will I be able to see my father?"

"Of course not," Flowers said. "Not if he's in Experimental, anyway. The only ones allowed to enter Experimental are doctors and attendants on duty."

"I understand. All right, I'll leave it up to you."

Again Flowers felt that quick, irrational flood of happiness. He had no reason to feel happy; he didn't want to feel happy—it would interfere with what he had to do. He shoved the feeling down, deep, as the walls of Medical Center opened and took them in.

They were lucky. There was no one around as Flowers parked the ambulance in the vast underground garage and led Leah cautiously to the subway. They waited in the shadows until an empty car swung into view.

"Move quickly," he said. "Trust me."

He led her onto the moving belt, holding her forearm in a sure grip. Even so, she swayed and almost fell. He pulled her up and led her swiftly after the car moving on the belt beside them. Just as they reached the end of the approachway, Flowers helped her into the car and swung himself after her.

He was sweating. The subway wasn't built for the blind.

Getting off was much less difficult. The sign above the archway said: EENT. They walked into an elevator and let it lift them to the fifth floor. Flowers watched from the concealment of a cross-corridor while Leah walked blindly down the hall, feeling her way to the glass enclosure of the duty office.

"Is anyone here?" she asked out of her darkness.

"There was a medic, but he had to leave. I'm from the Neosho County Hospital. . . ."

As Flowers faded down the hall, he saw the nurse come out of the office with a look of concern. He sighed. Leah was safe for the moment.

He walked through the dark halls wondering where everybody was. It was only eight o'clock in the evening.

The floor under his feet was yielding and resilient. He breathed in the hospital smells of anesthetic and alcohol, the old odors, omnipresent, eternal. They were his first memory of his father. It was a good smell. He filled his lungs with it, held it in tightly, as if he could hold on to everything he valued, if only he could keep the odor from escaping.

This was his place, his home. This was his job. This was his life. He had to believe that. Otherwise everything was worthless, seven years of study and labor were wasted, and a lifetime of dreams was turned into nightmare, and everything that was to come, the dedication, the rewards. . . .

Charley Brand looked up from his desk, surprised. "My God, man! Where've you been?"

"A long story," Flowers said wearily. "First, I've got to have some food and some rest."

"They'll have to wait. There's a royal request on your desk."

A message glowed on the plate set into the top of his desk. He read it with a cold, shrinking feeling.

Your presence is requested at the meeting of the

Wyandotte County Medical Society this evening and at the meeting of the Political Action Committee to follow.

J. B. Hardy, M.D.
Secretary

Flowers looked around the dormitory with frantic eyes; he had to discuss this with someone. "Where's Hal?"

"Do you think he'd miss a meeting?" Brand asked sardonically and added a good imitation of Mock's knowing voice. "'These things look good on your record.' Better run along. If you hurry you can still make the convoy."

It was more of a tradition than anything else—this convoy detail with the minesweepers snuffling ahead, the tanks lumbering heavily on either side, and helicopters hovering above. No one was foolish enough to attack anything stronger than a lone ambulance.

They drove north on Seventh Street Trafficway over the Armourdale Industrial District that flamed below them in the night, past the ruins of the old stockyards where no man went by night and few dared to go by day. Flowers looked out, unseeing, his fatigue and his hunger conquered by anxiety.

Why did the PAC want to see him?

Few medics and fewer doctors got summonses to appear before the committee. It was not an invitation to be envied. It was followed, frequently, by the person involved quietly collecting his personal belongings from the hospital and disappearing from the purview of medicine.

When the convoy pulled up in front of the courthouse and parked within the protection of the concrete pillboxes on the lawn and the antiaircraft emplacements on the roof, Flowers was still tormenting himself with possibilities.

As usual, the meeting was a bore. When the anxiety ebbed, Flowers dozed in his chair, jerking himself upright occasionally to hear a few fragments of the minutes of the last meeting, the treasurer's report, the mumbling of research records. . . .

There was a moving speech by the AMA field representative on the danger to ethical standards in new legislation pending before Congress. Its inevitable result was socialized medicine.

Funny, Flowers mused, how that Hydra was never scotched. Cut off one head and two more grew in its place. Doctors should know enough to cauterize the stump.

By unanimous voice vote, $325,000 was turned over to the Washington lobby for legislative action.

When the chairman of the Political Action Committee stood up, Flowers studied him curiously. He was a tall, fleshy man with bushy, black hair, crouching eyebrows, and a ruddy complexion. Flowers didn't know him. That wasn't unusual in a four-county census of 10,000 doctors.

According to the PAC, the political situation was under control at state and county levels. The Antivivisection Party had closed alliances with a number of quasi-religious groups during the last months, but this was expected to amount to no more than the usual annoyances. Everyone had been given a copy of the slate of the state and county candidates. They had all received PAC approval.

The slate was accepted without dissent. A sum of $553,000 was voted for campaign expenses.

There was more.

When the general meeting had been adjourned, Flowers wandered slowly toward the door of the room announced for the meeting of the PAC.

"Flowers?"

It was the chairman of the committee. Flowers followed him numbly into the big room. There were five doctors, the chairman taking his place in the middle. They sat solemn faced behind a long, heavy desk made of real wood darkened by centuries of use.

"You're in trouble, boy," the chairman began.

The doctor on the chairman's right leaned forward, a small memoreader in his hand. "Last night, while on an emergency call into the city, you turned over to the police an alleged shover named Crumm.

"Crumm was dismissed at nine A.M. He had a license. And the penicillin in the ampule tested a full three hundred thousand units."

"A typical Bone trick! He took out a license and backdated it. And they're lying about the penicillin. They couldn't sell it at that price; it was less than wholesale."

"If you had been listening to the reports tonight, you would have learned that penicillin is worthless. When it was first introduced, immune bacterial strains averaged five percent. Now they are ninety-five percent and still climbing."

Flowers thought of the money shoveled into research and production for antibiotics that developed more virulent bacterial strains for which newer and better antibiotics had to be discovered.

"How are we going to put a stop to it," Flowers asked, "if we don't punish them when we have a chance?"

The doctor smiled. "That's what the PAC is for. We've refused to renew John Bone's contract. That will bring him to his senses." His face hardened. "At least, we thought it would until today."

"What do you mean?" Flowers felt vaguely frightened.

"Until Bone released you this evening."

Flowers stared at the five immobile faces with a feeling of frozen horror. "He didn't release me. I escaped!"

"Now, Flowers, don't waste our time with stuff like that," the chairman said impatiently. "Men don't escape from John Bone. And we have evidence—a film of the examination and treatment you gave him!"

"But I did," Flowers broke in. "I used the supersonic anesthetizer and a hypodermic of neo-curare and I escaped—"

"Fantastic! After treating Bone—"

"I gave him sugar pills—"

"Just as bad. For Bone, they're as effective as anything else."

"Don't you see why Bone sent you the films? If I'd really treated him, he'd have held these films over my head as a blackmail threat."

The committee members exchanged glances. "We might be able to accept that," the chairman said, "except that we have other evidence to prove that you hold the Profession and its ethics rather lightly."

He switched on a recorder. Incredulously Flowers listened to his voice mouthing questions about medicine and fees and social problems. It had been skillfully edited. It was damning.

Hal, he thought, *Hal, why did you do it?*

But he knew why. Hal Mock was worried that he might not graduate. One less in the class was one more chance for Hal.

The chairman was speaking to him. "You will submit your resignation in the morning. As soon after that as possible, you will collect your personal effects and leave the Center. If you are ever discovered practicing medicine or treating the sick in any way . . ."

When it was finished, Flowers asked quietly, "What are you going to do with Doctor Russell Pearce?"

The chairman's eyes narrowed, and then he turned to the doctor on his right. "Doctor Pearce?" he said. "Why, he disappeared thirty years ago, didn't he? He must have died long ago. If he were alive, he'd be over one hundred and twenty-five. . . ."

Flowers stopped listening. Something had snapped inside him like a carbon-steel scalpel, and he didn't have to listen anymore. A man spends his life searching for the truth. If he's lucky he learns before he dies that no one has it all. We have little pieces, each of us, Flowers thought. The danger was in assuming our fragment was the whole. Medicine could not be both political and irresponsible. Dr. Pearce could not be both hero and villain.

Flowers had finally found his way to the back of the statue and learned—in time—that half an ideal is worse than none at all. *Father,* he thought, *you never got there. I'm sorry, Father.*

He turned and walked out of the room. There was a phone in the courthouse lobby. He called his number and waited and then spoke briefly and urgently into the pickup. While the chauffeur guided the ambulance back toward the Medical Center, he fished around in the black bag for a couple of amphetamine pills and ate them like candy.

But his feeling of exhilaration and purpose began minutes before the stimulant hit him. It was all very well to be an integral part of a great social and ethical complex, but occasionally a man had to do his own thinking. And then, of course, the great social and ethical complex had to watch out for itself.

He wasn't even disturbed to discover that he was being followed. He shook off the distant white jacket in the subway.

"Look," he said to the pharmacist on duty, "it must get pretty boring here at night. Don't you ever get an overwhelming yen for a cup of coffee?"

"I sure do."

"Go ahead," Flowers said. "I'll watch the pharmacy."

The pharmacist hesitated, torn between duty and desire. The decision to go resulted from a reluctance to appear timid before the medic.

As soon as he was gone, Flowers went straight through the pharmacy to the vault. The heavy door was ajar. In the farthest corner was a modest cardboard carton. Its contents had been estimated, conservatively, as worth $10,000,000. Flowers pocketed an ampule, hesitated, and removed the eleven others from their cotton nests—suddenly doubtful that the hospital should be trusted with them. . . .

"Thanks for the break," said the pharmacist gratefully a few minutes later.

Flowers waved carelessly as he left. "Any time."

At the barred door of Experimental Ward, the guard stopped him. "I don't see your name here anywhere," he growled, his finger moving down the duty list.

"No wonder," Flowers said, pointing his own finger. "They misspelled it. Powers instead of Flowers."

It worked. Inside he walked quickly past the blood bank with its rows of living factories, the organ bank with its surgery and automatic heart machines. . . . The part of the experimental rooms devoted to geriatrics was at the very end.

Dr. Pearce made scarcely a dent in the firm hospital mattress. Flowers shook him, but the smudged eyelids wouldn't open. He filled a hypodermic from the ampule in his jacket pocket and injected it into a vein.

Flowers waited anxiously in the near darkness. Finally Dr. Pearce's eyelids flickered. "Doctor Pearce," he whispered, "this is the medic. Remember?" Pearce nodded, barely perceptibly. "I'm going to try to get you out of here, you and Leah. She's here, too. Will you help?"

Pearce nodded again, stronger this time. Flowers brought the long cart beside the bed and lifted Pearce's bone-light body onto it. He pulled a sheet up over Pearce's face. "Here we go."

He engaged the clutch and guided the cart back the way he had come, past the rooms with their burdens of human tragedy, through the door, past the startled guard. The guard acted as if he were going to say something, but he waited too long.

When they were entering the elevator, Pearce whispered in a dust-dry voice, "What was the shot, Medic?"

"*Elixir vitae.* Isn't that justice?"

"Justice is hard to recognize when we see it so seldom."

"When did you have your last shot?"

"Thirty years ago."

So, Flowers thought, *I was wrong about that, too.* It wasn't the elixir keeping the old man alive. "You said you'd give Leah your eyes. Did you mean it?"

"Of course. Can you do it?"

The years had desiccated the body, but they hadn't dimmed the mind, Flowers thought. Pearce had realized instantly what Flowers meant. "I don't know," he admitted. "It's a chance. I'll have to do it all alone in haste. I could give her some from the bank, but she would hate it. With yours it would be different."

"A gift of love," Pearce whispered. "It can never be refused. It enriches him who gives and him who receives. That is how it should be done always, with love. Don't tell her. Afterward she'll understand, how it made me happy to give her what I could not give her as a father— the world of light. . . ."

*　　*　　*

The duty office was vacant. Flowers ran his finger down the room list until he found Leah's name. He found another cart, ran it silently into the room, and stopped beside the bed. "Leah?"

"Ben?" she said instantly.

For a moment her voice blunted the cold edge of his determination. It had been a long time since anyone had called him "Ben" like that. "Onto the cart. I've got your father. We're going to make a break for it."

"You'll be ruined."

"It was done for me," he said. "Funny. You have an ideal—maybe it looks like your father—and you think it exists inside you like a marble statue in a hidden niche. And one day you look and it isn't there anymore. You're free."

The cart was rolling toward the elevator. On the floor below he guided the cart into the EENT operating room. As it bumped gently against the cart on which Pearce was lying, Leah put out a hand, touched her father's arm, and said, "Russ!"

"Leah!"

For a moment the exchange of names stabbed Flowers with jealousy; he felt left out, alone. "You were right," Leah said, and she put out another hand to catch hold of Flowers and pull him close. "He is the man. Better even than we thought."

"Find a great deal of happiness, children," Pearce said.

Flowers chuckled. "I think you two planned the whole thing."

Leah blushed slowly. *She's really beautiful,* Flowers thought in sudden surprise. "No, we only hoped it," she said.

Flowers injected the anesthetic, felt her fingers relax, droop away. Motionless, he stared at her face and then held up his hands in front of his eyes. They were trembling. He looked around at the gleaming whiteness of the walls, the delicate microsurgical tools, the suturing machine, the bandages, and he knew how easy it would be to slip, to make the fatal mistake.

"Courage, Medic," said Pearce. His voice was getting stronger. "You've studied for seven years. You can do this simple thing."

He took a deep breath. Yes, he could do it. And he went at it, as it should be done—with love.

"Medic Flowers," said the hidden speaker in the ceiling, "report to the dormitory. Medic Flowers . . ."

They had discovered that Pearce was missing. The old man talked to him while his hands were busy and helped take his mind off the terrifying consequences. He told Flowers why he had walked out on his class thirty years before.

"It suddenly came to me—the similarity between medicine and religion. We fostered it with our tradition building, our indecipherable prescriptions, our ritual. Gradually the public had come to look upon us as miracle workers. The masses called the new medicines wonder drugs because they didn't know how they worked. Religion and medicine—both owed their great periods to a pathological fear of death. Death is not so great an enemy."

Flowers made depth readings of the cloudy corneas and set them into the microsurgical machine.

"Oh, the doctors weren't to blame. We were a product of our society just as John Bone is a product of his. But we forgot an ancient wisdom which might have given us the strength to resist. 'A sound mind in a sound body,' the Greeks said. And even more important, 'Nothing in excess.'"

Flowers positioned the laser scalpel over Leah's right eye.

"Anything in excess will ruin this society or any other. Even the best of things—too much wealth, too much piety, too much health. We made a fetish of health, built it shrines in our medicine cabinets, built great temples for worship."

The beam slipped into the eye without resistance, slicing away the cornea.

"The life span can be extended to a reasonable length without overburdening the society. Then we run into the law of diminishing returns, and it takes just as much again to push it a year further, and then six months, three months, a week, a day. There is no end, and our fear is such that no one can say, 'Stop! We're healthy enough.'"

The scalpel retracted and moved to the left eye.

"The lives we were saving were peripheral: the very young, the very old, and the constitutional inadequates. We repealed natural selection, saved the weak to reproduce themselves, and told ourselves that we were healthier. It was a kind of suicide. It was health out of bottles. When the bottles break, the society will die."

Both corneas were gone. Flowers looked at his watch. It was taking too long. He turned to Pearce.

"No anesthetic," Pearce said. As the microsurgical machine came over his face, he went on, "We called it humanitarian, but it was only another name for folly. Medicine became dependent upon the very thing it was destroying. Vast technologies were vital to its maintenance, but that level of civilization fostered its own diseases."

The empty sockets were bandaged.

"We destroyed the cities with our doomsayings, and we amassed a disproportionate amount of capital with our tax exemptions, our subsidies, our research grants. Like religion again, in medieval Europe, when piety accumulated wealth exempt from levies."

The corneas were in place.

"It couldn't last in Europe, and it can't last here. Henry the Eighth found an excuse to break with the Pope and appropriate the Church lands. In France it helped bring the Revolution. And thus this noble experiment will end. In ice or fire, by the degeneration of technology below the level necessary to sustain it, or by rebellion. And that's why I went into the city."

The suturing machine fused the edges of the cornea in a neat graft.

"That's where the future will be made, where the people are surviving because they are strong. There we are learning new things—the paranormal methods of health that are not so new after all, but the age-old methods of healers. Their merit is that they do not require complexity and technology, but only a disciplined mind that can discipline the body. When the end comes, the fine spacious life in the country will end like the mayfly. The city will survive and grow again. Outside they will die of diseases their bodies have forgotten, of cancer they cannot resist, of a hundred different ailments, for which the medicine has been lost."

As the bandages were fastened over Leah's eyes, the speaker in the ceiling spoke again. "Emergency squads report to stations. Heavily armed forces are attacking St. Luke's."

The time for caution was past. Flowers taped together the cart legs and guided them across the hall into the elevator. They dropped to the subway level. Clumsily Flowers maneuvered the two carts across the approachway into one of the cars and swung himself aboard after them.

In seconds the garage would be swarming with the emergency squads.

Another speaker boomed: "Snipers on buildings along Main Street are shelling St. Luke's with five-inch mortars. No casualties reported. Emergency squads, on the double."

"Has it started already?" Pearce asked softly.

Unseen, Flowers smiled grimly.

As they reached the garage, men were racing past them. No one paid any attention to the medic guiding the two carts. Flowers stopped at the first unoccupied ambulance, opened the back, and lifted Leah's unconscious body onto one of the stretchers. He lifted Pearce onto the other one. He slammed the door shut and ran around to the front.

Just as the engine caught, a startled medic raced up and pounded futilely against the door. Flowers pulled away from him in a burst of speed.

The ambulance was only one vehicle among many; they streamed from the Center, ambulances, half-tracks, tanks. At Southwest Trafficway, Flowers edged out of the stream and turned north. North into the city.

John Bone was waiting beside the garage door under City Hall. "Okay," he told Coke, "you can call off the diversion now. Come on in," he said to Flowers.

"Said the spider to the fly," Flowers said, smiling. "No, thanks. You'll get healed, and better than I can do. But not now."

Bone's face wrinkled angrily. "By whom?"

"These," Flowers said, waving his hand toward the back of the ambulance.

"An old man? A blind girl?"

"A blind old man, and a girl who might see. Yes. They can do more for you than I can. We'll get along, Bone."

Bone grimaced. "Yes. Yes, I suppose we will."

Leah was stirring. Flowers reached back and put a hand on her forehead. She grew quiet. He turned back to Bone and stripped off his white jacket and tossed it to the political boss of the city. "Here, maybe this will do you some good. You can have the ambulance, too, when it's taken us home."

Home. He smiled. He had thrown in his lot with the city. He had even forgotten his filters. There was brutality in the city, but you could tame it, put its misdirected vitality to use. But the only thing to do with an ideal that has outworn its necessity is to turn your back on it, to leave it behind.

People can't be divided into two groups: There aren't people, and people in white jackets. A doctor is only a man with special skills. But a healer is something more than a man. They would make the beginning, the old man, and the blind girl who might see, and the medic who had found a new ideal. "I spent seven years learning to be a doctor," Flowers said. "I guess I can spend seven years more learning how to heal."

PART V
IMMORTAL

The clinic was deserted.

Harry Elliott smothered a yawn as he walked slowly toward the draped operating table under the cold, glareless light at the back of the big room tiled in anti-septic white and flooded with invisible, germ-killing ultraviolet. He lit the candelabra of Bunsen burners standing on each side of the table and turned on the ventilators under the mural of Immortality slaying Death with a syringe. The air, straight from the Medical Center, was pure, disease-free, and aromatic with the hospital incense of anesthetic and alcohol.

Science, surgery, and salvation—the clinic had something for everybody.

It was going to be another ordinary day, Harry decided. Soon would come the shrill cacophony of six o'clock, and the factories would release their daily human floods into the worn channels between the high walls. For an hour or two, then, he would be busy.

But it was a good shift. He was busy only between six and curfew. Other times he could sneak a view of the *Geriatrics Journal* or flip a few reels of text over the inner surface of his glasses. He didn't need them for seeing—if he had he would have used contact lenses—but they were handy for viewing and they made a man look professional and older.

At twenty-four that was important to Harry. . . .

Sunday was bad. But then Sunday was a bad day for everybody.

He would be glad when it was over. One more week and he would be back on duty inside. Six more months and he would have his residency requirements completed. As soon as he passed his boards—it was unthinkable that he would not pass—there would be no more clinics.

It was all very well to administer to the masses—that was what the oath of Hippocrates was about, partly—but a doctor had to be practical. There just wasn't enough medical care to go around. Curing an ear infection here, a case of gonorrhea there, was like pouring antibiotics into the river. The results were unnoticeable.

With those who had a chance at immortality, it was different. Saving a life meant something. It might even mean a reprieve for himself, when he needed it. And reprieves had been stretched into immortality.

The prognosis, though, was unfavorable. A man's best hope was to make something of himself worth saving. Then immortality would be voted him by a grateful electorate. That was why Harry had decided to specialize in geriatrics. Later, when he had more leisure and laboratory facilities, he would concentrate on the synthesis of the *elixir vitae*. Success would mean immortality not only for himself but for everybody. Even if he did not succeed within a lifetime, if his research was promising, there would be reprieves.

But it was the synthesis that was important. The

world could not continue to depend upon the Cartwrights. They were too selfish. They preferred to hide their own accidental immortality rather than contribute harmless amounts of blood at regular intervals. If Fordyce's statistical analysis of Locke's investigations was correct, there were enough Cartwrights alive to grant immortality to 50,000 mortals—and that number would increase geometrically as more Cartwrights were born. One day a baby would inherit life as its birthright, not death.

If the Cartwrights were not so selfish . . . As it was, there had been only enough of them discovered to provide immortality for a hundred to two hundred persons; nobody knew exactly how many. And the tame Cartwrights were so infertile that their numbers increased very slowly. They could contribute only a limited quantity of the precious blood. From this could be extracted only a small amount of the gamma globulin that carried the immunity factor. Even at closely calculated minimal dosages, the shots could not be stretched beyond a small group of essential persons, because the immunity to death was passive. It was good for no more than thirty to forty days.

But once the blood protein was synthesized . . .

Harry had an idea of how it might be done—by taking apart the normal gamma globulin molecule and then putting it back together again, DNA fragment by fragment. With radiation and the new quick freeze, absolute, he could do it. Once he got his hands on a research grant and laboratory facilities . . .

He walked slowly toward the street entrance, past the consultation rooms with their diagnostic couches on both sides of the long clinic hallway. He paused between the giant Aesculapian staffs that supported the lintel of the doorway, just before he reached the moving curtain of air that kept out the heat of summer, the cold of winter, and the dust and disease of the city. At this stage in his career, it was folly to think of research grants. They were for older, proven researchers, not for callow residents, nor even eager young specialists.

The clinic was built out from the Medical Center wall. Opposite was the high wall of a factory that made armored cars for export to the suburbs. That's where the Center got its ambulances. A little farther along the Medical Center wall was a second smaller outbuilding. On its roof was a neon sign: BLOOD BOUGHT HERE. Beside its door would be another, smaller sign: WE ARE NOW PAYING $50 A PINT.

In a few minutes the blood-tank technicians would be busy inserting needles into scarred antecubital veins as the laborers were set free by the quitting whistles. They would pour through the laboratory, spending their life resources prodigally, coming back, many of them, to give another pint before two weeks had elapsed, much less two months. No use trying to keep track of them. They would do anything: trade identity cards, scuff up their inner arms so that the previous needle hole would not show, swear that the scars were from antibiotic shots. . . .

And then they would gulp down their orange juice—some of the children did it mostly for that because they had never tasted orange juice before—grab their fifty dollars and head for the nearest shover of illicit antibiotics and nostrums. Or they would give it to some neighborhood leech for rubbing salve on some senile invalid or for chanting runes over some dying infant.

Well, they were essential. He had to remember that. They were a great pool of immunities. They had been exposed to all the diseases bred of poverty, ignorance, and filth from which the squires had been protected. The squires needed the citizens' gamma globulins, their antigens. The squires needed the serums manufactured in citizen bodies, the vaccines prepared from their reactions.

A remarkable teacher had once shocked him into awareness by saying, "Without filth there is no cleanliness; without disease there is no health." Harry remembered that in his contacts with the citizens. It helped.

Past the blood bank, the Center wall curved away. Beyond was the city. It was not dying; it was dead.

Wooden houses had subsided into heaps of rotten lumber. Brick tenements had crumbled; here and there a wall tottered against the sky. Aluminum and magnesium walls were dented and pierced. Decay was everywhere.

But, like green shoots pushing through the forest's mat of dead leaves, the city was being born again. A two-room shack was built with scavenged boards. A brick bungalow stood behind tenement ruins. Metal walls became rows of huts.

The eternal cycle, Harry thought. *Out of death, life. Out of life, destruction. Only man could evade it.*

All that remained of the original city were the walled factories and the vast hospital complexes. Behind their protective walls, they stood tall and strong and faceless. On the walls, armored guard houses glinted in the orange-red fire of the declining sun.

As Harry stood there, the whistles began to blow—all tones and volumes of them, making a strange, shrill counterpoint, suited to sunset in the city. It was primitive and stirring, like a savage ceremony to propitiate the gods and ensure the sun's return.

The gates rolled up and left openings in the factory walls. Laborers spilled out into the street: all kinds of them, men and women, children and ancients, sickly and strong. Yet there was a sameness to them. They were ragged and dirty and diseased; they were the city dwellers.

They should have been miserable, but they were usually happy. They would look up at the blue sky, if the smog had not yet crept up from the river, and laugh, for no reason at all. The children would play tag between their parents' legs, yelling and giggling. Even the ancients would smile indulgently.

It was the healthy squires who were sober and concerned. Well, it was natural. Ignorance can be happy; the citizens need not be concerned about good health or immortality. It was beyond them. They could appear on a summer day like the mayfly and flutter about gaily and die. But knowledge had to worry; immortality had its price.

Remembering that always made Harry feel better.

Seeing the great hordes of citizens with no chance for immortality made him self-conscious about his advantages. He had been raised in a suburban villa not far from the city's diseases and carcinogens. From infancy he had received the finest of medical care. He had been through four years of high school, eight years of medical school, and almost three years of residency training.

That gave him a head start toward immortality. It was right that he should pay for it with concern.

Where do they all come from? he thought. *They must breed like rabbits in those warrens. Where do they all go to? Back into the wreckage of the city, like the rats and the vermin.*

He shuddered. *Really, they are almost another race.*

Tonight, though, they weren't laughing and singing. Even the children were silent. They marched down the street soberly, almost the only sound the tramp of their bare feet on the cracked pavement. Even the doors of the blood bank weren't busy.

Harry shrugged. Sometimes they were like this. The reason would be something absurd—a gang fight, company trouble, some dark religious rite that could never really be stamped out. Maybe it had something to do with the phases of the moon.

He went back into the clinic to get ready. The first patient was a young woman. She was an attractive creature with blond hair worn long around her shoulders and a ripe body—if you could ignore the dirt and the odor that drifted even into the professional chamber behind the consultation room.

He resisted an impulse to have her disrobe. Not because of any consequences—what was a citizen's chastity? A mythical thing like the unicorn. Besides, they expected it. From the stories the other doctors told, he thought they must come to the clinic for that purpose. But there was no use tempting himself. He would feel unclean for days.

She babbled as they always did. She had sinned against nature. She had not been getting enough sleep. She had not been taking her vitamins regularly. She had bought illicit terramycin from a shover for a bladder infection. It was all predictable and boring.

"I see," he kept muttering. And then, "I'm going to take a diagnosis now. Don't be frightened."

He switched on the diagnostic machine. A sphygmomanometer crept up snakelike from beneath the Freudian couch and encircled her arm. A mouthpiece slipped between her lips. A stethoscope counted her pulse. A skullcap fitted itself to her head. Metal caps slipped over her fingertips. Bracelets encircled her ankles. A band wrapped itself around her hips. The machine punctured, withdrew samples, counted, measured, listened, compared, correlated. . . .

In a moment it was over. Harry had his diagnosis. She was anemic; they all were. They couldn't resist that fifty dollars.

"Married?" he asked.

"Nah," she said hesitantly.

"Better not waste any time. You're pregnant."

"Prag-nant?" she repeated.

"You're going to have a baby."

A joyful light broke across her face. "Aw! Is that all! I thought maybe it was a too-more. A baby I can take care of nicely. Tell me, Doctor, will it be boy or girl?"

"A boy," Harry said wearily. *The slut!* Why did it always irritate him so?

She got up from the couch with a lithe, careless grace. "Thank you, Doctor. I will go tell Georgie. He will be angry for a little, but I know how to make him glad."

There were others waiting in the consultation rooms, contemplating their symptoms. Harry checked the panel: a woman with pleurisy, a man with cancer, a child with rheumatic fever. . . . But Harry stepped out into the clinic to see if the girl dropped anything into the donation box as she passed. She didn't. Instead, she paused by the shover hawking his wares just outside the clinic door.

"Get your aureomycin here," he ranted, "your penicillin, your terramycin. A hypodermic with every purchase. Good health! Good health! Don't let that infection cost you your job, your health, your life. Get your filters, your antiseptics, your vitamins. Get your amulets, your good-luck charms. I have here a radium needle which has already saved thirteen lives. And here is an ampule of *elixir vitae*. Get your ilotycin here. . . ."

The girl bought an amulet and hurried off to Georgie. A lump of anger burned in Harry's throat.

The throngs were still marching silently in the street. In the back of the clinic, a woman was kneeling at the operating table. She took a vitamin pill and a paper cup of tonic from the dispensary.

Behind the walls the sirens started. Harry turned toward the doorway. The gate in the Medical Center wall rolled up.

First came the outriders on their motorcycles. The people in the street scattered to the walls on either side, leaving a lane down the center of the street. The outriders brushed carelessly close to them—healthy young squires, their nose filters in place, their goggled eyes haughty, their guns slung low on their hips.

That would have been something, Harry thought enviously—to have been a company policeman. There was a dash to them, a hint of violence. They were hell on wheels. And if they were one-tenth as successful with women as they were reputed to be, there was no woman—from citizen through technician and nurse up to their suburban peers—who was immune to their virility.

Well, let them have the glamour and the women. He had taken the safer and more certain route to immortality. Few company policemen made it.

After the outriders came an ambulance, its armored ports closed, its automatic 40-millimeter gun roaming restlessly for a target. More outriders covered the rear. Above the convoy a helicopter swooped low.

Something glinted in the sunlight, became a line of small round objects beneath the helicopter, dropping in an arc toward the street. One after another they broke with fragile, popping sounds. They strung up through the convoy.

Like puppets when the puppeteer has released the strings, the outriders toppled to the street, skidding limply as their motorcycles slowed and stopped on their single wheels.

The ambulance could not stop. It rolled over one of the fallen outriders and crashed into a motorcycle, bulldozing it out of the way. The 40-millimeter gun jerked erratically to fix its radar sight on the helicopter, but the plane was skimming the rooftops. Before the gun could get the range the plane was gone.

Harry smelled something sharply penetrating. His head felt swollen and light. The street tilted and then straightened.

In the midst of the crowd beyond the ambulance an arm swung up. Something dark sailed through the air and smashed against the top of the ambulance. Flames splashed across it. They dripped down the sides, ran into gun slits and observation ports, were drawn into the air intake.

A moment followed in which nothing happened. The scene was like a frozen tableau—the ambulance and the motorcycles balanced in the street, the outriders and some of the nearest citizens crumpled and twisted on the pavement, the citizens watching, the flames licking up toward greasy, black smoke. . . .

The side door of the ambulance fell open. A medic staggered out, clutching something in one hand, beating at flames on his white jacket with the other.

The citizens watched silently, not moving to help or hinder. From among them stepped a dark-haired man.

His hand went up. It held something limp and dark. The hand came down against the medic's head.

No sound came to Harry over the roar of the idling motorcycles and ambulance. The pantomime continued, and he was part of the frozen audience as the medic fell and the man stooped, patted out the flames with his bare hands, picked the object out of the medic's hand, and looked at the ambulance door.

A girl stood there, Harry noticed. From this distance Harry could tell little more than that she was dark-haired and slender.

The flames on the ambulance had burned themselves out. The girl remained in the doorway, not moving. The man beside the fallen medic looked at her, started to hold out a hand, stopped, let it drop, turned, and faded back into the crowd.

Less than two minutes had passed since the sirens began.

Silently the citizens pressed forward. The girl turned and went back into the ambulance. The citizens stripped the outriders of their clothing and weapons, looted the ambulance of its black bag and medical supplies, picked up their fallen fellows, and disappeared.

It was like magic. One moment the street was full of them. The next moment they were gone. The street was empty of life.

Behind the Medical Center walls the sirens began again.

It was like the release from a spell. Harry began running down the street, his throat swelling with shouts. There were no words to them.

Out of the ambulance came a young boy. He was slim and small—no more than seven years old. He had blond hair, cut very short, and dark eyes in a tanned face. He wore a ragged T-shirt that once might have been white and a pair of blue jeans cut off above the knees.

He reached an arm back into the ambulance. A yellowed claw came out to meet it, and then an arm. The arm was a gnarled stick encircled with ropy blue veins like lianas. It was attached to a man on stiff, stiltlike legs. He was very old. His hair was thin, white silk. His scalp and face were wrinkled parchment. A tattered tunic fell from bony shoulders, around his permanently bent back, and was caught in folds around his loins.

The boy led the old man slowly and carefully into the ruined street, because the man was blind, his eyelids flat and dark over empty sockets. The old man bent painfully over the fallen medic. His fingers explored the medic's skull. Then he moved to the outrider who had been run over by the ambulance. The man's chest was crushed; a pink froth edged his lips as punctured lungs gasped for breath.

He was as good as dead. Medical science could do nothing for injuries that severe, that extensive.

Harry reached the old man, seized him by one bony shoulder. "What do you think you're doing?" he asked.

The old man didn't move. He held to the outrider's hand for a moment and then creaked to his feet. "Healing," he answered in a voice like the whisper of sandpaper.

"That man's dying," Harry said.

"So are we all," said the old man.

Harry glanced down at the outrider. Was he breathing more easily, or was that illusion?

The stretcher bearers reached them.

Harry had a difficult time finding the dean's office. The Medical Center covered hundreds of city blocks, and it had grown under a strange stimulus of its own. No one had ever planned for it to be so big, but it had sprouted an arm here when demand for medical care and research outgrew the space available, a wing there, and arteries through and under and around. . . .

He followed the glowing guidestick through the unmarked corridors, and tried to remember the way. But it was useless. He inserted the stick into the lock on an armored door. The door swallowed the stick and opened. As soon as Harry had entered, the door swung shut and locked. He was in a bare anteroom. On a metal bench bolted to the floor along one wall sat the boy and the old man from the ambulance. The boy looked up at Harry curiously, and then his gaze returned to his folded hands. The old man rested against the wall.

A little farther along the bench was a girl. She looked like the girl who had stood in the doorway of the ambulance, but she was smaller than he had thought and younger. Her face was pale. Only her blue eyes were vivid as they looked at him with a curious appeal and then faded. His gaze dropped to her figure; it was boyish and unformed, clad in a simple brown dress belted at the waist. She was no more than twelve or thirteen years old, he thought.

The reception box had to repeat the question twice: "Name?"

"Doctor Harry Elliott," he said.

"Advance for confirmation."

He went to the wall beside the far door and put his right hand against the plate set into it. A light flashed into his right eye, comparing retinal patterns.

"Deposit all metal objects in the receptacle," the box said.

Harry hesitated and then pulled his stethoscope out of his jacket pocket, removed his watch, emptied his trouser pockets of coins and pocketknife and hypospray.

Something clicked. "Nose filters," the box said.

Harry put those into the receptacle, too. The girl was watching him, but when he looked at her, her eyes moved away. The door opened. He went through the doorway. The door closed behind him.

Dean Mock's office was a magnificent room, thirty feet long and twenty feet wide. It was decorated in mid-Victorian style. The furniture all looked like real antiques, especially the yellow-oak rolltop desk and the mahogany instrument cabinet.

The room looked rich and impressive. Personally, though, Harry preferred Twentieth Century Modern. Its clean chromium-and-glass lines were aesthetically pleasing; moreover, they were from the respectable early days of medical science—that period when mankind first began to realize that good health was not merely an accident, that it could be bought if men were willing to pay the price.

Harry had seen Dean Mock before but never to speak to. His parents couldn't understand that. They thought he was the peer of everyone in the Medical Center because he was a doctor. He kept telling them how big the place was, how many people it contained: 75,000, 100,000—only the statisticians knew how many. It didn't do any good; they still couldn't understand. Harry had given up trying.

The dean didn't know Harry. He sat behind the rolltop desk in his white jacket and studied Harry's record cast up on the frosted glass insert. He was good at reading as if he were simply glancing down, but you couldn't deceive a man who had studied like that for ten years in this Center alone.

The dean's black hair was thinning. He was almost eighty years old now, but he didn't look it. He came of good stock, and he had had the best of medical care. He was good for another twenty years, Harry estimated, without longevity shots. By that time, surely, with his position and his accomplishments, he would be voted a reprieve.

Once, when a bomb had exploded in the power room, some of the doctors had whispered in the safe darkness that Mock's youthful appearance had a more reasonable explanation than heredity, but they were wrong. Harry had searched the immortality lists, and Mock's name wasn't on them.

Mock looked up quickly and caught Harry staring at him. Harry glanced away, but not before he had seen in Mock's eyes a look of—what?—fright? Desperation?

Harry couldn't understand it. The raid had been daring, this close to the Center walls, but nothing new. There had been raids before; there would be raids again. Any time there is something valuable, lawless men will try to steal it. In Harry's day it happened to be medicine.

Mock said abruptly, "Then you saw the man? You could recognize him if you saw him again, or if you had a good solidograph?"

"Yes, sir," Harry said. Why was Mock making such a production out of it? He had already been over this with the head resident and the chief of the company police.

"Do you know Governor Weaver?" Mock asked.

"An Immortal?" Mock might as well have asked if he knew God.

"No, no," Mock said impatiently. "Do you know where he lives?"

"In the governor's mansion. Forty miles from here, almost due west."

"Yes, yes," Mock said. "You're going to carry a message to him, a message. The shipment has been hijacked. Hijacked." Mock had developed a nervous habit of repeating words. Harry had to listen intently to keep from being distracted. "It will be a week before another shipment is ready, a week. How we will get it to him I don't know. I don't know." The last statement was muttered to himself.

Harry tried to make sense out of it. Carry a message to the governor? "Why don't you call him?" he said, unthinking.

But the question only roused Mock out of his introspection. "The underground cables are cut. Cut. No use repairing them. Repairmen get shot. And even if they're fixed, they're only cut again the next night. Radio and television are jammed. Get ready. You'll have to hurry to get out the southwest gate before curfew."

"A pass will get me through," Harry said, uncomprehending. Was Mock going insane?

"Didn't I tell you? Tell you?" Mock passed the back of his hand across his forehead as if to clear away cobwebs. "You're going alone, on foot, dressed as a citizen. A convoy would be cut to pieces. To pieces. We've tried. We've been out of touch with the governor for three weeks. Three weeks! He must be getting impatient. Never make the governor impatient. It isn't healthy."

For the first time Harry really understood what the dean was asking him to do. The governor! He had it in his power to cut half a lifetime off Harry's personal quest for immortality. "But my residency—"

Mock looked wise. "The governor can do you more good than a dozen boards. More good."

Harry caught his lower lip between his teeth and counted off on his fingers. "I'll need nose filters, a small medical kit, a gun—"

Mock was shaking his head. "None of those. Out of character. If you reach the governor's mansion, it will be because you pass as a citizen, not because you defend yourself well or heal up your wounds afterward. And a day or two without filters won't reduce your life expectancy appreciably. Well, Doctor? Will you get through?"

"As I hope for immortality!" Harry said fervently.

"Good, good. One more thing. You'll take along with you the people you saw in the anteroom. The boy's name is Christopher; the old man calls himself Pearce. He's some kind of neighborhood leech. The governor has asked for him."

"A leech?" Harry said incredulously.

Mock shrugged. His expression said that he considered the exclamation impertinent, but Harry could not restrain himself, and he said, "If we made an example of a few of these quacks—"

"The clinics would be more crowded than they are now. Now. They serve a good purpose. Besides, what can we do? He doesn't claim to be a physician. He calls himself a healer. He doesn't drug, operate, advise, or manipulate. Sick people come to him and he touches them. Touches them. Is that practicing medicine?"

Harry shook his head.

"What if the sick people claim to be helped? Pearce claims nothing. Nothing. He charges nothing. Nothing. If the sick people are grateful, if they want to give him something, who is to stop them?"

Harry sighed. "I'll have to sleep. They'll get away."

Mock jeered, "A feeble old man and a boy?"

"The girl's lively enough."

"Marna?" Mock reached into a drawer and brought out a hinged silver circle. He tossed it to Harry. Harry caught it and looked at it.

"It's a bracelet. Put it on."

It looked like nothing more than a bracelet. Harry shrugged, slipped it over his wrist, and clamped it shut.

For a moment it seemed too big, and then it tightened. His wrist tingled where the bracelet touched him.

"It's tuned to the one on the girl's wrist. Tuned. When the girl moves away from you, her wrist will tingle. The farther she goes, the more it will hurt. After a little she will come back. I'd put bracelets on the boy and the old man, but the bracelets only work in pairs. Pairs. If someone tries to remove the bracelet forcibly, the girl will die. Die. It links itself to the nervous system. The governor has the only key."

Harry stared at Mock. "What about mine?"

"The same. For you it's a warning device."

Harry took a deep breath and looked down at his wrist. The silver gleamed now like a snake's flat eyes.

"Why didn't you have one on the medic?"

"We did. We had to amputate his arm to get it off." Mock turned to his desk and started the microfilmed reports flipping past the window again. In a moment he looked up and seemed startled that Harry had not moved. "Still here? Get started. Wasted too much time now if you're going to beat curfew."

Harry turned and started toward the door through which he had come.

"Watch out for ghouls," Dean Mock called after him. "And mind the headhunters."

By the time they reached the southwest gate, Harry had evolved a method of progress for his little group that was mutually unsatisfactory.

"Hurry up," he would say. "There's only a few minutes left before curfew."

The girl would look at him and look away. Pearce, already moving more rapidly than Harry had expected, would say, "Patience. We'll get there."

None of them would speed up. Harry would walk ahead rapidly, outdistancing the others. His wrist would begin to tingle, then to smart, to burn, and to hurt. The farther he left Marna behind, the worse his pain grew. Only the thought that her wrist felt just as bad sustained him.

After a little the pain would begin to ebb. He knew then, without looking, that she had broken. When he would turn, she would be twenty feet behind him, no closer, willing to accept that much pain to keep from coming nearer to him.

Then he would have to stop and wait for the old man. Once she walked on past, but after a little she could stand the pain no more, and she returned. After that she stopped when he did.

Her surrender was a small triumph for Harry, but something to strengthen him when he started thinking about the deadly thing on his wrist and the peculiar state of the world, in which the Medical Center had been out of touch with the governor's mansion for three weeks, in which a convoy could not get through, in which a message had to be sent by a messenger on foot.

Under other conditions Harry might have thought Marna a lovely thing. She was slim and graceful, her skin was clear, her features were regular and pleasing, and the contrast between her dark hair and her blue eyes was striking. But she was young and spiteful and linked to him by a hateful condition. They had been thrown together too intimately too soon, and, besides, she was only a child.

They reached the gate with only a minute to spare.

On either side of them the chain-link double fence stretched as far as Harry could see. There was no end to it, really; it completely encircled the town. At night it was electrified, and savage dogs roamed the space between the fences.

Somehow citizens still got out. They formed outlaw bands that attacked defenseless travelers. That would be one of the dangers.

The head guard at the gate was a dark-skinned, middle-aged squire. At sixty he had given up any hopes for immortality; he intended to get what he could out of this life. That included bullying his inferiors.

He looked at the blue, daylight-only pass, and then at Harry. "Topeka? On foot?" He chuckled. It made his big belly shake until he had to cough. "If the ghouls don't get you, the headhunters will. The bounty on heads is twenty dollars now. Outlaw heads only—but then, heads don't talk. Not if they're detached from bodies. Of course, that's what you're figuring on doing—joining a wolf pack." He spat on the sidewalk beside Harry's foot.

Harry jerked back his foot in revulsion. The guard's eyes brightened.

"Are you going to let us through?" Harry asked.

"Let you through?" Slowly the guard looked at his wristwatch. "Can't do that. Past curfew. See?"

Automatically Harry bent over to look. "But we got

here before curfew—" he began. The guard's fist hit him just above the left ear and sent him spinning away.

"Get back in there and stay in there, you filthy citizens!" the guard shouted.

Harry's hand went to his pocket where he kept the hypospray, but it was gone. Words that would blast the guard off his post and into oblivion trembled on his lips, but he dared not utter them. He wasn't Dr. Elliott anymore, not until he reached the governor's mansion. He was Harry Elliott, citizen, fair game for any man's fist, who should consider himself lucky it was only a fist.

"Now," the guard said suggestively, "if you were to leave the girl as security—" He coughed.

Marna shrank back. She touched Harry accidentally. It was the first time they had touched, in spite of a more intimate linkage that joined them in pain and release, and something happened to Harry. His body recoiled automatically from the touch, as it would from a scalding sterilizer. Marna stiffened, aware of him.

Harry, disturbed, saw Pearce shuffling toward the guard, guided by his voice. Pearce reached out, his hand searching. He touched the guard's tunic, then his arm, and worked his way down the arm to the hand. Harry stood still, his hand doubled into a fist at his side, waiting for the guard to hit the old man. But the guard gave Pearce the instinctive respect due age and only looked at him curiously.

"Weak lungs," Pearce whispered. "Watch them. Pneumonia might kill before antibiotics could help. And in the lower left lobe, a hint of cancer—"

"Aw, now!" The guard jerked his hand away, but his voice was frightened.

"X ray," Pearce whispered. "Don't wait."

"There—there ain't nothing wrong with me," the guard stammered. "You—you're trying to scare me." He coughed.

"No exertion. Sit down. Rest."

"Why, I'll—I'll—" He began coughing violently. He jerked his head at the gate. "Go on," he said, choking. "Go out there and die."·

The boy Christopher took the old man's hand and led him through the open gateway. Harry caught Marna's upper arm—again the contact—and half helped her, half pushed her through the gate, keeping his eye warily on the guard. But the man's eyes were turned inward toward something far more vital to himself.

As soon as they were through, the gate slammed down behind them and Harry released Marna's arm as if it were distasteful to hold it. Fifty yards beyond, down the right-hand lanes of the disused six-lane divided highway, Harry said, "I suppose I ought to thank you."

Pearce whispered, "That would be polite."

Harry rubbed his head where the guard had hit him. It was swelling. He wished for a medical kit. "How can I be polite to a charlatan?"

"Politeness does not cost."

"Still—to lie to the man about his condition. To say—cancer—" Harry had a hard time saying it. It was a bad word—it was the one disease, aside from death itself, for which medical science had found no final cure.

"Was I lying?"

Harry stared sharply at the old man and then shrugged. He looked at Marna. "We're all in this together. We might as well make it as painless as possible. If we try to get along together, we might even all make it alive."

"Get along?" Marna said. Harry heard her speak for the first time; her voice was low and melodious, even in anger. "With this?" She held up her arm. The silver bracelet gleamed in the last red rays of the sun.

Harry said harshly, raising his wrist, "You think it's any better for me?"

Pearce whispered, "We will cooperate, Christopher and I—I, Doctor Elliott, because I am too old to do anything else, and Christopher because he is young and discipline is good for the young."

Christopher grinned. "Grampa used to be a doctor before he learned how to be a healer."

"Pride dulls the senses and warps the judgment," Pearce said softly.

Harry held back a comment. Now was no time to argue about medicine and quackery. The road was deserted. The once magnificent pavement was cracked and broken. Grass sprouted tall and thick in the cracks. The weeds stood like young trees along both edges, here and there the big, brown faces of sunflowers, fringed in yellow, nodding peacefully.

Beyond were the ruins of what had once been called the suburbs. The distinction between them and the city had been only a line drawn on a map; there had been no fences then. When they had gone up, the houses outside had soon crumbled.

The real suburbs were far out. First it was turnpike time to the city that had become more important than distance; then, helicopter time. Finally time had run out for the city. It had become so obviously a sea of carcinogens and disease that the connection to the suburbs had been broken. Shipments of food and raw materials went in and shipments of finished materials came out, but nobody went there anymore—except to the medical centers. They were located in the cities because their raw material was there: the blood, the organs, the diseases, the bodies for experiment. . . .

Harry walked beside Marna, ahead of Christopher and Pearce, but the girl didn't look at him. She walked on, her eyes straight ahead, as if she were alone. Harry said finally, "Look, it's not my fault. I didn't ask for this. Can't we be friends?"

She glanced at him just once. "No!"

His lips tightened, and he dropped away. He let his wrist tingle. What did he care if a thirteen-year-old girl disliked him?

The western sky was fading from scarlet into lavender and purple. Nothing moved in the ruins or along the road. They were alone in an ocean of desolation. They might have been the last people on a ruined earth.

Harry shivered. Soon it would be hard to keep to the road. "Hurry," he said to Pearce, "if you don't want to spend the night out here with the ghouls and the headhunters."

"There are worse companions," Pearce whispered.

By the time they reached the motel, the moonless

night was completely upon them and the old suburbs were behind. The sprawling place was dark except for a big neon sign that said MOTEL, a smaller sign that said VA-CANCY, and, at the gate in the fence that surrounded the whole place, a mat that said WELCOME. On a frosted glass plate were the words *Push button.*

Harry was about to push the button when Christopher said urgently, "Doctor Elliott, look!" He pointed toward the fence at the right with a stick he had picked up half a mile back.

"What?" Harry snapped. He was tired and nervous and dirty. He peered into the darkness. "A dead rabbit."

"Christopher means the fence is electrified," Marna said, "and the mat you're standing on is made of metal. I don't think we should go in here."

"Nonsense," Harry said sharply. "Would you rather stay out here at the mercy of whatever roams the night? I've stopped at these motels before. There's nothing wrong with them."

Christopher held out his stick. "Maybe you'd better push the button with this."

Harry frowned, took the stick, and stepped off the mat. "Oh, all right," he said ungraciously. At the second try, he pushed the button.

The frosted glass plate became a television eye. "Who rings?"

"Four travelers bound for Topeka," Harry said. He held up the pass in front of the eye. "We can pay."

"Welcome," said the speaker. "Cabins thirteen and fourteen will open when you deposit the correct amount of money. What time do you wish to be awakened?"

Harry looked at his companions. "Sunrise," he said.

"Good night," said the speaker. "Sleep tight."

The gate rolled up. Christopher led Pearce around the welcome mat and down the driveway beyond. Marna followed. Irritated, Harry jumped over the mat and caught up with them.

A single line of glass bricks along the edge of the driveway glowed fluorescently to point out the way they should go. They passed a tank trap and several machine-gun emplacements, but the place was deserted.

When they reached Cabin 13, Harry said, "We won't need the other one; we'll stay together." He put three twenty-dollar uranium pieces into the coin slot.

"Thank you," the door said. "Come in."

As the door opened, Christopher darted inside. The small room held a double bed, a chair, a desk, and a floor lamp. In the corner was a small partitioned bathroom with an enclosed shower, a lavatory, and a toilet. The boy went immediately to the desk, removed a plastic menu card from it, and returned to the door. He helped Pearce enter the room and then waited by the door until Harry and Marna were inside. He cracked the menu card into two pieces. As the door swung shut, he slipped one of the pieces between the door and the jamb. As he started back toward Pearce, he stumbled against the lamp and knocked it over. It crashed and went out. They were left with only the illumination from the bathroom light.

"Clumsy little fool!" Harry said.

Marna was at the desk, writing. She turned and

handed the paper to Harry. He edged toward the light and looked at it. It read:

Christopher has broken the eye, but the room is still bugged. We can't destroy the bugs without too much suspicion. Can I speak to you outside?

"That is the most ridiculous—" Harry began.

"This seems adequate," Pearce whispered. "You two can sleep in fourteen." His blind face was turned intently toward Harry.

Harry sighed. He might as well humor them. He opened the door and stepped into the night with Marna. The girl moved close to him, put her arms around his neck and her cheek against his. Without his volition, his arms went around her waist. Her lips moved against his ear; a moment later he realized that she was speaking.

"I do not like you, Doctor Elliott, but I do not want us all killed. Can you afford another cabin?"

"Of course, but—I'm not going to leave those two alone."

"It would be foolish for us not to stick together. Please, now. Ask no questions. When we go in fourteen, take off your jacket and throw it casually over the lamp. I'll do the rest."

Harry let himself be led to the next cabin. He fed the door. It greeted them and let them in. The room was identical with 13. Marna slipped a piece of plastic between the door and the jamb as the door closed. She looked at Harry expectantly.

He shrugged, took off his jacket, and tossed it over the lamp. The room took on a shadowy and sinister appearance. Marna knelt, rolled up a throw rug, and pulled down the covers on the bed. She went to the wall phone, gave it a little tug, and the entire flat vision plate swung out on hinges. She reached into it, grabbed something, and pulled it out. There seemed to be hundreds of turns of copper wire on a spool.

Marna went to the shower enclosure, unwinding wire as she went. She stood outside the enclosure and fastened one end of the wire to the hot-water faucet. Then she strung it around the room like a spider's web, broke it off, and fastened the end to the drain in the shower floor. She threaded the second piece of wire through the room close to but not touching the first wire.

Careful not to touch the wires, she reached into the shower enclosure and turned on the hot-water faucet. It gurgled, but no hot water came out. She tiptoed her way out between the wires, picked up the throw rug, and tossed it on the bed.

"Well, 'night," she said, motioning Harry toward the door and gesturing for him to be careful of the wires. When Harry reached the door without mishap, Marna turned off the lamp and removed the jacket.

She let the door slam behind them and gave a big sigh of relief.

"Now you've fixed it!" Harry whispered savagely. "I can't take a shower, and I'll have to sleep on the floor."

"You wouldn't want to take a shower anyway," Marna said. "It would be your last one. All of them are wired.

You can have the bed if you want it, although I'd advise you to sleep on the floor with the rest of us."

Harry couldn't sleep. First it had been the room, shadowed and silent, and then the harsh breathing of the old man and the softer breaths of Christopher and Marna. As a resident, he was not used to sleeping in the same room with other persons.

Then his arm had tingled—not much, but just enough to keep him awake. He had got out of bed and crawled to where Marna was lying on the floor. She, too, had been awake. Silently he had urged her to share the bed with him, gesturing that he would not touch her. He had no desire to touch her, and if he had, he swore by Hippocrates that he would restrain himself. He only wanted to ease the tingling under the bracelet so that he could go to sleep.

She motioned that he could lie on the floor beside her, but he shook his head. Finally she relented enough to move to the floor beside the bed. By lying on his stomach and letting his arm dangle, Harry relieved the tingling and fell into an uneasy sleep.

He had dreams. There was one in which he was performing a long and difficult lung resection. The microsurgical controls slipped in his sweaty fingers; the laser beam sliced through the aorta. The patient started up on the operating table, the blood spurting from her heart. It was Marna. She began to chase him down long hospital halls.

The overhead lights kept getting farther and farther

apart until Harry was running in complete darkness through warm, sticky blood that rose higher and higher until it closed over his head.

Harry woke up, smothering, fighting against something that enveloped him completely, relentlessly. There was a sound of scuffling nearby. Something spat and crackled. Someone cursed.

Harry fought, futilely. Something ripped. Again. Harry caught a glimpse of a grayer darkness, struggled toward it, and came out through a long cut in the taut blanket, which had been pulled under the bed on all four sides.

"Quick!" Christopher said, folding up his pocketknife. He headed for the door, where Pearce was already standing patiently.

Marna picked up a metal leg that had been unscrewed from the desk. Christopher slipped the chair out from under the doorknob and silently opened the door. He led Pearce outside, and Marna followed. Dazedly Harry came after her.

In Cabin 14 someone screamed. Something flashed blue. A body fell. Harry smelled the odor of burning flesh.

Marna ran ahead of them toward the gate. She rested the ferrule of the desk leg on the ground and let the metal bar fall toward the fence. The fence spat blue flame, which ran, crackling, down the desk leg. The leg glowed red and sagged as the metal softened. Then everything went dark, including the neon sign above them and the light at the gate.

"Help me!" Marna panted.

She was trying to lift the gate. Harry put his hands underneath and pulled. The gate moved a foot and stuck.

Up the drive someone yelled hoarsely, without words. Harry strained at the gate. It yielded at last and then rolled up smoothly. He raised his hand to hold it up while Marna got through, and then Pearce and the boy. Harry edged under and let the gate drop.

A moment later the electricity flickered on again. The desk leg melted through and dropped away.

Harry looked back. Coming toward them was a motorized wheelchair. In it was something lumpy and monstrous, a nightmarish menace—until Harry recognized it for what it was: a basket case, a quadruple amputee complicated by a heart condition. An artificial heart-and-lung machine rode on the back of the wheelchair like a second head. Behind galloped a gangling scarecrow creature with hair that flowed out behind. It wore a dress in imitation of a woman. . . .

Harry stood transfixed, watching, fascinated, while the wheelchair stopped beside one of the gun emplacements. Wires reached out from one of the chair arms like Medusan snakes, inserted themselves into control plugs. The machine gun started to chatter. Something plucked at Harry's sleeve.

The spell was broken. He turned and ran into the darkness.

Half an hour later he was lost. Marna, Pearce, and the boy were gone. All he had left was a tired body, an arm that burned, and a wrist that hurt worse than anything he could remember.

He felt his upper arm. His sleeve was wet. He brought his fingers to his nose. Blood. The bullet had creased him.

He sat disconsolately on the edge of the turnpike, the darkness around him as thick as soot. He looked at the fluorescent dial of his watch. Three-twenty. A couple of hours until sunrise. He sighed and tried to ease the pain in his wrist by rubbing around the bracelet. It seemed to help. In a few minutes it dropped to a tingle.

"Doctor Elliott," someone said softly.

He turned. Relief and something like joy flooded through his chest. There, outlined against the dim starlight, were Christopher, Marna, and Pearce.

"Well," Harry said gruffly, "I'm glad you didn't try to escape."

"We wouldn't do that, Doctor Elliott," Christopher said.

"How did you find me?" Harry asked.

Marna silently held up her arm.

The bracelet. Of course. He had given them too much credit, Harry thought sourly. Marna sought him out because she could not help herself, and Christopher, because he was out here alone with a senile old man to take care of and he needed help.

Although, honesty forced him to admit, it had been he and not Christopher and Pearce who had needed help back there a mile or two. If they had depended on him, their heads would be dangling in the motel's freezer, waiting to be turned in for the bounty. Or their still-living bodies would be on their way to some organ bank somewhere.

"Christopher," Harry said to Pearce, "must have been apprenticed to a bad-debt evader."

Pearce accepted it for what it was: a compliment and an apology. "Dodging the collection agency traps and keeping out of the way of the health inspector," he whispered, "makes growing up in the city a practical education. . . . You're hurt."

Harry started. How did the old man know? Even with eyes, it was too dark to see more than silhouettes. Harry steadied himself. It was an instinct, perhaps. Diagnosticians got it sometimes, he was told, after they had been practicing for years. They could smell disease before the patient lay down on the couch. From the gauges they got only confirmation.

Or maybe it was simpler than that. Maybe the old man smelled the blood with a nose grown keen to compensate for his blindness.

The old man's fingers were on his arm, surprisingly gentle. Harry pulled his arm away roughly. "It's only a crease."

Pearce's fingers found his arm again. "It's bleeding. Find some dry grass, Christopher."

Marna was close. She had made a small, startled movement toward him when Pearce had discovered his wound. Harry could not accept her actions for sympathy; her hate was too tangible. Perhaps she was wondering what she would do if he were to die.

Pearce ripped the sleeve away.

"Here's the grass, Grampa," Christopher said.

How did the boy find dry grass in the dark? "You

aren't going to put that on the wound!" Harry said quickly.

"It will stop the bleeding," Pearce whispered.

"But the germs—"

"Germs can't hurt you—unless you let them."

Pearce put the grass on the wound and bound it with the sleeve. "That will be better soon."

He would take it off, Harry told himself, as soon as they started walking. Somehow, though, it was easier to let it alone now that the harm was done. After that he forgot about it. When they were walking again, Harry found himself beside Marna. "I suppose you got your education dodging health inspectors in the city, too?" he said dryly.

She shook her head. "No. There's never been much else to do. Ever since I can remember I've been trying to escape. I got free once." Her voice was filled with remembered happiness. "I was free for twenty-four hours, and then they found me."

"But I thought—" Harry began. "Who are you?"

"Me? I'm the governor's daughter."

Harry recoiled. It was not so much the fact, but the bitterness with which she spoke that shocked him.

Sunrise found them on the turnpike. They had passed the last ruined motel. Now, on either side of the turnpike, were rolling, grassy hills, valleys filled with trees, and the river winding muddily beside them, sometimes so close they could have thrown a stone into it, sometimes turning beyond the hills out of sight.

The day was warm. Above them the sky was blue, with only a trace of fleecy cloud on the western horizon. Occasionally a rabbit would hop across the road in front of them and vanish into the brush on the other side. Once they saw a deer lift its head beside the river and stare at them curiously.

Harry stared back with hunger in his eyes.

"Doctor Elliott," Christopher said.

Harry looked at him. In the boy's soiled hand was an irregular lump of solidified brown sugar. It was speckled with lint and other unidentifiable additions, but at the moment it was the most desirable object Harry could imagine. His mouth watered, and he swallowed hard. "Give it to Pearce and the girl. They'll need their strength. And you, too."

"That's all right," Christopher said. "I have more." He held up three other pieces in his other hand. He gave one to Marna and one to Pearce. The old man bit into his with the stubs that served him as teeth.

Harry picked off the largest pieces of foreign matter, and then could restrain his hunger no longer. He couldn't remember a more satisfying breakfast.

They kept walking, not moving rapidly but steadily. Pearce never complained. He kept his bent old legs tottering forward, and Harry gave up trying to move him faster. They passed a hydroponic farm with an automated canning factory close beside it. No one moved around either building. Only the belts turned, carrying the tanks toward the factory to be harvested, or away from it refilled with nutrients, replanted with new crops.

"We should get something for lunch," Harry said. It would be theft, but it would be in a good cause. He could get his pardon directly from the governor.

"Too dangerous," Christopher said.

"Every possible entrance," Marna said, "is guarded by spy beams and automatic weapons."

"Christopher will get us a good supper," Pearce whispered.

They saw a suburban villa on a distant hill, but no one moved around it. They plodded on along the grass-grown double highway toward Lawrence.

Suddenly, Christopher said, "Down! In the ditch beside the road!"

This time Harry moved quickly, without questions. He helped Pearce down the slope—the old man was very light—and threw himself into the ditch beside Marna. A minute later they heard motors race by not far away. After they passed, Harry risked a glance above the top of the ditch. A group of motorcycles dwindled on the road toward the city. "What was that?" Harry asked, shaken.

"Wolf pack!" Marna said, hatred and disgust mingled in her voice.

"But they looked like company police," Harry said.

"When they grow up they will be company policemen," Marna said. "Company police are only wolf packs with badges."

"I thought the wolf packs were made up of escaped citizens," Harry said.

Marna looked at him scornfully. "Is that what they tell you?"

"A citizen," Pearce whispered, "is lucky to stay alive when he's alone. A group of them wouldn't last a week."

They got back up on the turnpike and started walking again. Christopher led Pearce nervously. He kept turning to look behind them and glancing from side to side. Soon Harry was edgy, too.

"Down!" Christopher shouted.

Something whistled a moment before Harry was struck a solid blow in the middle of the back as he was throwing himself to the pavement. It knocked him hard to the ground. Marna screamed.

Harry rolled over, wondering if his back was broken. Christopher and Pearce were on the pavement beside him, but Marna was gone.

A rocket blasted a little ahead and above them. Then another. Pearce looked up. A powered glider zoomed toward the sky. Marna was dangling from it, her body twisting and struggling to get free. From a second glider swung empty talons—padded hooks that had closed around Marna and had almost swooped up Harry.

Harry got to his knees, clutching his wrist. It was beginning to send stabs of pain up his arms, like the prelude to a symphony of anguish. The only thing that kept him from falling to the pavement in writhing torment was the black anger that surged through his veins and fought off weakness. He shook his fist at the turning gliders, climbing on smoking jets.

"Doctor Elliott!" Christopher said urgently.

Harry looked toward the voice with blurred eyes. The boy was in the ditch again. So was the old man.

"They'll be back! Get down!" Christopher said.

"But they've got Marna!" Harry said.

"It won't help if you get killed."

One glider swooped like a hawk toward a rabbit. The other, carrying Marna, continued to circle as it climbed. Harry rolled toward the ditch. A line of chattering bullets chipped at the pavement where he had been.

"I thought," he gasped, "they were trying to abduct us."

"They hunt heads, too," Christopher said.

"Anything for a thrill," Pearce whispered.

"I never did anything like that," Harry moaned. "I never knew anyone who did."

"You were busy," Pearce said.

It was true. Since he had been four years old he had been in school constantly, the last part of that time in medical school. He had been home only for a brief day now and then; he scarcely knew his parents anymore. What would he know of the pastimes of young squires? But this—this wolf-pack business! It was a degradation of life that filled him with horror.

The first glider was now a small cross in the sky; Marna, a speck hanging from it. It straightened and glided toward Lawrence. The second followed.

Suddenly Harry began beating the ground with his aching arm. "Why did I dodge? I should have let myself be captured with her. She'll die."

"She's strong," Pearce whispered, "stronger than you or Christopher, stronger than almost anyone. But sometimes strength is the cruelest thing. Follow her. Get her away."

Harry looked at the bracelet from which pain lanced up his arm and through his body. Yes, he could follow her. As long as he could move, he could find her. But feet were so slow against glider wings.

"The motorcycles will be coming back," Christopher said. "The gliders will have radioed them."

"But how do we capture a motorcycle?" Harry asked. The pain wouldn't let him think clearly.

Christopher had already pulled up his T-shirt. Around his thin waist was wrapped turn after turn of nylon cord. "Sometimes we fish," he said. He stretched the cord across the two-lane pavement in the concealment of grass grown tall in a crack. He motioned Harry to lie flat on the other side. "Let them pass, all but the last one," he said. "Hope that he's a straggler, far enough behind so that the others won't notice when we stand up. Wrap the cord around your waist. Get it up where it will catch him around the chest."

Harry lay beside the pavement. His left arm felt like a swelling balloon, and the balloon was filled with pain. He looked at it once, curiously, but it was still the same size.

After an eternity came the sound of motors, many of them. As the first ones passed, Harry cautiously lifted his head. Yes, there was a straggler. He was about a hundred feet behind the others; he was speeding now to catch up.

The others passed. When the straggler got within twenty feet, Harry jumped up, bracing himself against the impact. Christopher sprang up at the same instant. The young squire had time only to look surprised before he hit the cord. The cord pulled Harry out into the middle of the pavement, his heels skidding. Christopher had wrapped his end around the trunk of a young tree.

The squire smashed into the pavement. The motorcycle slowed and stopped. Beyond, far down the road, the others had not looked back.

Harry untangled himself from the cord and ran to the squire. He was about as old as Harry, and as big. He had a harelip and a withered leg. He was dead. His skull was crushed. Harry closed his eyes. He had seen men die before, but he had never been the cause of it. It was like breaking his Hippocratic oath.

"Some must die," Pearce whispered. "It is better for the evil to die young."

Harry stripped quickly and got into the squire's clothes and goggles. He strapped the pistol onto his hip and turned to Christopher and Pearce. "What about you?"

"We won't try to escape," Pearce said.

"I don't mean that. Will you be all right?"

Pearce put a hand on the boy's shoulder. "Christopher will take care of me. And he will find you after you have rescued Marna."

The confidence in Pearce's voice strengthened Harry. He did not pause to question that confidence. He mounted the motorcycle, settled himself into the saddle seat, and turned the throttle. The motorcycle took off violently.

It was tricky, riding on one wheel, but he had had experience on similar vehicles in the subterranean Medical Center thoroughfares.

His arm hurt, but it was not like it had been before when he was helpless. Now it was a guidance system. As he rode, he could feel the pain lessen. That meant he was getting closer to Marna.

It was night before he found her. The other motorcycles had completely outdistanced him, and he had swept past the side road several miles before the worsening pain warned him. He cruised back and forth before he finally located the curving ramp that led across the cloverleaf ten miles east of Lawrence.

From this a ruined asphalt road turned east, and the pain in Harry's arm had dropped to an ache. The road ended in an impenetrable thicket. Harry stopped just before he crashed into it. He sat immobile on the seat, thinking.

He hadn't considered what he was going to do when he found Marna; he had merely taken off in hot pursuit, driven partly by the painful bracelet on his wrist, partly by his concern for Marna and the pain she was feeling as well as her likely fate.

Somehow—he could scarcely trace back the involutions of chance to their source—he had been trapped into leading this pitiful expedition from the Medical Center to the Governor's mansion. Moment by moment it had threatened his life—and not, unless all his hopes were false, just a few years but eternity. Was he going to throw it away here on a quixotic attempt to rescue a girl from the midst of a pack of cruel young wolves?

But what would he do with the thing on his wrist?

What of the governor? What would remain of his life if he showed up at the governor's mansion without his daughter? And what of Marna? He discovered that the last concern overshadowed all the rest and silently cursed the emotions that were dooming him to a suicide mission.

"Ralph?" someone asked out of the darkness, and the decision was taken out of his hands.

"Yeth," he lisped. "Where ith everybody?"

"Usual place—under the bank."

Harry moved toward the voice, limping. "Can't thee a thing."

"Here's a light."

The trees lighted up, and a black form loomed in front of Harry. Harry blinked once, squinted, and hit the squire with the edge of his palm on the fourth cervical vertebra. As the man dropped, Harry picked the everlight out of the air, and caught the body. He eased the limp form into the grass and felt the neck. It was broken, but the squire was still breathing. He straightened the head so that there would be no pressure on nerve tissue, and looked up.

Light glimmered and flickered somewhere ahead. There was no movement, no sound; apparently no one had heard him. He flicked the light on, saw the path, and started through the young forest.

The campfire was built under a clay overhang so that it could not be seen from above. Roasting over it was a whole young deer being slowly turned on a spit by one of the squires. Harry found time to recognize the empty ache in his midriff for what it was: hunger.

The rest of the squires sat in a semicircle around the fire. Marna was seated on the far side, her hands bound behind her. Her head was raised; her eyes searched the darkness around the fire. What was she looking for? And then he answered his own question—she was looking for him. She knew by the bracelet on her wrist that he was near.

He wished that he could signal her, but that was impossible. He studied the squires: One was an albino, a second had artificial lungs attached to his back, a third had an external skeleton of stainless steel. The others may have had physical impairments that Harry could not see—all except one, who seemed older than the rest and leaned against the edge of the clay bank. He was blind, but inserted surgically into his eye sockets were electrically operated binoculars. He carried a power pack on his back with leads to the binoculars and to what must have been an antenna embedded in his coat.

Harry edged cautiously around the forest edge beyond the firelight toward where Marna was sitting.

"First the feast," the albino gloated, "then the fun."

The one who was turning the spit said, "I think we should have the fun first—then we'll be good and hungry."

They argued back and forth, good-naturedly for a moment and then, as others chimed in, with more intensity. Finally the albino turned to the one with the binoculars. "What do you say, Eyes?"

In a deep voice Eyes said, "Sell the girl. Young parts are worth top prices."

"Ah," said the albino slyly, "but you can't see what a pretty little thing she is, Eyes. To you she's only a pattern of white dots against a gray kinescope. To us she's cream and pink and blue and—"

"One of these days," Eyes said in a calm voice, "you'll go too far."

"Not with her, I won't—"

A stick broke under Harry's foot. Everyone stopped talking and listened. Harry eased his pistol out of its holster.

"Is that you, Ralph?" the albino said.

"Yeth," Harry said, limping out into the edge of the firelight, but keeping his head in the darkness, his pistol concealed at his side.

"Can you imagine?" the albino said. "The girl says she's the governor's daughter."

"I am," Marna said clearly. "He will have you cut to pieces slowly for what you are going to do."

"But I'm the governor, dearie," said the albino in a falsetto, "and I don't give a—"

Eyes interrupted. "That's not Ralph. His leg's all right."

Harry cursed his luck. The binoculars were equipped to pick up X-ray reflections as well as radar. "Run!" he shouted in the silence that followed.

His first shot was for Eyes. The man was turning so that it struck his power pack. He began screaming and clawing at the binoculars that served him for eyes. But Harry wasn't watching. He was releasing the entire magazine into the clay bank above the fire. Already loosened by the heat from the fire, the bank collapsed, smothering the fire and burying several of the squires sitting close to it.

Harry dived to the side. Several bullets went through the space he had just vacated. He scrambled for the forest and started running. He kept slamming into trees, but he picked himself up and ran again. In one of the collisions he lost his everlight. Behind, the pursuit thinned and died away.

He ran into something that yielded before him. It fell to the ground, something soft and warm. He tripped over it and toppled, his fist drawn back.

"Harry!" Marna said.

His fist turned into a hand that went out to her, pulled her tight. "Marna!" he whispered. "I didn't know. I didn't think I could do it. I thought you were—"

Their bracelets clinked together. Marna, who had been soft beneath him, suddenly stiffened, pushed him off. "Let's not get slobbery about it," she said angrily. "I know why you did it. Besides, they'll hear us."

Harry drew a quick, outraged breath and then let it come out in a sigh. What was the use? She'd never believe him—why should she? He wasn't sure himself. Now that it was over and he had time to realize the risks he had taken, he began to shiver. He sat there in the dark forest, his eyes closed, and tried to control his shaking.

Marna put her hand out hesitantly and touched his arm. She started to say something, stopped, and the moment was past.

"B-b-brat-tt!" he said. "N-n-nasty—un-ungrate-ful b-b-brat!" And then the shakes were gone.

She started to move. "Sit still!" he whispered. "We've got to wait until they give up the search."

At least he had eliminated the greatest danger: Eyes with his radar, X-ray, maybe infrared vision that was just as good by night as by day.

They sat in the darkness and waited, listened to the forest noises. An hour passed. Harry was going to say that perhaps it was safe to move, when he heard something rustling nearby. Animal, or human enemy? Marna, who had not touched him again or spoken, clutched his upper arm with a panic-strengthened hand. Harry doubled his fist and drew back his arm.

"Doctor Elliott?" Christopher whispered. "Marna?"

Relief surged over Harry like a warm, life-giving current. "You wonderful little imp! How did you find us?"

"Grampa helped me. He has a sense for that. I have a little, but he's better. Come."

Harry felt a small hand fit itself into his.

Christopher led them through the darkness. At first Harry was distrustful, and then, as the boy kept them out of bushes and trees, he moved more confidently. The hand became something he could trust. He knew how Pearce felt, and how bereft he must be now.

Christopher led them a long way before they reached another clearing. A bed of coals glowed dimly beneath a bower built from bent green branches and stuffed with leaves. Pearce sat near the fire, slowly turning a spit fashioned from another branch. It rested on two forked sticks. On the spit two skinned rabbits were golden brown and sizzling.

Pearce's sightless face turned as they entered the clearing. "Welcome back," he said.

Harry felt a warmth inside him that was like coming home. "Thanks," he said. His voice was husky.

Marna fell to her knees in front of the fire, raising her hands to it to warm them. Rope dangled from them, frayed in the center where she had methodically picked it apart while she had waited by another fire. She must have been cold, Harry thought, and I let her shiver through the forest while I was warm in my jacket. But it was too late to say anything.

When Christopher removed the rabbits from the spit, they almost fell apart. He wrapped four legs in damp green leaves and tucked them away in a cool hollow between two tree roots. "That's for breakfast," he said.

The four of them fell upon the remainder. Even without salt, it was the most delicious meal Harry had ever eaten. When it was finished, he licked his fingers, sighed, and leaned back on a pile of old leaves. He felt more contented than he could remember being since he was a child. He was a little thirsty, because he had refused to drink from the brook that ran through the woods close to their improvised camp, but he could stand that. A man couldn't surrender all his principles. It would be ironic to die of typhoid so close to his chance at immortality. That the governor would confer immortality upon him—or at least put him into a position where he could earn it—he did not doubt. After all, he had saved the governor's daughter. Marna was a pretty little thing. It was too bad she was still a child. An alliance with the governor's fam-

ily would not hurt his chances. Perhaps in a few years—
He pushed the notion away. Marna hated him.

Christopher shoveled dirt over the fire with a large piece of bark. Harry sighed again and stretched luxuriously. Sleeping would be good tonight.

Marna had washed at the brook. Her face was clean and shining. "Will you sleep here beside me?" Harry asked her, touching the dry leaves. He held up his bracelet apologetically. "This thing keeps me awake when you're very far away."

She nodded coldly and sat down nearby—but far enough so that they did not touch. Harry said, "I can't understand why we've run across so many teratisms. I can't remember ever seeing one in my practice at the Medical Center."

"You were in the clinics?" Pearce asked. And without waiting for an answer he went on, "Increasingly, the practice of medicine becomes the treatment of defectives, genetic monstrosities. In the city they would die; in the suburbs they are preserved to perpetuate themselves. Let me look at your arm."

Harry started. Pearce had said it so naturally that for a moment he had forgotten that the old man couldn't see. The old man's gentle fingers untied the bandage and carefully pulled the matted grass away. "You won't need this anymore."

Harry put his hand wonderingly to the wound. It had not hurt for hours. Now it was only a scar. "Perhaps you really were a doctor. Why did you give up practice?"

Pearce whispered, "I grew tired of being a technician.

Medicine had become so desperately complicated that the relationship between doctor and patient was not much different from that between mechanic and equipment." '

Harry objected. "A doctor has to preserve his distance. If he keeps caring, he won't survive. He must become callous to suffering, inured to sorrow, or he couldn't continue in a calling so intimately associated with them."

"No one ever said," Pearce whispered, "that it was an easy thing to be a doctor. If he stops caring, he loses not only his patient but his own humanity. But the complication of medicine had another effect. It restricted treatment to those who could afford it. Fewer and fewer people grew healthier and healthier. Weren't the rest human, too?"

Harry frowned. "Certainly. But it was the wealthy contributors and the foundations that made it all possible. They had to be treated first so that medical research could continue."

Pearce whispered, "And so society was warped all out of shape; everything was sacrificed to the god of medicine—all so that a few people could live a few years longer. Who paid the bill?

"And the odd outcome was that those who received care grew less healthy, as a class, than those who had to survive without it. Premies were saved to reproduce their weaknesses. Faults that would have proved fatal in childhood were repaired so that the patient reached maturity. Nonsurvival traits were passed along. Physiological inadequates multiplied, requiring greater care—"

Harry sat upright. "What kind of medical ethics are those? Medicine can't count the cost or weigh the value. Its business is to treat the sick—"

"Those who can afford it. If medicine doesn't make decisions about the rationing of care, then something else will: power or money or groups. One day I walked out on all that. I went among the citizens, where the future was, where I could help without discrimination. They took me in; they fed me when I was hungry, laughed with me when I was happy, cried with me when I was sad. They cared, and I helped them as I could."

"How?" Harry asked. "Without a diagnostic machine, without drugs or antibiotics."

"The human mind," Pearce whispered, "is still the best diagnostic machine. And the best antibiotic. I touched them. I helped them to cure themselves. So I became a healer instead of a technician. Our bodies want to heal themselves, you know, but our minds give counter-orders and death instructions."

"Witch doctor!" Harry said scornfully.

"Yes. Always there have been witch doctors. Healers. Only in my day have the healer and the doctor become two persons. In every other era the people with the healing touch were the doctors. They existed then; they exist now. Countless cures are testimony. Only today do we call it superstition. And yet we know that some doctors, no wiser or more expert than others, have patients with a far greater recovery rate. Some nurses—not always the best-looking ones—inspire in their patients a desire to get well.

"It takes you two hours to do a thorough examination; I can do it in two seconds. It may take you months or years to complete a treatment; I've never taken longer than five minutes."

"But where's your control?" Harry demanded. "How can you prove you've helped them? If you can't trace cause and effect, if no one else can duplicate your treatment, it isn't science. It can't be taught."

"When a healer is successful, he knows," Pearce whispered. "So does his patient. As for teaching—how do you teach a child to talk?"

Harry shrugged impatiently. Pearce had an answer for everything. There are people like that, so secure in their mania that they can never be convinced that the rest of the world is sane. Man had to depend on science—not on superstition, not on faith healers, not on miracle workers. Or else he was back in the Dark Ages.

He lay back in the bed of leaves, feeling Marna's presence close to him. He wanted to reach out and touch her, but he didn't.

Else there would be no law, no security, no immortality. . . .

The bracelet woke him. It tingled. Then it began to hurt. Harry put out his hand. The bed of leaves beside him was warm, but Marna was gone.

"Marna!" he whispered. He raised himself on one elbow. In the starlight that filtered through the trees above, he could just make out that the clearing was empty of everyone but himself. The places where Pearce and the boy had been sleeping were empty. "Where is everybody?" he said, more loudly.

He cursed under his breath. They had picked their time and escaped. But why, then, had Christopher found them in the forest and brought them here? And what did Marna hope to gain? Make it to the mansion alone?

He started up. Something crunched in the leaves. Harry froze in that position. A moment later he was blinded by a brilliant light.

"Don't move!" said a high-pitched voice. "I will have to shoot you. And if you try to dodge, the Snooper will follow." The voice was cool and precise. The hand that held the gun, Harry thought, would be as cool and accurate as the voice.

"I'm not moving," Harry said. "Who are you?"

The voice ignored him. "There were four of you. Where are the other three?"

"They heard you coming. They're hanging back, waiting to rush you."

"You're lying," the voice said contemptuously.

"Listen to me!" Harry said urgently. "You don't sound like a citizen. I'm a doctor—ask me a question about medicine, anything at all. I'm on an urgent mission. I'm taking a message to the governor."

"What is the message?"

Harry swallowed hard. "The shipment was hijacked. There won't be another ready for a week."

"What shipment?"

"I don't know. If you're a squire, you've got to help me."

"Sit down."

Harry sat down.

"I have a message for you. Your message won't be delivered."

"But—" Harry started up.

From somewhere behind the light came a small explosion—little more than a sharply expelled breath. Something stung Harry in the chest. He looked down. A tiny dart clung there between the edges of his jacket. He tried to reach for it and couldn't. His arm wouldn't move. His head wouldn't move, either. He toppled over onto his side, not feeling the impact. Only his eyes, his ears, and his lungs seemed unaffected. He lay there, paralyzed, his mind racing.

"Yes," the voice said calmly, "I am a ghoul. Some of my friends are headhunters, but I hunt bodies and bring them in alive. The sport is greater. So is the profit. Heads are worth only twenty dollars; bodies are worth more than a hundred. Some with young organs like yours are worth much more.

"Go, Snooper. Find the others."

The light went away. Something crackled in the brush and was gone. Slowly Harry made out a black shape that seemed to be sitting on the ground about ten feet away.

"You wonder what will happen to you," the ghoul said. "As soon as I find your companions, I will paralyze them, too, and summon my stretcher. They will carry you to my helicopter. Then, since you came from Kansas City, I will take you to Topeka."

A last hope died in Harry's chest.

"That works best, I've found," the high-pitched voice continued. "Avoids complications. The Topeka hospital I do business with will buy your bodies, no questions asked. You are permanently paralyzed, so you will never feel any pain, although you will not lose consciousness. That way the organs never deteriorate. If you're a doctor, as you said, you know what I mean. You may know the technical name for the poison in the dart; all I know is that it was synthesized from the poison of the digger wasp. By use of intravenous feeding, these eminently portable organ banks have been kept alive for years until their time comes. . . ."

The voice went on, but Harry stopped listening. He was thinking that he would go mad. They often did. He had seen them lying on slabs in the organ bank, and their eyes had been quite mad. Then he had told himself that the madness was why they had been put there, but now he knew the truth. He would soon be one of them.

Perhaps he would strangle before he reached the hospital, before they got a breathing tube down his throat and the artificial respirator on his chest and the tubes into his arms. They strangled sometimes, even under care.

He would not go mad, though. He was too sane. His mind might last for months.

He heard something crackle in the brush. Light flashed across his eyes. Something moved. Bodies thrashed. Someone grunted. Someone else yelled. Something went *pouf!* Then the sounds stopped, except for someone panting.

"Harry!" Marna said anxiously. "Harry! Are you all right?"

The light came back as the squat Snooper shuffled into the little clearing again. Pearce moved painfully through the light. Beyond him was Christopher and Marna. On the ground near them was a twisted creature. Harry couldn't figure out what it was, and then he realized it was a dwarf, a gnome, a man with thin, little legs and a twisted back and a large, lumpy head. Black hair grew sparsely on top of the head, and the eyes looked out redly, hating the world.

"Harry!" Marna said again, a wail this time.

He didn't answer. He couldn't. It was a momentary flash of pleasure, not being able to answer, and then it was buried in a flood of self-pity.

Marna picked up the dart gun and threw it deep into the brush. "What a filthy weapon!"

Reason returned to Harry. They had not escaped after all. Just as he had told the ghoul, they had only faded away so that they could rescue him if an opportunity came. But they had returned too late.

The paralysis was permanent; there was no antidote. Perhaps they would kill him. How could he make them understand that he wanted to be killed?

He tried to speak through his eyes.

Marna had moved to him. She cradled his head in her lap. Her hand moved restlessly, smoothing his hair.

Carefully Pearce removed the dart from his chest and shoved it deep into the ground. "Be calm," he said. "Don't give up. There is no such thing as permanent paralysis. If you will try, you can move your little finger." He held up Harry's hand, patted it.

Harry tried to move his finger, but it was useless. What was the matter with the old quack? Why didn't Pearce kill him and get it over with? Pearce kept talking, but Harry did not listen. What was the use of hoping? It only made the pain worse.

"A transfusion might help," Marna said.

"Yes," Pearce agreed. "Are you willing?"

"You know what I am?"

"Of course. Christopher, search the ghoul. He will have tubing and needles on him for emergency treatment of his victims." Pearce spoke to Marna again. "There will be some commingling. The poison will enter your body."

Marna's voice was bitter. "You couldn't hurt me with cyanide."

There were movements and preparations. Harry couldn't concentrate on them. Things blurred. Time passed like the movement of a glacier.

As the first gray light of morning came through the trees, Harry felt life moving painfully in his little toe of his left foot. It was worse than anything he had ever experienced, a hundred times worse than the pain from the bracelet. The pain spread to his other toes, to his feet, up his legs and arms toward his trunk. He wanted to plead with Pearce to restore the paralysis, but by the time his throat relaxed, the pain was almost gone.

When he could sit up, he looked around for Marna. She was leaning against a tree trunk, her eyes closed, looking paler than ever. "Marna!" he said. Her eyes opened wearily; an expression of joy flashed across them as they focused on him, and then they clouded.

"I'm all right," she said.

Harry scratched his left elbow where the transfusion needle had been inserted. "I don't understand—you and Pearce—you brought me back from that—but—"

"Don't try to understand," she said. "Just accept it."

"It's impossible," he muttered. "What are you?"

"The governor's daughter."

"What else?"

"A Cartwright," she said bitterly.

His mind recoiled. One of the Immortals! He was not surprised that her blood had counteracted the poison. Cartwright blood was specific against any foreign substance. He thought of something. "How old are you?"

"Seventeen," she said. She looked down at her slender figure. "We mature late, we Cartwrights. That's why Weaver sent me to the Medical Center—to see if I was fertile. A fertile Cartwright can waste no breeding time."

There was no doubt: She hated her father. She called him Weaver. "He will have you bred," Harry repeated stupidly.

"He will try to do it himself," she said without emotion. "He is not very fertile; that is why there are only three of us—my grandmother, my mother, and me. Then, too, we have some control over conception—particularly after maturity. We don't want his children, even though they might make him less dependent on us. I'm afraid"—her voice broke—"I'm afraid I'm not mature enough to prevent conception."

"Why didn't you tell me before?" Harry demanded.

"And have you treat me like a Cartwright?" Her eyes glowed with anger. "A Cartwright isn't a person, you know. A Cartwright is a walking blood bank, a living fountain of youth, something to be possessed, used, guarded, but never really allowed to live. Besides"—her head dropped—"you don't believe me. About Weaver."

"But he's the governor!" Harry exclaimed. He saw her face and turned away. How could he explain? You had a job and you had a duty. You couldn't go back on those. And then there were the bracelets. Only the governor had the key. They couldn't go on for long linked together like that. They would be separated again, by chance or by force, and he would die.

He got to his feet. The forest reeled for a moment, and then settled back. "I owe you thanks again," he said to Pearce.

"You fought hard to preserve your beliefs," Pearce whispered, "but there was a core of sanity that fought with me, that said it was better to be a whole man with crippled beliefs than a crippled man with whole beliefs."

Harry stared soberly at the old man. He was either a real healer who could not explain how he worked his miracles, or the world was a far crazier place than Harry had ever imagined. "If we start moving now," he said, "we should be in sight of the mansion by noon."

As he passed the dwarf, he looked down, stopped, and looked back at Marna and Pearce. Then he stooped, picked up the misshapen little body, and walked toward the road.

The helicopter was beside the turnpike. "It would be only a few minutes if we flew," he muttered.

Close behind him Marna said, "We aren't expected. We would be shot down before we got within five miles."

Harry strapped the dwarf into the helicopter seat. The ghoul stared at him out of hate-filled eyes. Harry started the motor, pressed the button on the autopilot marked *Return*, and stepped back. The helicopter lifted, straightened, and headed southeast.

Christopher and Pearce were waiting on the pavement when Harry turned. Christopher grinned suddenly and held out a rabbit leg. "Here's breakfast."

They marched down the turnpike toward Lawrence.

The governor's mansion was built on the top of an L-shaped hill that stood tall between two river valleys. Once it had been the site of a great university, but taxes for supporting such institutions had been diverted into more vital channels. Private contributions had dwindled as the demands of medical research and medical care had intensified. Soon there was no interest in educational fripperies, and the university died.

The governor had built his mansion there some seventy-five years ago when Topeka became unbearable. Long before that it had become a lifetime office—and the governor would live forever.

The state of Kansas was a barony—a description that would have meant nothing to Harry, whose knowledge of history was limited to the history of medicine. The governor was a baron, and the mansion was his keep. His vassals were the suburban squires; they were paid with immortality or its promise. Once one of them had received an injection, he had two choices: remain loyal to the governor and live forever, barring accidental death, or die within thirty days.

The governor had not received a shipment for nearly four weeks. The squires were getting desperate.

The mansion was a fortress. Its outer walls were five-foot-thick prestressed concrete faced with five-inch armor plate. A moat surrounded the walls; it was stocked with piranha. An inner wall rose above the outside one. The paved, unencumbered area between the two could be flooded with napalm. Inside the wall were concealed guided-missile nests.

The mansion rose, ziggurat fashion, in terraced steps. On each rooftop was a hydroponic farm. At the summit of the buildings was a glass penthouse; the noon sun turned it into silver. On a mast towering above, a radar dish rotated.

Like an iceberg, most of the mansion was beneath the surface. It went down through limestone and granite a mile deep. The building was almost a living creature; automatic mechanisms controlled it, brought in air, heated and cooled it, fed it, watered it, watched for enemies and killed them if they got too close. . . .

It could be controlled by a single hand. At the moment it was.

The mansion had no entrance. Harry stood in front of the walls and waved his jacket. "Ahoy, the mansion! A message for the governor from the Medical Center. Ahoy, the mansion!"

"Down!" Christopher shouted.

An angry bee buzzed past Harry's ear and then a whole flight of them. Harry fell to the ground and rolled. In a little while the bees stopped.

"Are you hurt?" Marna asked quickly.

Harry lifted his face out of the dust. "Poor shots," he said grimly. "Where did they come from?"

"One of the villas," Christopher said, pointing at the scattered dwellings at the foot of the hill.

"The bounty wouldn't even keep them in ammunition," Harry said.

In a giant, godlike voice the mansion spoke: "Who comes with a message for me?"

From his prone position, Harry shouted, "Doctor Harry Elliott. I have with me the governor's daughter, Marna, and a leech. We're under fire from one of the villas."

The mansion was silent. Slowly then a section of the inside wall swung open. Something flashed into the sunlight, spurting flame from its tail. It darted downward. A moment later a villa lifted into the air and fell back, a mass of rubble.

Over the outer wall came a crane arm. From it dangled a large metal car. When it reached the ground a door opened.

"Come into my presence," the mansion said.

The car was dusty. So was the penthouse where they were deposited. The vast swimming pool was dry; the cabanas were rotten; the flowers and bushes and palm trees were dead.

In the mirror-surfaced central column, a door gaped at them like a dark mouth. "Enter," said the door.

The elevator descended deep into the ground. Harry's stomach surged uneasily; he thought the car would never stop, but eventually the doors opened. Beyond was a spacious living room, decorated in shades of brown. One entire wall was a vision screen.

Marna ran out of the car. "Mother!" she shouted. "Grandmother!" She raced through the apartment. Harry followed her more slowly.

Six bedrooms opened off a long hall. At the end of the hall was a nursery. On the other side of the living room were a dining room and a kitchen. Every room had a wall-wide vision screen. Every room was empty.

"Mother?" Marna said again.

The dining-room screen flickered. Across the huge screen flowed the giant image of a creature who lolled on a pneumatic cushion. It was a thing incredibly fat, a sea of flesh rippling and surging. Although it was naked, its sex was a mystery. The breasts were great pillows of fat, but there was a sprinkling of hair between them. Its face, moon though it was, was small on the fantastic body; in the face, eyes were stuck like raisins.

It drew sustenance out of a tube; then, as it saw them, it pushed the tube away with one balloonlike hand. It giggled; the giggle was godlike.

"Hello, Marna," it said in the mansion's voice. "Looking for somebody? Your mother and your grandmother thwarted me, you know. Sterile creatures! I connected them directly to the blood bank; now there will be no delay about blood—"

"You'll kill them!" Marna gasped.

"Cartwrights? Silly girl! Besides, this is our bridal night, and we would not want them around, would we, Marna?"

Marna shrank back into the living room, but the creature looked at her from that screen, too. It turned its raisin eyes toward Harry. "You are the doctor with the message. Tell me."

Harry frowned. "You—are Governor Weaver?"

"In the flesh, boy." The creature chuckled. The chuckle sent waves of fat surging across its body and back again.

Harry took a deep breath. "The shipment was hijacked. It will be a week before another shipment is ready."

Weaver frowned and reached a stubby finger toward something beyond the camera's range. "There!" He looked back at Harry and smiled the smile of an idiot. "I just blew up Dean Mock's office. He was inside it at the time. It's justice, though. He's been sneaking shots of elixir for twenty years."

"Elixir? But—!" The information about Mock was too unreal to be meaningful; Harry didn't believe it. It was the mention of the elixir that shocked him.

Weaver's mouth made an O of sympathy. "I've disillusioned you. They tell you the elixir has not been synthesized. It was. Some one hundred years ago by a doctor named Russell Pearce. You were planning on synthesizing it, perhaps, and thereby winning yourself immortality as a reward. No—I'm not telepathic. Fifty out of every one hundred doctors dream that dream. I'll tell you, Doctor—I am the electorate. I decide who shall be immortal, and it pleases me to be arbitrary. Gods are always arbitrary. That is what makes them gods. I could give you immortality. I will; I will. Serve me well, Doctor, and when you begin to age, I will make you young again. I could make you dean of the Medical Center. Would you like that?"

Weaver frowned again. "But no—you would sneak elixir, like Mock, and you would not send me the shipment when I need it for my squires." He scratched between his breasts. "What will I do?" he wailed. "The loyal ones are dying off. I can't give them their shots, and their children are ambushing their parents. Whitey crept up on his father the other day; sold him to a junk collector. Old hands keep young hands away from the fire. But the old ones are dying off, and the young ones don't need the elixir, not yet. They will, though. They'll come to me on their knees, begging, and I'll laugh and let them die. That's what gods do, you know."

Weaver scratched his wrist. "You're still shocked about the elixir. You think we should make gallons of it, keep everybody young forever. Now think about it! We know that's absurd, eh? There wouldn't be enough of anything to go around. And what would be the value of immortality if everybody lived forever?" His voice changed suddenly, became businesslike. "Who hijacked the shipment? Was it this man?"

A picture flashed on the lower quarter of the screen.

"Yes," Harry said. His brain was spinning. Illumination and immortality, all in one breath. It was coming too fast. He didn't have time to react.

Weaver rubbed his doughy mouth. "Cartwright! How can he do it?" There was a note of godlike fear in the voice. "To risk—forever. He's mad—that's it, the man is mad. He wants to die." The great mass of flesh shivered; the body rippled. "Let him try me. I'll give him death." He looked at Harry again and scratched his neck. "How did you get here, you four?"

"We walked," Harry said tightly.

"Walked? I don't believe it."

"Ask a motel manager just this side of Kansas City, or a pack of wolves that almost got away with Marna, or a ghoul that paralyzed me. They'll tell you we walked."

Weaver scratched his mountainous belly. "Those wolf packs. They can be a nuisance. They're useful, though. They keep the countryside tidy. But if you were paralyzed, why is it you are here instead of waiting to be put to use on some organ-bank slab?"

"The leech gave me a transfusion from Marna." Too late Harry saw Marna motioning for him to be silent.

Weaver's face clouded. "You've stolen my blood! Now I can't bleed her for a month. I will have to punish you. Not now, but later, when I have thought of something fitting the crime."

"A month is too soon," Harry said. "No wonder the girl is pale if you bleed her every month. You'll kill her."

"But she's a Cartwright," Weaver said in astonishment, "and I need the blood."

Harry's lips tightened. He held up the bracelet on his wrist. "The key, sir?"

"Tell me," Weaver said, scratching under one breast, "is Marna fertile?"

"No, sir." Harry looked levelly into the eyes of the governor of Kansas. "The key?"

"Oh, dear," Weaver said. "I seem to have misplaced it. You'll have to wear the bracelets yet a bit. Well, Marna. We will see how it goes tonight, eh, fertile or no? Find something suitable for a bridal night, will you? And let us not mar the occasion with weeping and moaning and screams of pain. Come reverently and filled with a great joy, as Mary came unto God."

"If I have a child," Marna said, her face white, "it will have to be a virgin birth."

The sea of flesh surged with anger. "Perhaps there will be screams tonight. Yes. Leech! You—the obscenely old person with the boy. You are a healer."

"So I have been called," Pearce whispered.

"They say you work miracles. Well, I have a miracle for you to work." Weaver scratched the back of one hand. "I itch. Doctors have found nothing wrong with me, and they have died. It drives me mad."

"I cure by touch," Pearce said. "Every person cures himself; I only help."

"No man touches me," Weaver said. "You will cure me by tonight. I will not hear of anything else. Otherwise I will be angry with you and the boy. Yes, I will be very angry with the boy if you do not succeed."

"Tonight," Pearce said, "I will work a miracle for you."

Weaver smiled and reached for a feeding tube. His dark eyes glittered like black marbles in a huge dish of custard. "Tonight, then!" The image vanished from the screen.

"A grub," Harry whispered. "A giant white grub in the heart of a rose. Eating away at it, blind, selfish, and destructive."

"I think of him," Pearce said, "as a fetus who refuses to be born. Safe in the womb, he destroys the mother, not realizing that he is thereby destroying himself." He turned slightly toward Christopher. "There is an eye?"

Christopher looked at the screen. "Every one."

"Bugs."

"All over."

Pearce said, "We will have to take the chance that he will not audit the recordings, or that he can be distracted long enough to do what must be done."

Harry looked at Marna and then at Pearce and Christopher. "What can we do?"

"You're willing?" Marna said. "To give up immortality? To risk everything?"

Harry grimaced. "What would I be losing? A world like this—"

"What is the situation?" Pearce whispered. "Where is Weaver?"

Marna shrugged helplessly. "I don't know. My mother and grandmother never knew. He sends the elevator. There are no stairs, no other exits. And the elevators are controlled from a console beside his bed. There are thousands of switches. They also control the rest of the building, the lights, water, air, heat, and food supplies. He can release toxic or anesthetic gases or napalm. He can set off charges not only here but in Topeka and Kansas City, or send rockets to attack other areas. There's no way to reach him."

"You will reach him," Pearce whispered.

Marna's eyes lighted up. "If there were some weapon I could take . . . But there's an inspection in the elevator—magnetic and fluoroscopic detectors."

"Even if you could smuggle in a knife, say," Harry said, frowning, "it would be almost impossible to hit a vital organ. And even though he isn't able to move his body, his arms must be fantastically strong."

"There is, perhaps, one way," Pearce said. "If we can find a piece of paper, Christopher will write it out for you."

The bride waited near the elevator doors. She was dressed in white satin and old lace. The lace was pulled up over the bride's head for a veil. In front of the living-room screen, in a brown velour Grand Rapids over-stuffed chair, sat Pearce. At his feet, leaning against his bony knee, was Christopher.

The screen flickered, and Weaver was there, grinning his divine-idiot's grin. "You're impatient, Marna. It pleases me to see you so eager to rush into the arms of your bridegroom. The wedding carriage arrives."

The doors of the elevator sighed open. The bride stepped into the car. As the doors began to close, Pearce got to his feet, pushing Christopher gently to one side, and said, "You seek immortality, Weaver, and you think you have found it. But what you have is only a living death.

I am going to show you the only real immortality. . . ."

The car dropped. It plummeted to the tune of the wedding march from Lohengrin. Detectors probed at the bride and found only cloth. The elevator began to slow. After it came to a full stop, the doors remained closed for a moment, and then, squeaking, they opened.

The stench of decay flowed into the car. For a moment the bride recoiled, and then she stepped forward out of the car. The room had once been a marvelous mechanism: a stainless-steel womb. Not much bigger than the giant pneumatic mattress that occupied the center, the room was completely automatic. Temperature regulators kept it at blood heat. Food came directly from the processing rooms through the tubes without human aid. Sprays had been installed for perfumed water to sweep dirt and refuse to collectors around the edge of the room that would dispose of it. An overhead spray washed the creature who occupied the mattress. Around the edges of the mattress, like a great circular organ with ten thousand keys, was a complex control console. Directly over the mattress, on the ceiling, was a view screen.

Some years before, apparently, a water pipe had broken, through some shift in the earth, after a small leak or a hard freeze had made the rock swell. The cleansing sprays no longer worked, and the occupant of the room either was afraid to have intruders trace the trouble, or he no longer cared.

The floor was littered with decaying food, with food containers and wrappers, with waste matter. As the bride stepped into the room, a multitude of cockroaches scattered. Mice scampered into hiding places.

The bride pulled the long white-satin skirt up above her hips. She unwound a thin, nylon cord from her waist. A loop was fastened into the end. She shook it out until it hung free.

Weaver, she saw, was watching the overhead screen with almost hypnotic concentration. Pearce was saying, "Aging is not a physical disease; it is mental. The mind grows tired and lets the body die. Only half the Cartwrights' immunity to death lies in their blood; the other half is their unflagging will to live.

"You are one hundred fifty-three years old. I tended your father, who died before you were born. I gave him, unwittingly, a transfusion of Marshall Cartwright's blood."

Weaver whispered, "But that would make you—" His voice was thin and high; it was not godlike at all. It was ridiculous coming from that vast mass of flesh.

"Almost two hundred years old," Pearce said. His voice was stronger, richer, deeper—no longer a whisper. "Without even a transfusion of Cartwright blood, even an injection of the *elixir vitae*. The effective mind can achieve conscious control of the autonomic nervous system, of the very cells that make up the bloodstream and the body."

The bride craned her neck to see the screen on the ceiling. Pearce looked different. He was taller. His legs were straight and muscular. His shoulders were broader. As the bride watched, muscle and flesh and fat built up beneath his skin, firming it, smoothing out wrinkles. The facial bones receded beneath young flesh and skin. Silky white hair thickened and grew darker.

"You wonder why I stayed old," Pearce said, and his voice was resonant and powerful. "It is something one does not use for oneself. It comes through giving, not taking."

His sunken eyelids grew full, paled, opened. And Pearce looked out at Weaver, tall, strong, and straight— no more than thirty, surely. There was power latent in that face—power leashed, under control. Weaver recoiled from it.

Then, onto the screen, walked Marna.

Weaver's eyes bulged. His head swiveled toward the bride. Harry tossed off the veil and swung the looped cord lightly between two fingers. The importance of his next move was terrifying. The first throw had to be accurate, because he might never have a chance for another. His surgeon's fingers were deft, but he had never thrown a lariat. Christopher had described how he should do it, but there had been no chance to practice.

And if he were dragged within reach of those doughy arms, a hug would smother him. And in that startled moment, Weaver's head lifted with surprise and his hand stabbed toward the console. Harry flipped the cord. The loop dropped over Weaver's head and tightened around his neck.

Quickly Harry wrapped the cord several times around his waist and pulled it tight with his right hand. Weaver jerked against it, tightening it further. The thin cord disappeared into the neck's soft flesh. Weaver's stubby fingers clawed at it, tearing the skin, as his body thrashed on the mattress.

He had, Harry thought crazily, an Immortal at the end of his fishing line—a great white whale struggling to free itself so that it could live forever, smacking the pneumatic waves with fierce lunges and savage tugs. It seemed as unreal as a nightmare.

Weaver, by some titanic effort, had turned over. He had his hands around the cord now. He rose onto soft, flowing knees and pulled at the cord, dragging Harry forward toward the mattress. Weaver's eyes were beginning to bulge out of his pudding-face.

Harry dug his heels into the floor. Weaver came up, like a whale leaping its vast bulk incredibly out of the water, and stood, shapeless and monstrous, his face purpling. Then, deep inside, the heart gave up, and the body sagged. It flowed like a melting wax image back to the mattress on which it had spent almost three-quarters of a century.

Harry dazedly unwrapped the cord from his hand and waist. It had cut deep into the skin; blood welled out. He didn't feel anything as he dropped the cord. He shut his eyes and shuddered.

After a period of time that he never remembered, he heard someone calling him. "Harry!" It was Marna's voice. "Are you all right? Harry, please!"

He took a deep breath. "Yes. Yes, I'm all right."

"Go to the console," said the young man who had been Pearce. "You'll have to find the right controls, but they should be marked. And then we've got to get out of here ourselves. Marshall Cartwright is outside, and I think he's getting impatient."

Harry nodded, but still he waited. It would take a strong man to go out into a world where immortality was a fact rather than a dream. He would have to live with it and its problems. And they would be greater than anything he had imagined.

He moved forward to begin the search.